THE SECRET LIVES OF MURDERERS' WIVES

THE SECRET LIVES OF MURDERERS' WIVES

ELIZABETH ARNOTT

BERKLEY
NEW YORK

BERKLEY
An imprint of Penguin Random House LLC
1745 Broadway, New York, NY 10019
penguinrandomhouse.com

Copyright © 2026 by Lunar Books Ltd.
Penguin Random House values and supports copyright. Copyright fuels creativity, encourages diverse voices, promotes free speech, and creates a vibrant culture. Thank you for buying an authorized edition of this book and for complying with copyright laws by not reproducing, scanning, or distributing any part of it in any form without permission. You are supporting writers and allowing Penguin Random House to continue to publish books for every reader. Please note that no part of this book may be used or reproduced in any manner for the purpose of training artificial intelligence technologies or systems.

BERKLEY and the BERKLEY & B colophon are registered trademarks of
Penguin Random House LLC.

Book design by George Towne
Interior art: Cooking knife icon vector logo © Nilamsari/Shutterstock

Library of Congress Cataloging-in-Publication Data
Names: Arnott, Elizabeth, author
Title: The secret lives of murderers' wives / Elizabeth Arnott.
Description: New York : Berkley, 2026.
Identifiers: LCCN 2025018551 (print) | LCCN 2025018552 (ebook) |
ISBN 9780593952993 (hardcover) | ISBN 9780593953006 (ebook)
Subjects: LCGFT: Detective and mystery fiction | Thrillers (Fiction) | Novels | Fiction
Classification: LCC PR6116.O5548 S43 2026 (print) | LCC PR6116.O5548 (ebook)
LC record available at https://lccn.loc.gov/2025018551
LC ebook record available at https://lccn.loc.gov/2025018552

Printed in the United States of America
1st Printing

The authorized representative in the EU for product safety and compliance is
Penguin Random House Ireland, Morrison Chambers, 32 Nassau Street,
Dublin D02 YH68, Ireland, https://eu-contact.penguin.ie.

For Joni and D

THE SECRET LIVES OF MURDERERS' WIVES

ONE

BERRYVIEW, CALIFORNIA, 1966

There's something about hot weather that makes Beverley Lightfoot think of finding her husband's clothes in the trash.

It was sweltering, just like today, when she locked eyes with a skinny coyote, lifted the lid of her neighbor's garbage can and saw her husband's shirt—the plaid one she'd got him for his thirty-fifth birthday—flecked with old eggshells, discarded coffee grounds and bloodstains.

She blinks away the image, tilts the rearview mirror and splays her hands across the steering wheel, lifting her fingers to inspect nails she carefully painted just this morning, an innocuous carnation pink. She frowns, leans in, sure she can see the polish bubbling in the heat.

The surrounding sidewalks are fringed with gasping palms and packed tightly with bodies in capri pants and sleeveless sweaters. This type of insistent heat—so stubborn that it radiates from the buildings, the crosswalks—sends folks' heads into a spin, especially in Berryview, where there is no coastal breeze, not even the mildest gust to shoo off the muggy stink of summer.

It has been this way for weeks: a meteorological standoff, the papers running headlines of record temperatures alongside stories of planes bombing Hanoi. CITY SWELTERS! they cry hysterically. THOUSANDS MORE KILLED IN 'NAM.

Salesmen have taken the weather as a cue to knock on Beverley's door. They come with freestanding fans, with bulky Coleman coolers, with ice machines balanced on their hips, their damp hair palmed back, their grins twitching with the knowledge that they have access to treasure. Once Beverley has politely dismissed them, she will lean out of the porch. In every manicured front yard, behind white fences and blowsy hibiscus, she will see the same thing: men standing wide legged, with open shirts—just like the one she found in the trash that day—soaked through by the spray of their garden sprinklers.

Beverley adjusts her white sunglasses to repel the glare of the parking lot. Slick asphalt and expensive cars—she'd expected nothing but wealth today. She shifts in the driver's seat of her Cortina, her thighs tacky against the old vinyl. Her dress—cream twill, belted narrow at the waist, tied with a silk bow at the neck—is already damp with sweat. There's nothing she can do about it now; she only hopes the spotlights won't be too bright when she makes it inside.

She checks her rearview mirror again. The sun is spiking through the trees, glancing off windows, a blazing wash of light. Her teeth find the soft insides of her cheeks and bite down hard. She resents the oafish predictability of her own memory, as if she's some dumb Pavlovian mutt thinking of helicopter blades and red flashing lights whenever the temperature rises above ninety degrees.

She reaches forward and snaps off the car radio, then pulls the bow from her neck, purses her lips and blows a stream of hot air down to her chest. *Twill. Really? In this heat? Bravo, Beverley.*

She'd taken the dress from the back of the closet and had it dry-cleaned especially. Deciding on her outfit had been a ritual enacted over several days—hours in front of the mirror, holding each garment against her body to study it. She had to consider whether it struck the right balance. Nothing too stern. Nothing playful, for obvious reasons. Nothing short. No cleavage. Absolutely no red.

She'd layered on makeup before removing it bit by bit as if a sweep of blush in the wrong shade of peach or mascara applied too thickly was the thing people would focus on, the thing that would validate their hunch that they had been right about her all along.

Outside the car window, a well-dressed crowd streams toward the entrance of the hotel. Silver badges and tenderly polished buttons glint in the sun. There are hundreds surging in: run-of-the-mill cops, detectives and sheriffs, and wives in their own uniform—pearls, skimmer dresses and earrings plump as Christmas tree baubles. Beverley glances down at her legs, sighs. There's a snag in her new pantyhose.

She checks her makeup once more, and the car fills with her mother's voice. *With a face as round as yours, Beverley, you really should reconsider whether bangs are the best option.* Mascara has congealed beneath her bottom lashes, and her new Coty lipstick is bleeding out from the corners of her mouth. She looks unhinged.

She grabs for her purse and pulls out a tissue, realizing as she does that her hands are trembling. In fact, her whole body is vibrating, her veins electric with dread. She dabs the sides of her mouth, reaches for the lipstick to reapply, unsure which is worse, the infernal heat or the infernal nerves. There will be people inside, important people, and they'll all be watching her, listening only to her, thinking to themselves, *Of course she knew*, or *She didn't know? The woman's a floozy, a total waste of space.*

If there's one thing Beverley has learned over the past five years, it's that other women think they would know if their husband were out doing what Beverley's husband had been out doing. They wouldn't, but they like to comfort themselves with the notion just the same. Beverley has the grace to allow them that.

She glances at her reflection again, lipstick poised, and instantly she sees *him* across the parking lot. She shrinks down as far as she can, her shoulders brushing her earlobes.

"Shit." She loses her grasp on the lipstick, and it tumbles into the footwell. "Shit, shit, shit!" She realizes, with horror, that it has swiped a crimson smear across the front of her dress.

Risking another glance, she judges that Roger Greaves is some way across the lot. Even from this distance, she can recognize his silver hair, swept to one side, his crisp, pressed uniform and his imposing height. His wife, Enid, clings to his elbow.

Beverley holds her breath as the couple passes the car at a distance and pushes through the double doors of the hotel. Her eyes linger on the sandwich board out front, with words scrawled in chalk.

3RD JULY
LAPD GALA EVENING
WELCOME OFFICERS AND THEIR FAMILIES

Hurriedly, she presses powder onto her face, trying to beat back the blush that crawls upward from her neck.

If she doesn't go in now, she'll never go in.

If she doesn't go in, they'll know it's because she's got something to hide.

Before she can stop herself, she reaches toward the glove box and nudges it open. She pulls Henry's old hip flask from the compartment. She knows she shouldn't still use it, but it feels like a small act of rebellion to sip from the steel. The liquor's warm, and it burns exquisitely as it goes down. After a while, she notices that she's sitting a little taller in her seat. When that familiar TV static arrives in her gut, she puts the flask away, tucks a loose strand of hair behind her ear and steps out of the car.

Outside, the air is thick enough to slice. Her fingertips crackle as she checks each of her car doors in turn, then repeats the well-worn routine. She resists the urge to check a third time. If she doesn't go in now, they will start to make connections that aren't there. They will tell her story for her.

She turns toward the gold-framed entrance doors, but something makes her pause. A young woman steps out of a Plymouth Barracuda and slams the driver's-side door behind her. Her Mary Janes slap the asphalt as she hurries toward the entrance.

"Excuse me." Beverley bolts after her. "Miss, excuse me. Wait!" She draws level and seizes her shoulder.

The girl—a Jean Shrimpton type, sleeveless turtleneck, late twenties, just like Beverley—turns and raises a plucked eyebrow.

"I'm sorry for the hollering, but you forgot to lock your car." Beverley smiles.

"Oh." The woman's hands flicker to her collarbone, brushing a crucifix so delicate that it's almost translucent. "Thank God," she exhales. "I thought you were going to sell me insurance or something."

Beverley forces a laugh. "Just wanted to help."

The woman smiles as if Beverley has said something odd. "I'm sure it's fine," she eventually replies, then half turns back to the gala, waves a pretty little hand. "There must be three hundred cops in that building right there. This is the safest parking lot in the city right now."

She may be pretty, but pretty doesn't keep you alive.

Beverley fixes her own smile in place. "If you don't lock your car, someone could climb in and conceal himself behind the driver's seat."

The woman blinks at her, visibly appalled.

"It's always safer to lock your car."

The woman's eyes have narrowed to disgusted slits. Without a word, she stalks back to her car, locks it pointedly and then shoulders past Beverley into the hotel, her purse clutched to her chest.

T**HE BALLROOM IS** crammed with a hothouse fug. Ushers have distributed paper fans, and the wives flap them, lifting ponytails from their necks, revealing clasps of expensive auction-house jewelry. The space is cotton-wooled with chatter, the low baritone of men telling unprompted stories about themselves—broad shoulders, brilliantined hair, a heady waft of Aramis. Some of the officers are in uniform. Others smooth the lapels of tuxedo jackets, fix bow ties.

It's dark, a welcome contrast with the migraine blare of the sun outside. The walls are veiled with black drapes. Chandeliers jitter above in a wash of kaleidoscopic glass. Beverley glances down, fingers the lipstick stain on the front of her dress. *Well, that's it.* She is absolutely making it worse.

Perhaps she should have asked Margot to accompany her, or even Elsie. That would have given people a spectacle. *You want a murderer's wife, ladies and gentlemen? Here. Have three.*

She moves through the room, her eyes trained on the floor, and hopes nobody recognizes her from the papers.

Beverley has always envied the officers and their wives. For them, murder is merely six letters scrawled in a hastily written report. It's discussed over meat loaf at the dinner table. It's crime-scene evidence shut away in a locker at the end of the day.

A waiter with Lee Marvin eyebrows glides past and she plucks a glass of champagne from his tray, then stretches behind her to grab another. Clutching one tightly in each fist, she turns to face the wall and downs the first in several gulps, discarding the glass on a nearby table. She tips the other to her lips, then thinks better of it; she'll keep hold of it so her hands have something to do.

"Mrs. Lightfoot."

She almost jumps out of her skin. The young guy in front of her looks like something from a TV commercial. He is about the same age as Beverley, much younger than most of the officers in the room. She can't help but imagine him playing tennis, all tanned legs and snug white shorts.

"It's Miss Edwards now, actually," she says, holding his gaze longer than feels comfortable. She refuses to use *Mrs.* Mrs. Edwards is her mother.

"Miss Edwards." He shows his teeth, and she feels the tips of her ears growing hot. "Our speakers are invited to relax backstage." He has two beads of sweat above his lip. "There's a room, a bit quieter, where you can wait, if you'd like, before your"—he blinks a few times—"appearance."

She nods as he leaves. After a moment, she sets off in the direction of the stage. Down its right edge, flanked by high, black partition walls, she finds a corridor and steps into it gratefully. The thrum of the ballroom is immediately muffled, barks of laughter and machismo dulled to a quiet, ignorable buzz. She pauses in the darkness and takes a breath, moving a hand to the tight muscles at the back of her neck, tipping her chin upward, draining the nerves.

Her skin suddenly prickles.

Someone is watching her.

She can feel it like the soft scrape of fingernails.

"Good to see you again, Mrs. Lightfoot."

The prickling stops. She knows that gruff voice. She turns.

"Chief Cornwell." Her shoulders tense. "You surprised me."

"Probably shouldn't do that, right?" He raises an eyebrow but does not smile. Tom Cornwell was never the sort of guy to smile—not when he caught Henry, not when he accused Beverley of knowing more than she let on. "How have you been?"

"You know..." She shrugs.

He nods, runs his fingers down either side of his mustache. "So, you ready for this?" He gestures to the stage.

No, she wants to reply. She'll never be ready. But if she doesn't do this, he and others will continue to suspect her of having protected Henry, of shielding his crimes long before they came to light.

"As I'll ever be, I guess." She pictures herself up there, in front of all those scrutinizing faces, and she reaches for the wall to keep herself upright.

"It's a good thing you're doing." Cornwell purses his lips briefly, as if it pains him to be polite. "It's going to help a lot of people."

"Sure." She closes her eyes, battling the part of her that wants to tear down the corridor and race back out into the parking lot. But she has little time for escape fantasies. Cornwell glances at his watch just as the feedback squeal of a tapped microphone rips through the air.

TWO

"LADIES AND GENTLEMEN," the emcee's voice booms, "welcome to the LAPD's annual family-and-friends gala evening, 1966."

Beverley feels as if her heart has dislodged itself and oozed down into her stomach. "To get us started, please welcome"—someone has stuffed sandpaper into her mouth—"Chief Tom Cornwell, head of the California Major Crimes Investigation Unit."

The crowd applauds.

She slips into a spot at the side of the stage that is crammed with shadows but has a clear sight line to the audience. People watch intently, low light refracting off their diamond jewelry, as Cornwell strolls into the spotlight. It occurs to Beverley that men like Tom Cornwell have no cause to be nervous, because they are so often the default heroes, so often able to control the narrative, to tell others what they should be thinking of them.

So, what does that make her? A villain? An accomplice? It has been almost five years since it all happened, but she has still not figured out quite where she fits into the story. A wife? Sure. A woman existing in a torturous duality? Most certainly. Someone close enough to a killer to know the smell of their neck, the sighing noise they make in their sleep, the fact that their bottom-left canine tooth is black from a run-in with a baseball bat. But someone so close to a killer that she could not step back and see it, so wrapped up in the mundanity of her life that she was very easily played.

"Ladies and gentlemen," Cornwell begins. Beverley sees shoulders straighten at his imposing voice, the same voice that questioned her, that bombarded her with the horrific intricacies of Henry's crimes. "Thank you for having me here tonight to celebrate another year of successes at the Los Angeles Police Department and beyond." Still no smile. "I'm proud to have the opportunity to speak about one of the most pivotal moments in my career."

It's about him. It's always been about him.

"Five years ago, after an investigation that demanded unprecedented resources, the support of every county sheriff's office in the state and the hard work of my staff and my deputy, Roger Greaves, I placed handcuffs around the wrists of Henry Lightfoot, a man who terrorized the good residents of California for over three years. A brutal spree that earned him the name the Heatwave Killer." He pauses, and it takes a moment for the audience to realize they are expected to clap.

What must it be like, Beverley wonders, to stand before a roomful of people and demand that they applaud you? Cornwell fixes his tie, flexes his jaw, basking in the sound, before quieting the room with his hands.

"I can still remember"—the audience is transfixed—"the way my heart raced when my fingers brushed his skin. It was like touching pure evil."

Beverley swallows.

"And, actually"—he raises a finger—"while that might have been the most pivotal point in my career"—he glances briefly into the shadows—"my proudest moment is right now, right here"—he points to his feet—"tonight, because tonight I am blessed to be welcoming a remarkable woman to this stage."

She could leave. She could turn and run before anyone could stop her.

"Mrs. Beverley Lightfoot, ladies and gentlemen."

It's Edwards now. Miss Edwards.

"Wife of the Heatwave Killer."

Ex-wife.

"The woman who worked openly with the police to help secure a conviction for her husband."

Define openly.

Suddenly the lights are on her, and she sways a little, dizzy from the ambush. She squints, her hearing blunted by white noise, flashes of the afternoon it happened hot in her skull. The handcuffs. The helicopters. *Bandstand* on the television. Teenagers dancing to Neil Sedaka's "Little Devil"; she still remembers the song. Images reel by. The sunlight, golden at that hour, slanting in through the window. The heat of the casserole dish through her oven mitts, the ones with rabbits. Ceramic smashing into a hundred pieces on the floor.

"We can chase criminals all we want," Cornwell continues, "but only brave women like Beverley Lightfoot know what it's like to share a life with one, and with *that* sort of information, that sort of insight into the lives of murderers, shared by women like this one right here, we can help build a picture of these dangerous men and what they do behind closed doors."

She can smell him then—Henry—what he used to smell like when he crawled back into their bed late at night. She swears the scent still lingers in her nostrils, Old Spice and engine oil. She'd slide herself over to where he lay and curl herself across his back like the shell of a pill bug.

"So, without any further ado, here's introducing to the stage the remarkable Mrs. Beverley Lightfoot."

The applause is deafening. She can see, among a celestial burst of brightness, the whites of their watching eyes. Somehow, she steps toward the microphone at the center of the stage. As she nears it, she reaches out for it. The seams of her dress are digging in at the base of her neck. The bow is too tight. She pictures neat, red indentations in her skin.

She'd wanted to help—that's all—to try to stop there being more victims. That is why she had said yes. That is why she is here. But she is finding it almost impossible to remember how to speak.

Someone clears their throat.

She gulps. "Good evening." The microphone shrieks. She recoils, glances to the side of the stage and sees Cornwell watching her intently.

She steps to the microphone again, not too close this time. Lowering her eyelids against the light, she takes a deep, audible breath.

"Good evening, ladies and gentlemen. My name is Beverley . . . Lightfoot. I was the wife of Henry James Lightfoot, who, between 1957 and 1961, killed seven women in the Bay Area of California. This is my story."

THE APPLAUSE IS a roar as she leaves the stage. She is not quite sure how she has done it, but she has, and were she not so numb from the effort, she might consider that it has gone well.

Cornwell nods reluctantly as she moves past. Then he turns his head as an officer calls out from the bottom of the steps.

"We're headed back to the precinct, Chief," the man says, eyes lingering on the lipstick stain on Beverley's dress. "There's been an incident." He assesses her as if weighing whether she should hear what he is about to say. "We've got a body. You're not going to want to miss this one. It's . . . unusual."

THREE

"Have you tried bleach?" Margot calls from her reclined position atop a pool float. Her head is pounding, the sun casting bright cobweb patterns through her eyelids. She flops an arm to the side and allows her fingers to graze the water's cool surface, quivering blue and gold. She really shouldn't have drunk so much last night, but she didn't know that Tony Curtis would show, and he's always a devil with the Gibsons.

She paddles her way to the ladder, pulls herself out of the water and stands for a while, allowing the day's molten heat to dry her limbs. By her toes, a tiny salamander idles, licks its eye. The air is replete with heat-woozy honeysuckle and a chemical whiff of chlorine. The kitchen doors have been pulled wide, and the tinny sounds of the Beatles leak out from the radio. "Paperback Writer." She hates that cutesy song. She wraps a towel around her waist, sits, wonders if someone might fetch her some Tylenol if she looks pathetic enough.

"She's right," says Elsie. "Lipstick should shift with bleach. Just soak it, hang it on the line. It'll dry in no time."

"Kids, stay where I can see you!" Beverley hollers suddenly. Margot's head snaps up with a crick. Benjamin and Audrey, who have been chasing each other relentlessly around the lawn, freeze and nod dumbly at their mother. "I *really* don't think I should be airing my dirty laundry for the neighbors." Bev turns back to them, adjusting the straps of her polka-dot one-piece. "It's not a good look for me."

"Honey, I'd be more worried about that creep at number forty-four ogling your underwear." Margot pulls a copy of the *LA Times* from her purse and rests her sunglasses on the top of her head.

"That's not nice." Elsie's British accent barbs the admonishment. "We don't judge people like that."

"We do if they are creeps," Margot replies, overly loudly, turning the pages of the newspaper. "That's when we do judge, Elsie."

Margot glances at Beverley, hoping for a laugh, but her friend seems distracted, probably thinking about what happened at the gala last night. She was so nervous in the run-up to it. In fact, Bev's been nervous about everything of late. She wasn't jittery like this when they met, four years ago. When Margot first laid eyes on Beverley, she'd felt a stab of jealousy. Bev was younger than her, but that wasn't really the issue. She was also beautiful, with that maddening sort of beauty that just seems to happen. Beverley didn't even need to try. Her whole family looked like something from the pages of *Ladies' Home Journal*; it was all too easy to picture them gathered at a bowling alley or slurping through straws at a malt shop. Margot worked hard on her own appearance—getting her hair set, wearing makeup, investing in the expensive face creams she'd heard Liz Taylor used. It was a cultivation, a tending to a garden that could so very easily turn. Bev had baggage, sure, and it extended way beyond the fact that her husband was a killer. Margot had clocked it a mile off: daddy issues, the need for a man to control her. That was why, Margot knew, Bev was most rattled by her husband's being put behind bars. Never mind what he did to that girl with a fire poker. There was now no one left to tell her what to do.

When Margot and Elsie arrived at her house a couple of hours ago, Bev had told them that things had wound down early at the gala; a bunch of officers had been called back to their precinct because a body had been discovered nearby.

Margot should ask more questions, but she's keen not to dwell on corpses today—not with this hangover.

"Jesus, I'm melting." She pours more mint julep from the jug, pokes at it with the swizzle stick and then downs it in three open-throated gulps. She glances at Bev again, sighs.

"You still thinking about last night?" She'll indulge her. "It sounds like you did a great job."

"I should never have done it." Bev shakes her head, lips tight. "All that attention. All that gossip. The neighbors have all been talking about it, about us—I know it."

"Well, if we did what everyone thought we should do, Bev, we'd be spending the rest of our days prostrate in church."

Margot has never felt guilty about what her husband did. What was guilt but a useless artifact from the past? She reaches for the cocktail jug and pours herself another large measure. "I will not go gentle into that good night!" she cries as she pours.

The radio announcer signals the lunchtime news bulletin, and Margot notices Beverley shift to hear it better.

"And screw the neighbors. Who cares if people gossip?" Margot continues over the headlines. "I've got nothing to hide."

"Do they know who we are?" Elsie asks, pulling her shawl around her shoulders. "The neighbors?"

"They probably think we're some sort of *fabulous* divorcées club." Margot reaches for the sun lotion and squirts it across her chest.

"More like a survivors' club," says Elsie.

"What? That's depressing." Beverley frowns.

"Exactly. Stop that. I don't want to be depressed," says Margot, lighting a cigarette. "In fact, I want to make margaritas. Beverley, where's your salt?" She stands, tosses the newspaper onto the table.

"Most men who kill murder their wives or partners," Elsie continues. "We're still here, so technically we are survivors."

Margot rolls her eyes.

"We *are*," Elsie urges. "We're victims in all this, too. Don't forget that."

"Sorry, but this"—Margot circles the air in front of her face with a finger—"is not what a victim looks like."

Elsie huffs loudly. She always was a prude. They'd met only at Beverley's request. Bev and Elsie had been exchanging letters about their husbands for months, and Beverley thought it would do Margot good to meet someone else in the same situation as theirs.

It is true, though. Criminals' wives—victims of their husbands' indiscretions—sometimes had a certain *look*. Margot could see it in newspaper articles and rolling coverage on the TV. Especially those wives who loyally followed their husbands to court, adamant that their Joe/Bob/Frank could never be responsible for such abominable acts. *He was such a kind man,* they'd parrot in interviews after trials that laid out in scrupulous, incontestable detail how their husbands had slaughtered multiple people. *He never raised a fist at home.*

"We're not simpering wives. We learned the truth; we got mad; we moved on," says Margot.

"Is this really moving on?" Beverley asks doubtfully. "I just had to relive everything in front of a roomful of cops."

"Well, I'm drinking cocktails at two thirty in the afternoon. I've moved on," Margot replies.

"I made melon balls." Elsie shrugs weakly.

When the air has turned lilac, the amber trails of the fading sun smearing across the skyline, Margot helps Beverley clear up in the kitchen. The children are in bed and Elsie has left for the drive back to Burbank, but the TV's still on in the living room, Ronald Reagan's voice, bemoaning beatniks and radicals, filtering through the walls.

"Did you decide what to do about the anniversary, by the way?" Margot asks, tightening an apron covered in little brown rabbits around her waist. "Five years—that's a milestone, right?"

"What did you do for yours?" Beverley asks, wiping her hands on a dishcloth before tossing it on the mint-green countertop. Behind her, the matching refrigerator, covered in children's artwork, emits a faltering hum.

It felt like both minutes and years since the truth about Margot's husband, Stephen, had come out. She turns and leans back against the sink, pulling on yellow rubber gloves, a cigarette clasped between her teeth. "Drank about ten Manhattans and passed out on the couch."

"Margot . . ."

"All right, all right. I went to church."

There is a short silence.

"Margot Green! Church?"

Margot knows she does not belong at church. She is not church. She is Hollywood mansions and fuchsia chiffon. But the truth is, she hadn't known what to do when five years rolled round for her, either.

"Hated every second of it, of course," Margot continues, changing her mind about the hideous apron and unlacing it with a tug. "But that was years ago now." She tosses the apron on the counter and waves a hand dismissively after it. "Just do whatever feels right—even if that's nothing."

"Well, there is something."

Margot pauses, intrigued.

Beverley reaches behind the bread bin and pulls out an envelope. "I got this. Someone left it on my windshield last night, after the gala."

Margot pulls off the gloves, reaches for the envelope and reads.

"They want you to go on TV?" She looks up from the letter. "For the anniversary?"

"Just a local network. Nothing major."

"That *is* major. What are you going to do?"

"I'm going to ignore it, obviously." Beverley seems to have rehearsed the answer. "I can't go on television. I barely got through last night."

Margot tucks the letter back into the envelope and studies her friend. "You know you don't have to do this, Bev—any of it."

"What do you mean?" Bev's hand goes to her neck, a habit of hers.

"The radio's been on all day. The TV, too. And your scrapbook, with all the news stuff..." Margot knows Beverley keeps every newspaper article she comes across about crime, kidnapped women, shithead husbands...

"I don't want to miss anything important."

"Right. But you do know you are not personally responsible for the safety of other women just because of what your husband did, don't you?" Margot fixes her eye. "It's not your fault."

Beverley briefly looks taken aback, and then the radio flicks over to the evening news. Margot sees her straighten to attention once more. It must be exhausting to be so hyperaware all the time.

"We cannot keep bad people from doing bad things."

Bev blinks up at her, blue eyes wide, clear and determined. "Can't we?"

FOUR

THE CLACKERS ARE already in the office. Elsie attempts to arrive before them most days to prove how dedicated she is to her position, but it is as if they sleep in the walls, an army of robots assembling as soon as the lights spring on. Even if Elsie somehow got in before the sun came up—arriving, her eyes red ringed and sore, as the tobacconists set out their stalls—the women would be at their desks, straight backed in pastel pussy bows, clack, clack, clacking away at their typewriters.

When Elsie was made assistant to the newspaper's editor, Paul Hunter, she thought that she'd made it, that she was a step closer to her dream of one day writing for the *Los Angeles Signal*. She knew she was smart enough, hardworking enough, that she had more qualifications than most of the men in the office. She had notebooks crammed full of story ideas, sample columns, corrections she would make to previous days' articles. Perhaps she could have a little section to oversee. Books? Theater? Instead, she finds herself infuriatingly stuck, fetching coffee, typing letters, sourcing Dodgers tickets for Paul's most valuable contacts.

She takes a seat at her desk. It's neat, with just a few books lined up—Joan Didion, Katherine Anne Porter, Truman Capote—her typewriter always clean. A newspaper lies open to the crossword, almost complete. As her colleagues flow in, her mind scratches away at the final clue. *Capital of Albania.* She's sure she knows it.

She greets the morning's arrivals with a smile, a "Good morning, Charles," a gracious acceptance of the work they sling on her pile.

"Tell Hunter I'm still waiting for his notes on the Bobby Seale story. Did they get lost somewhere?"

"I need to switch my meeting with Paul from eleven forty-five to three fifteen. You think you can remember that, sweetie? It's important. I've got Gregson on my case."

Yes, Sweetie could remember it. Sweetie would run rings around the rest of them if she were given the chance—although she could never show that she felt herself worthy of more than just an assistant's job. She could never mark herself out like that. Promising young women didn't get on well at the *Signal*. Forget sloppiness with a typewriter; the worst thing you could be labeled as at this office was a firecracker. *Ah.* Elsie reaches for a pen, scrawls the letters *T-I-R-A-N-A*.

Paul Hunter arrives just after nine, and Elsie is intrigued to see that there is a woman with him. She is tall. Her hair, unlike that of the other women in the office, is not pin curled or frozen with Aqua Net. It is wild, frizzy, loose around her shoulders. She is not dressed like the Clackers or the assistants, either. She is not even wearing a skirt or heels or makeup. She has a pantsuit on. The men will lose their minds at a pantsuit.

"All right, listen up, everybody." Hunter claps his hands until the hubbub dies down. Above, an industrial light bulb flickers as a bluebottle fries.

"This is Patricia Fowler, our new reporter." He seems to gesture specifically to the pantsuit. "We're lucky to have her on board. She'll be an asset to the team."

Patricia looks as if she is about to speak, but Paul places a firm hand on her wrist.

"She has a ton of experience, most recently at the *Times*."

The Clackers raise their eyebrows. Patricia, Elsie notices, is glaring at Paul's hand on hers.

"She'll be working with Mattson and Hope on news, assisting Heston on crime and running the domestic column, of course."

Elsie resists the urge to scoff. How come *this* woman has been brought in as a reporter and she's still running around after Paul Hunter? Elsie is smart enough to do a reporter's job; she knows she is. Sure, she doesn't have this Patricia's experience at the *Times*, but what else can she have that Elsie doesn't?

"Straight to it, then," Hunter barks. "Department heads: in my office."

Elsie longs to be called into the morning meeting—to be offered a seat at the table, to be in the thick of it, floating her own story ideas. *How about something on women's roles in the anti-war movement across the state? What about a profile on Bobbi Gibb, the woman who snuck in and ran the Boston marathon alongside all those men?* Instead, she watches as several identical figures file into Paul's office, their trousers the color of burned toast, their pallid bald spots deprived of sunlight. Then suddenly, to Elsie's astonishment, Hunter stands and beckons her in through the doorway. She inhales sharply, scrapes back her chair so fast that it screeches. Perhaps this is it. Perhaps the hiring of Patricia has opened his eyes. Perhaps he *finally* has a story that needs her considered female perspective. Even if it's predictable—maternity statistics, women's health, some Hollywood wedding—she'll do it.

By the time she reaches the door, he has sat down again, and the group is discussing the headlines. Selman, the deputy news chief, is listing the day's top stories: missing women, civil rights marches, John Lennon hates Jesus.

She clears her throat.

"Yes, Elsie?" Hunter says briskly, shuffling a thick stack of papers. She could read them, sure, offer her opinion, correct his grammar. She feels her fingers start to twitch but resists reaching out for the documents.

He glances up. "I'm meeting Halliday later. My cabinet's looking dry. I need scotch. Fetch, please." He waves her off.

Her shoulders sink.

"Elsie?" Hunter seems annoyed that she is still standing in the doorway.

"Right away, Mr. Hunter." She pulls the door closed behind her, shutting out the rising laughter from inside.

LATER, WHEN THE afternoon lull is seeping in, Elsie returns with the liquor.

She knocks for Hunter and, finding his office empty, crosses to his desk and places the brown paper package in the middle of it. As she turns to leave, the telephone rings. She pauses. The call must have come directly to him rather than to the general number, which Elsie usually answers before patching the caller through. Still, she should answer the call. It could be important, and she doesn't want to be yelled at for missing a message.

"Paul Hunter's office."

The man at the other end of the line is abrupt, says he's from the county sheriff's department.

"It's about the Jane Doe from the gala," he says. "Blondie. Get him to call me. I'm around until six."

Elsie scratches down the details, tucks the message underneath the bottle of scotch and tries to ignore the prickle in her fingers. This must be the same body that Bev told them about last night. She pictures the story moving through the newsroom—silt along the channels of a river. Hunter will return from his meeting and find the message; he will call the sheriff's department, then open his door wide to call in the reporters for an urgent meeting. Patricia Fowler might even be admitted. Elsie will be forced to sit outside while everything happens behind that closed door.

She'll get lost outside it all.

A Jane Doe. She knows what the term means: an unidentified female body. Elsie pauses at the threshold of Hunter's office, her fingers flexing almost imperceptibly at her side. She could change all this; for once, she could be the one in the office who is first on the story.

She turns, strides back to the desk, picks up the note and places it firmly in her pocket.

FIVE

"PASS ME MY smokes, will you, Bev?"

Beverley lifts her head from Roger's chest and reaches across to the nightstand, hands the box over, resists the urge to take one for herself. Being in this bed with Roger Greaves always sets her slightly on edge. It's the same bed she shared with her husband, with the same faded floral sheets, the indentation of Henry's limbs still deep in the old mattress. Sometimes, at night, when Roger's gone and she's alone, she eyeballs the shape as if it's the chalk outline of a body at a crime scene. She supposes it is, really—the lingering aftermath of a death.

After everything happened, she hadn't wanted to leave her home, as Margot had, across the country, from New York to LA, or as Elsie had, from a shitty house in the Haight to an even shittier apartment in Burbank. The catch is that she still feels Henry in the walls, in the fabric of the couch, in the old, clouded tumblers at the back of the cupboard.

She returns to Roger's warmth, bringing her ear to his heartbeat, drowning out "Strangers in the Night" on the bedside radio. The sheets are mussed at their ankles, her knee hooked over his thigh. Clothes lie discarded on the floor. Roger's police badge, always removed with the greatest care, sits next to a blister pack of Valium Beverley snuck from her mother's bathroom cabinet. The room is heavy with humidity, but she won't have the window open, and by now Roger knows better than to ask. Her skin tingles with the rock-pool damp of cooling sweat. The smell of the act hangs low in the air.

Beverley uses the opportunity to ask about the body found on the night of the gala. She can't quite put her finger on it, but there's something about the timing, the fact that Beverley was there when Cornwell found out, that makes her feel connected to it in a way. Roger usually has no qualms about sharing the details of cases with Beverley. She chooses to believe that's because he trusts her, and not because she is so inconsequential that he knows she would have nothing to do with the information anyway.

"Oh, that." The words are squashed in his throat as he swallows smoke. "Cornwell's got his eyes on the Kings for it." He exhales.

"Who?"

"You must have heard of the Kings." He leans on an elbow, fixes his flinty eyes on her. "What with all that digging you do, the newspapers."

She can't help but feel that he's mocking her.

"They're a gang," he explains. "Slick. Dangerous. This is just the sort of thing they'd do."

"But who was it?"

"The Kings, Bev."

"No, who was it that was murdered?"

"Oh." Roger draws on his cigarette again; it makes the dimples in his cheeks sink deeper. He holds two fingers of his left hand in the air. "A—quote, unquote—good-time girl."

"Roger."

"Not my quote!" He laughs.

"Roger."

"I'm sorry, Bev, but these women put themselves in vulnerable positions. What do they expect?"

She grows hot. "I think it's fair to expect not to be killed, Roger."

He pauses, then laughs regretfully, shakes his head. "Point taken." He reaches over, trails his fingers across the tops of her arms.

They're quiet for a while.

"You're a remarkable woman, Bev. You know that," he says eventually as he leans back on the pillow. "To have the strength to talk about this stuff..."

She didn't feel remarkable. She felt exhausted and cheap. She hated being the other woman. She knew what they were doing was wrong, but it had been five years now since she'd first seen Roger and Tom Cornwell, with her husband in handcuffs, helicopters circling overhead. She had not known then, of course, that they would become entangled in one another's lives, that Cornwell would remain a looming presence, that Roger would become a familiar routine for her—as a consequence not of any intense passion or attraction but of physics, two points drawn to each other in a steady, unswerving way. And so it went: Roger stopping by after work, once the kids were in bed, when Enid thought he was working late. They'd make love; they'd talk; they'd drink. Beverley would talk about the children—how the other mothers waiting for the school bus would shame her; how her own mother, so adroit at criticism, liked to tell her that her children would be ruined by what their father had done. Henry was the reason Beverley's son never slept at night, Alice said. Henry was the reason he wet the bed, lashed out. Roger liked to take the chance to reminisce, to tell stories. He'd speak about his time in the military, about the travels he'd made as a young man, about his childhood in Chicago. She'd drift off, soothed by the low timbre of his voice, the comforting presence of someone there in the room.

Once Roger has gone, she locks the door behind him, then clicks into the monotony of her nighttime routine. First, she checks all the windows and grabs the flashlight from beside the radio. She opens the back door but does not step out into the yard. The moon has retreated; the night is clear, crammed with stars, the twitch of heat still alive in the air. She flicks on the flashlight and roams the shadows with the beam, focusing on corners and any shrubs she hasn't cut back quite far enough. When she's satisfied, she turns it off and shuts the door, locking it, then trying the handle. She makes her way to the entrance hall and stands at one end of the sideboard there. Leaning her whole body weight against it, she pushes it along the wall until its edge is at the front exterior wall. Then she swivels it, as best she can, ninety degrees, so it is flush against the front door, sealing everything off from the outside world. After that, she goes to the living room, grabs a glass vase and three heavy books. She returns to the sideboard, places the books on top of one another and then finishes with the vase. If anyone even tries to open the door in the middle of the night, the glass will smash and Beverley will be alerted.

Then she pours herself a drink and retrieves the box from the pantry.

Inside the box is a scrapbook, the size of a large photo album, ring bound and well-worn. She opens it and flips through the pages. Newspaper clippings are stuck neatly throughout. She runs her fingers over the first and hovers them over the picture: Henry working a grill at a backyard party, tongs in hand, hamburger meat sizzling away. The editors had clearly chosen a picture intended to make him look like your average Joe, but Henry was never average, at least not physically—that thick, black hair; those eyes that looked as if they had been whittled from stone simply to gaze at her, eyes that would bore in so that she felt forever pinned by him. She remembers the picture being taken. It was the Fourth of July and they'd invited Beverley's mother and a few of Henry's coworkers from the air-conditioning company over for a barbecue. The yard was strung with stars and stripes and the weather was fine, bees idling around the jasmine. She'd worn a sleeveless blouse with heart-shaped buttons. She remembers fiddling with them while the wives tried to engage her in conversation about potato salad. She'd been distracted. She and Henry had argued just before he struck the pose for the camera. She had bought the wrong frankfurters from the grocery store, and Henry had called her out in front of everybody. When they'd turned away, he had administered his punishment. She flexes her wrist now, as if she can still feel the sting of the tongs, still hear the hissing of her own flesh. She trails her fingertips over her skin. There is a patch where it has lightened, been toughened by scar tissue, grown harder over the years.

She smooths the edges of the clipping. The headline—THE HEATWAVE KILLER UNMASKED—still leaves her numb. She flips quickly through the rest of the book, each article detailing a different crime, a different murderer, cases from the Bay Area to San Diego. Elsie's ex-husband is in there: Albert Moss, the community college teacher who trailed women home after his classes. There are all sorts of men trapped between the pages—men who bludgeoned women to death with hammers, loners who stalked girls from their cars late at night. Beverley never liked to overlook anything. If a woman went missing in Sacramento, she'd add a clipping to the book. If a husband shot his former lover in Santa Maria, she'd neatly score the story out from the newspaper, find a fresh new space, fix it to the page.

She scans more articles, murderers allotted paragraph upon paragraph while their victims are sidelined to passing whispers of acknowledgment. When the women *are* given space, it is to make clear that they had brought their own murders upon themselves. By making themselves known. By staying out late. By kissing the guy. By wearing the short dress. By not taking self-defense classes. By being pretty. By not being pretty enough. By being fat. By being short. By being striking and loud and ambitious. Women brought death upon themselves simply by being women, it seemed. Avoiding death was just an expected part of life for them—the constant mental calculations, the weighing up of choices, of risk.

She turns to a clean page and pulls scissors and a tube of Elmer's Glue-All from the box. Then she goes to the pile of papers on the countertop and picks up the copy of the *LA Times* that Margot had left behind on the patio.

She is flipping quickly past stories of space missions and civil rights marches when a small photograph toward the back of the paper makes her pause. She smooths out the page so she can examine the article more carefully. She wasn't sure if the story would have been picked up yet, but here it is: a grainy crime-scene shot—a gurney with a body bag laid out on top; police tape; the glow of lights on the sidewalk.

POLICE WORKING TO IDENTIFY MYSTERY VICTIM

The article beneath the photograph is perfunctory, scant on details, but Beverley immediately knows this is the victim from the night of the gala, the woman Roger had referred to as a good-time girl. A woman working as a prostitute, Beverley supposes, but nevertheless a woman just like she was, whose identity has now been lost, plastered over, replaced with the stark image of a body bag and the rear wheels of waiting police cars.

The moment jolts back into Beverley's mind—the coarse blare of the spotlights, Tom Cornwell's eyes widening, the officer at the bottom of the stairs.

She runs her fingers over the photograph, picturing uniformed men in muttered discussion, tense looks; a woman's fragile body left on the sidewalk, abandoned, life snuffed out. Having been in the area, so close, on the night the woman was killed, Bev can't help but feel like part of her story.

It's unusual. That's what Cornwell's officer had said. *You're not going to want to miss this one.* She clearly remembers that now. But Roger didn't mention anything unusual about it tonight. Nothing unusual is mentioned in the article, either.

She lifts the paper, holds it a little closer, studies the photograph again.

What are they hiding?

SIX

Elsie had received an agitated call from Beverley, who'd remembered what the police had said about the body of the Jane Doe. She'd then asked Elsie if she knew anything about a gang known as the Kings, if she might be able to find out more about them at work.

She had been surprised that Beverley was taking such an interest in the case, but then she'd remembered the scrapbook, Beverley's need to collect and categorize bad news—as if keeping on top of awful things was a way to stay in control, to stop more awful things from happening. There was clearly something up with this murder, more to the story, something the police were concealing. So Elsie was interested, too. And wasn't it her job as a journalist—well, okay, a journalist's assistant—to find out what was being hidden?

She already knows the cops have given the woman a nickname, "Blondie"—that's what the county sheriff had said on the phone—but she knows she'll get no further information by asking them anything directly. She's already tried, of course—called the number from the note that she'd stashed in her pocket, received nothing in return but a slammed-down phone and a dial tone.

She takes a sip from her third stale coffee of the morning and ignores her pounding caffeine headache. She scours the office floor for Robert Heston, the *Signal*'s chief crime reporter. She needs more information about this Jane Doe, and she knows Heston could be a way to get it—if she asks delicately enough.

But Robert Heston is not an early-morning sort of guy. Robert Heston chain-smokes Chesterfields and smells as if he has been out drinking all night, every night—because that is exactly what he has been doing. His skin is pale, and there are large bags under his eyes. She has never once seen the man look rested. His hair is dull. His expression is often vacant, uninterested. Elsie thinks he is the most inspirational man in this office.

An hour or so—and two more coffees—later, the reporter finally lopes in. Elsie waits for him to take a seat, her teeth buzzing from the caffeine. She watches as, instead of reaching for his notebook or his typewriter, he leans his forearms on his desk, collapses his head into them and groans. He must be hungover again. Elsie cuts a glance over her shoulder, but she knows Hunter's not in yet—not that he'd punish Heston for arriving at work in this state. Heston is the best crime reporter in California; Elsie knows he's at the *Signal* only because he got fired from the *Times* for getting wasted at the Christmas party and urinating on the editor's desk. Before that, he broke the story of the Elmwood Avenue Killer. He got the only interview with Jack Ruby's attorney. He scooped everyone else in the city when he exposed police wrongdoing in the Toogood case—an officer had ignored vital evidence in the Klan's murder of a civil rights activist. His editor would have been pissed about that—Heston could have jeopardized the paper's relationship with the police with that exposé—but Heston won a Pulitzer, so who was anyone to argue?

The man is a stellar talent, a wordsmith, a genius. Right now, he appears to be drooling on his desk.

Elsie makes her way over and hovers at his shoulder, clears her throat. Heston does not move. She clears her throat again, more loudly. He slowly rolls over, peering up at her from under an elbow.

"What does he want?" he groans.

In her peripheral vision, Elsie notices Patricia Fowler watching them. She can't imagine Patricia ever turning up to the *Times* reeking of bourbon. In fact, she can't imagine many other reporters getting away with what Heston gets away with. She looks down at him and smiles politely. The veins in his eyes have burst, his hands are covered in scratches and she's pretty sure his shirt is stained with burger relish.

"Paul didn't . . . Mr. Hunter didn't send me." She straightens her shoulders. "I wanted to ask you something."

"What's that?" Heston flops back onto his forehead, then pushes himself up with his hands, shaking his head quickly and widening his eyes to sober up.

Elsie steels herself.

"I wondered if you'd heard anything about a Jane Doe—someone the LAPD might be referring to as Blondie, someone who might have some links to the Kings."

"To the what?" He straightens, and frowns at her. "Why are you asking about the Kings? You're a . . . secretary."

"Personal assistant."

She was a secretary once, when she first started at the *Signal*. She was fantastic at that job, a meticulous Clacker. She never let any errors slip through, as if her brain were a tightly strung net cast over the words, scooping up anything found wanting. She'd present her pages to the editors at regular intervals, her eyes shining, chest full. She'd long for them to appraise her work, to grade it as if writing a report card, to tell her she was at the top of the class. It was a need for constant validation that she'd had ever since she was a child growing up in England, her father far away, on the muddy beaches of France, for the bulk of her life, until he returned with a parasite, a malevolent rage inside that changed things forever.

"Get out of here," Heston orders. "Less questions."

"Fewer," Elsie tries to interject.

"More . . . typing, or whatever it is you do." He waves his hand, then returns his head to the desk.

Elsie turns away, forces a stage laugh; she doesn't want him to see that his words have scorched her. She makes her way back to her typewriter, then takes a seat, rearranging a stack of notepaper to keep her hands busy. Her eyes prickle with the threat of tears, which makes her even more frustrated. Why will they not treat her like one of their own? Yes, she's "just" a personal assistant, not a reporter, but she has proven herself to be good at her job. If only they would let her write, if only she could show them that she can do it . . .

She was primed for this job. After it all happened—after she discovered the extent of what Albert had been doing, just how many there were—she became ravenous for facts. When the trial and the sentence and the media frenzy had passed, any facts would do. She read encyclopedias, road atlases, phone books. She needed to know things—anything at all. That was when the puzzles started, too, when she found a taste for crosswords, for Martin Gardner's Mathematical Games column in *Scientific American*—an insatiable desire to solve, to put things in order, to trust her own brain again. After she learned of Albert's crimes, the grimy details of the world refracted into sharp focus. She saw the film of grime on everything—the peeling paint on otherwise beautiful buildings, the rats on the subway tracks, the discarded gum on the undersides of railings. She saw that muddy finish on people, too, could see their bad parts with only a glance.

In the office, she surveys the books on her desk, stories of men gone rotten, of the ways in which humans can so easily harm one another. Those who kill are often lionized in the press; Elsie knows that now. Revered, in a way, for their charisma, for the alien wit with which they can outsmart their victims. As if their brutal transgressions propel them to a different plane than the one the rest of society is on. But Albert was not really that smart. Albert was boring; he was awkward. Albert could never have been described as "magnetic." Eczema bloomed around his eyebrows and on his elbows, which were cracked and red. The back of his head was beginning to lose its hair, revealing a shining, freckled expanse of skin, like a monk's tonsure. There had been nothing dangerous about him, and everything dangerous about him at the same time. But it was easier for the police to cast him simply as otherworldly, wily, "different from us," because only that could explain why it took them so long to catch him.

"Hey." Someone is calling out to her in a hushed voice. "Hey, assistant girl."

She turns, and when she realizes it's Patricia, her cheeks betray her.

"Why are you asking about the Jane Doe?" she questions when Elsie hurries over. Patricia has a low voice for a woman, a drawl more than anything else; it stirs something strange in Elsie's stomach.

"I'm sorry," Elsie stammers. "You weren't supposed to hear that."

Patricia leans back and smiles. A suede jacket is slung over her chair. Elsie could never get away with a suede jacket.

"You looking for a story or something?" Patricia asks, the side of her mouth quirked.

Elsie falters, gives a fractured, unconvincing laugh. "I'm just a secretary. I mean, a personal assistant."

Patricia laughs drily. "If I'd accepted being *just a secretary*, I would have made my father very happy. And let me tell you, no one wants to do that less than me."

Is it a trap? What if Hunter is listening in?

"I can't help you unless you tell me why you're asking." There's something confrontational, schoolboyish about Patricia.

Elsie looks quickly around her again. Robert Heston, out of earshot, has a line of coffee cups arranged in front of him and he is downing them in quick succession.

"I heard there was something unusual about the body," Elsie ventures, trying to hold Patricia's gaze even though she feels entirely out of her depth.

"Okay." Patricia considers this, smiles again. "Well, firstly, the Jane Doe's not a Jane Doe anymore."

"What?"

"She's not blond, and she's not a hooker, despite what the cops want us to believe."

"How do you know that?" Elsie hates how eager she sounds, but this is gold; Patricia has the details she needs.

"Eh." Patricia waves a hand. "I used to help the crime guys at the *Times* when they were short-staffed. They let me in on it." She reaches for her coffee and takes a gulp. "I'm just enjoying making that guy's hangover worse." She gestures to Heston.

"What else do you know?" Elsie takes the seat next to Patricia, hoping she won't be put off by her zeal, and pulls out her notebook.

Patricia chuckles at the sight of Elsie with her pen poised, and taps the bottom of a pack of Lucky Strikes.

"Cheryl Herrera. She ran track." Patricia lights the cigarette, takes a drag. "Was about to go professional, by the sound of it."

"Herrera?" Elsie's pen moves fast. "How old?"

"Twenty-one. Final year of college."

Elsie pauses her scribbling, swallows. "How did she die?"

Patricia takes another long drag on the cigarette, blows out the smoke.

"Strangled."

Elsie grips her pen harder.

"Then whoever did it put an arrow through her eye."

Elsie's head whips up. "They . . . Sorry—*what?*" She cannot have heard that correctly.

"Mm-hmm." Patricia nods. "Right in the eyeball." She points at her own eye socket. "I'll eat my hat if it's the Kings. Too ostentatious."

Elsie wavers, unsure what to write in her notes, hypnotized by the image of an eyeball, an arrow. This must be what the police were talking about when they said there was something unusual about the body.

She frowns. "If she wasn't blond, why were the police calling her Blondie?"

"Yep. Not blond." Patricia flicks ash into the remains of her coffee. "Dark hair, olive skin." She looks briefly around the office, then tilts her head toward Elsie's. "But whoever did it put a wig on her—blond."

Elsie's mouth gapes. Is this what it feels like to be a reporter? To know what the police know but aren't telling anyone? It's like a drug in her system.

"How do I find out more about her—about Cheryl?" she asks.

Patti considers. "Buy me lunch and I'll get you an address."

Elsie bristles. She can't do that. It would be breaking the one rule she set for herself when she started at the *Signal*. No friendships. She can't let her colleagues get too close. They'd never understand how Albert hid it from her. They'd never understand how it makes you question yourself—that reckoning with your own sanity, what's happening inside your own brain. Plus, if they find out about her past, she'll be sacked, or shunned, her own story spread across the front page. No one would ever be convinced by an investigative journalist who'd failed to see what was happening right under her own nose.

She can't risk Patricia's finding out the truth about her. It would ruin everything she's worked for since Albert's arrest.

She should really wait for Hunter to get in. She should type his missives, fill his coffee cup.

But she's not letting anyone else have this story.

"Thank you, Patricia. Thank you. I'll just grab my coat."

"Please." The words come through a plume of fresh-puffed smoke: "It's Patti."

SEVEN

Margot reaches into the cooler and pulls out a beer. She opens it with her teeth, then leans back on her beach towel, shielding her eyes from the sun with her battered copy of *Valley of the Dolls*.

The day is sweltering, the mountains hunched around the lake doing little to ward off the glare from the water. The torched beach shrub is static, and she feels a slow trickle of sweat worming down the space between her shoulder blades. Duke is pooled in the shade of the parasol, panting audibly, his jowls hanging with slobber.

"An arrow? Holy moly." Margot takes a sip from the bottle, swallows. "That's not your average stab-and-go."

She hears Elsie tut.

It's been more than a week since Cheryl Herrera's body was found, on the night of the police gala, and Beverley has not stopped talking about it. Still, Margot supposes she doesn't really mind when the details are as juicy as this.

"It's got to mean something." Beverley pulls her swimsuit strap to the side and vigorously applies Coppertone sun cream beneath it. "It has to be some sort of message, right? Some cult thing? Who would do that?"

"How come you're so interested in this case, Bev?" Margot props herself up on an elbow.

"What do you mean?"

"Well, I get why Elsie's interested. That's a great story: an arrow in the eye. I'd read the hell out of that. But you?"

Bev sighs, shakes her head. "It's strange," she ventures after a pause, "but I feel sort of connected to her—to Cheryl."

"Okay," Margot replies dubiously. Bev's always been like this. Fatalistic. Seeing connections that aren't there, reading the daily horoscope in the newspaper. That's not Margot's style, but whatever you've got to do to get yourself through . . .

"I don't know, but the way they spoke about her, like she was some sort of spectacle, and the fact that it happened nearby, while I was up there talking about Henry—it all just feels weird."

"The universe sending you a message, Bev?" Margot gibes, regretting it when Bev doesn't smile in response.

"I just want to know who did this to her."

"I asked about that gang at work, Bev." Elsie pulls up the brim of her sun hat.

"Ah, there *is* someone alive under there," Margot quips. She does not get why Elsie insists on dressing like a nun. There's a decent figure beneath all that fabric. It's as if, Margot sometimes thinks, Elsie does whatever she can to avoid drawing the eyes of men, in order not to snag the attention of another bad apple.

"The Kings," Elsie continues, unfazed. "They're a street gang, started in Chicago but with offshoots across the country. Mainly, they deal in narcotics trafficking—cocaine, heroin, marijuana—but there are homicides, too. And gangs do leave warning signs and messages . . ."

"Interesting." Beverley wipes her lotioned hands on a towel.

"But why would a gang like that target a college student?" Margot asks.

"And it's such a visceral thing to do to a body," Bev muses, "to get an arrow and . . ." She trails off, eyes flicking briefly out to the water. "Isn't that odd? Kind of showy? I mean, that's not what Henry did, not what—" She glances at Margot and stops. Margot knows she's thinking about the kneecaps, the grim details of Stephen's crimes splashed across the news.

"The wig, too," Elsie agrees. "That's overkill"—she grimaces—"for want of a better word. I mean, it involves a lot of thinking, preparation, a lot of handling of the body. It's not like stabbing someone with a knife. It's not impulsive. It's as if whoever did it is some sort of professional."

"Is there a way of finding out if Cheryl had links to people like that, though?" Bev asks. "To these gangs?"

"I can do some more digging at work"—Elsie tucks a sweaty strand of hair under her hat—"but the crime guys didn't seem to think it was the Kings." She pauses briefly. "The wig, I think—it's not their style."

"Well, it's got to be someone out of their mind"—Margot reclines on her elbows—"to do a thing like that. Crazy." She swigs her beer, her eyes roving the beach. A group of state university students has assembled by the volleyball nets, all hard chests and mahogany limbs. They look like something from a Dr Pepper commercial. She turns her body toward them, waits for them to see her, for that familiar beat of warmth to spread across her skin. It's like a drug, knowing that she is being admired. She might be on the wrong side of thirty-five, but she can still draw glances. She'd felt the same thing when Stephen first put his eyes on her, from across the room at a dull political function at the Plaza. She'd gone there only because her friend Susie was waitressing and let her in through the back door. They'd thought Anouk Aimée might be there, and they were desperate to catch a glimpse of her. There were rumors that she was having an affair with the new district attorney. But she never showed, and Margot got stuck in conversation with some aide from Milwaukee who had dandruff and halitosis. She was sinking her fourth grasshopper when she felt a strange but not unpleasant sensation at the back of her skull. She turned to find its source and was met by the eyes of a handsome stranger. He was old. Not *old* old, but at least twenty years older than Margot. His suit was expensive, his hair was jet-black cut through with silver, and his eyes creased as he smiled and raised a glass to her. He was toasting her beauty, she knew, and while other women might have found it inappropriate, Margot basked in it, soaked it in. She couldn't let him know straightaway that she was interested, so she'd turned back to the guy with the bad hair and forced conversation about Eisenhower's coronary thrombosis for another few minutes. The stranger's eyes never left her back; she could feel them there.

Stephen took her home that evening, and she never left. The house was palatial, with Ford Thunderbirds in the driveway and columns around the front door that gave the whole place a Romanesque feel. It wasn't hard for Margot to act as if she belonged among the marble tiles and the Jackson Pollock paintings. She was used to being a social chameleon. How was anyone to know she wasn't rich—yet—and that her family did not have connections, or a beach house in the Hamptons? If she acted as if they did, then it could be so.

Cookie. That was what Stephen called her, showering her with gifts from the get-go—Italian lingerie, perfume, expensive jewelry whisked out from a sock drawer and presented with a flourish. In turn, Margot let Stephen watch her. She let him parade her around to his friends as if she were some rare, exotic bird. She was the consummate performer, acting the coquette, the party girl, the cozy girlfriend who'd massage his feet and fetch his slippers—whatever he desired. But when she caught him doing what he did, she was sure that she must have put in too many bad performances, that the lines on her face had started to show, that she'd failed to be entertaining enough for him. It enraged her to have been bested. For Margot, the worst thing about discovering that she was married to a killer was not the stories, the judgments, that came with it, but that it meant she was someone who could be duped.

"Margot." Her attention snaps back to the beach. Elsie is glaring at her expectantly, waggling a large silk scarf in her direction. "Your shoulders are burning."

She waves it away and sits up on her lounger. Shrieking comes from the water as one of the jocks lifts a girl easily onto his shoulders.

Bev is recounting the plan. "Elsie, you look further into the Kings, see if there's any connection with Cheryl's family. Margot, you and I will have a think about this arrow, see if there's any sort of symbolism to it, or any archery clubs in the area, anyone else who might have access to a weapon like that."

Margot nods, reaches for her beer. She's already caught one killer; she's sure she can do it again.

EIGHT

"DAMN IT." BEVERLEY grabs either side of the hedge trimmers and tries to pry them apart. The heat has a hold of everything, making the tool stubborn.

"Don't force it!" Beverley's mother hollers from her deck chair, positioned in the center of the front lawn to give her an acceptable view of Beverley at work. Alice takes a sip of her iced tea, crosses her knees, in slim white Jax pants, and peers over the top of her glasses. Her eyes are framed with sweeps of pale blue Avon eye shadow.

"You always force things." Alice flaps a hand. "They'll break, Beverley. You need to be more delicate."

Beverley's toes clench in her Chanel slip-ons; she can still feel the sand between them from the lake yesterday. She wishes she could do more to find out about Cheryl Herrera and her possible links to the Kings, but, unlike Elsie, she doesn't have access to an office full of crime reporters to draw on. She does, however, have her scrapbook. Maybe she could look through some of the old articles in there, see if any of them mentions an arrow.

The shears spring open suddenly. Beverley flinches, sighs and then wipes the sweat from her brow with her forearm. She scours the front yard, squinting in the glare of the sun. There's a lump in the grass, she notices. Meatball, the kids' pet tortoise, is forging a slow, determined path toward the road. She puts the shears down and gathers the tortoise in her arms, his shell alarmingly hot from the sun. She wishes she could get rid of the animal—Henry brought it home for Benjamin when he was tiny, one of his many impulsive acts, and whenever she sees it she can't help thinking of him—but you can't really burn a tortoise in the backyard like she did with the rest of her husband's possessions.

Alice watches silently as Beverley takes the creature inside and deposits him in the more secure surrounds of the kitchen. She leaves the door open when she returns, so she can hear the radio. The news bulletin will be on soon.

"Do you know what this song is called, Beverley, what they just said?" Alice scrunches her face in distaste. "Bev?"

But Beverley is distracted. The new neighbor across the street—Mr. Appleton, number forty-four, the man Margot joked would ogle Beverley's laundry—has opened his door and is making his way down his front path.

"Bev!" her mother calls again, incredulous. "It's called 'Let's Go Get Stoned.' Can you believe that?"

Mr. Appleton reaches his trash can, quickly surveys the street and then pulls the lid open, depositing what looks to be a bundle of blankets inside. He glances up and their eyes briefly meet, alarm flaming in Beverley's chest. But before she remembers her manners, before she can raise a forced hand in greeting, he has turned, hurrying with hunched shoulders back up the path.

"I've a right mind to call the station and complain." Alice reclines in her seat again, the ice in her tumbler clinking. "It's uncouth having the radio blaring out like this anyway. All the neighbors can hear. I'm *trying* to relax."

Her mother is not relaxing. Her mother has little interest in relaxing when she can observe Beverley's chores and deliver feedback instead.

Beverley picks up the shears and chews the side of her mouth. Mr. Appleton shuts the door behind him and she allows her eyes to linger on it, waiting to see if he'll open it again, peer out. But all is still, so she turns her attention back to her own front yard. It's looking good, neat. All the bushes are cut back, so there's nowhere for anything, or anyone, to lurk. The neatness, the tidiness, is a ritual she's been practicing ever since Henry was arrested. Neat and tidy keeps them safe.

"Did you call Ann Ember's son?" Alice asks, running her fingers over her set gray-blond hair, then checking her manicure. Alice's beauty has hardened into a brittle mask with age, although she is still clearly a woman who looks after herself, who smells of lotion and expensive perfume even while gardening. Beverley has seen pictures of her mother at her own age. They could be twins. Their smooth, clear skin so pale that their eyelids are almost translucent, laced with delicate purple veins; a dash of freckles across the nose; a sharply bowed top lip; full cheeks. How distressing it must be, Beverley sometimes thinks, when all you have to cling to is your looks, to have your former youth paraded in front of you, a reminder of everything that you have lost.

"I hope you've agreed on a date," Alice says. "He was really looking forward to hearing from you. Ann will be so disappointed if—"

Beverley tunes out the sound of her mother's voice. Alice has been trying to set her up with men for the past couple of years. She says it's damaging for the children not to have a male presence in their lives, that the neighbors would respect Beverley more if she had a partner. Beverley knows that it's wisest not to point out that she herself spent most of her childhood without a man in the house. Her father was unimaginative in his indiscretions, and before he left, Beverley stumbled upon him, more than once, with other women. A chaotic man, he was reliable in his cheating, and his cheating only. While Alice was busy in the kitchen during dinner parties, seeing to guests, arranging deviled eggs on trays, the skin of her neck blotchy from too many gimlets, he could be found with brassy blondes or feline brunettes in the bedroom he was supposed to share with his wife, trousers around his ankles, cigar dangling from beneath his mustache.

"I really haven't had a chance, Mom."

It's true. Beverley has been preoccupied, and not only with the Cheryl Herrera case. She had a call that rattled her yesterday—the producer from the news channel, following up on his letter, asking if she would appear on their morning show to mark the anniversary of Henry's arrest. Beverley had no idea how he'd found her number. She was supposed to have been delisted. She had stammered out an apology and slammed the phone down in panic.

Alice heaves a sigh. "You know"—she shifts forward on the deck chair, and Beverley knows she's in for it—"it's hurtful that you do not seize the opportunities I present to you, Beverley."

Beverley takes a breath.

"I'm sorry you think I'm a waste of space and that you don't need me—"

"I do need you, Mom." It always goes this way, Alice wounded and Beverley begging for forgiveness. *You want me to be unhappy because it means I'll never leave you.* That's what her mother said once, but Beverley knows that every word of the accusation was a truth about Alice herself.

Mrs. Akerman from a few doors down walks by with her chocolate dachshund. Beverley forces a smile. Alice springs up from her seat, almost curtsying as the woman strolls past.

"Good morning, Mrs. Akerman," Beverley calls.

The woman glances up, then snaps her attention back to the sidewalk, strides a little faster.

Alice purses her lips. "Now the neighbors know how you treat me."

Beverley is used to being ignored by the neighbors. They'd clung to her like curious birds in the aftermath of Henry's arrest. They were so sure, just as Beverley had been, that the police had arrested the wrong man.

Poor Beverley. Here's a casserole.

Poor Beverley. I'll just stop by for a cup of coffee, and we can have a good chat about it all.

They wanted gossip, of course, and they gawped wide-eyed as she described helicopter blades, officers streaming in, spreading dirt across the carpets, the mess the cadaver dogs made of the roses in the yard. When it became clear that Henry, the Heatwave Killer, had in fact murdered seven women, the birds retreated. Fast. Beverley was ostracized. If she was passing a neighbor as they were getting out of their car, they'd wait inside until she'd reached the end of the street. If someone was watering their lilacs and Beverley came out of her house to do the same, they'd put down their watering cans and slip wordlessly back inside. Accusations swirled around the street; everyone had an opinion. *She needs to go down as an accomplice,* she'd hear them whisper. *I don't understand how she's not as culpable as he is. There is no way in hell she didn't know.*

It was agonizing for Beverley to be a murderer's wife, to experience such a loss of control over her identity. It was a catastrophic detour from what she assumed her adulthood would bring. Her husband's crimes had forced on her social rules that she would forever have to obey. There was nothing she could do but keep her mouth shut, her eyes down and her business to herself.

"Who's that over there?" Alice calls, her attention caught by movement across the street.

Beverley looks. The curtains are twitching upstairs at number forty-four. Mr. Appleton disappears as soon as he sees them looking.

"Has the man never heard of a garden hose?" Alice crosses her legs and tuts.

She has a point. The plants in front of number forty-four are all dead or parched. Beverley hasn't seen her neighbor water the desert willow, deadhead the roses or mow the grass once since he moved in several weeks ago.

She glances back to the now-empty window, the now-still curtain, just as the sound of a breaking-news bulletin comes from the radio in the kitchen.

Beverley freezes. The newscaster's voice is lilting, suave. He is saying something about a woman, a body. This must be it. She expects to hear Cheryl Herrera's name publicly for the first time.

"*. . . body of twenty-year-old Fillmore cheerleader Emily Roswell,*" the newscaster is saying, "*pulled from the lake at Meadow Vine Golf Course late last night.*"

Beverley drops the shears and bolts inside. Her mother yells after her in protest.

"*Further details about Miss Roswell's death have not been revealed,*" the newscaster concludes.

Beverley's heart scuds. A strange buzzing sensation seizes her whole body.

A cheerleader.

Twenty years old.

Another murder.

She wipes her hands on her gardening apron and looks at the clock.

NINE

ON FIRST IMPRESSION, Las Espadas is just like one of those small, scrappy neighborhoods Elsie has seen in cop shows on TV. A little tired, but clinging on. No white picket fences. No cookie-cutter houses with front doors in flawless pigeon gray. Instead, there's traffic noise from the interstate. Potholed streets. Trash cans that are just a little too full.

There is already a crowd gathered outside the Herrera family's home, a community that has turned out in force to wish one of its own a final goodbye. Most people are knotted in groups; others sip drinks, finger shirt cuffs, not knowing where to look. A hundred or so yards away, a mourner hangs back, an outsider, just like Elsie, not sure through which entry point, or at what moment, to approach such an intimate scene.

There's a stall laid out in the Herreras' front yard. A large photograph of Cheryl—calm, wide eyes; thick, dark hair—has been placed atop a bunched white tablecloth. On a folding chair next to it, a young girl, perhaps a sister, sits with her hands clasped neatly on her lap.

Spread out across the tablecloth are candles for people to light and carry through the streets when the sun goes down.

It makes Elsie's chest tighten, the dignity of it, the coming together of a community in their grief.

She had hoped that by visiting, by finding out more about Cheryl and her family, she might start to fit together the very first pieces of the puzzle. She hadn't expected that being surrounded by so much loss, by people buried under the rubble of a dangerous man's actions, would affect her quite so much.

She glances up and sees a small man in a white T-shirt and a vest step out of the Herreras' front door. Elsie sucks in a breath. His is a face that has been weathered by grief. His polite smile—for neighbors who clasp his shoulder or take him in their arms as he passes—never quite reaches his eyes. Elsie knows this must be Cheryl's father.

The family will have had many visitors since Cheryl was killed, ten days ago—relatives attempting to console the inconsolable, neighbors carrying food and flowers, detectives, rubberneckers, those desperate to brush up against tragedy. There will be something uniting them all. She knows because she has felt it: the hum of people electrified by the relief that the universe didn't choose them, their sister, their daughter this time.

She makes her way through the crowd. Women are sobbing. Men are nodding, grave faced, their arms folded, their stomachs thrust forward, a posture that says, *We will not let this happen again.* Several of the younger mourners are in running gear. Elsie wonders if they might be from the same track team as Cheryl, makes a note of their kit.

Before she can hesitate further, she makes a beeline for Cheryl's father, then waits for a well-wisher to depart before she steps into view.

"Mr. Herrera, hi. I'm so very sorry for your loss." She holds out her hand and he takes it, but the grip is weak.

"My name is Elsie Parker. I'm a reporter with the *Tribune*."

She does not want to give her real name or reveal that she is actually from the *Signal*—not only because she does not want it getting back to Hunter that she broke rank, but because she is sure a grieving family would not let a lowly editor's assistant ask them questions about their dead daughter.

"Did Roachford not get everything he needs?" Mr. Herrera asks, not unkindly.

She pauses, wrong-footed. "Did . . . ?"

"Your colleague, Dom Roachford. Was there something else you needed to ask about Cherry?"

Of course someone else has been here. Any decent reporter in the area would have been here already. She scolds herself.

"Yes." She won't break the smile. "We just needed a couple of extra details for our story."

His eyes skitter around her face, checking for cracks.

"We just hope that getting the word out there will encourage anyone who knows anything to come forward."

It feels cheap—truly cheap—lying to a bereaved father. But, she hurriedly reminds herself, this is the only way she is going to get what she needs. And it is for a good cause. It's for Cheryl.

"Come on in." He nods over his shoulder, toward the front door. "We just want to catch whoever did this."

Tragedy has snatched all warmth from the house. There are people on the couch, drinking tea, their eyes ringed with red. Others are gathered in the kitchen, mouths turned downward, hair done nicely.

In the living room, condolence cards line the mantelpiece. There's an overspill of lilies in a thick glass vase, their stamens drooping so low that orange pollen has begun to collect on the carpet. There are ornaments on the shelves, little ceramic animals that Elsie's mother used to collect, too. Family photos hang on the walls. The tasseled cushions have been plumped especially for today's guests. The household certainly doesn't look, Elsie thinks, like the sort that would have links to a dangerous gang like the Kings.

She eyes the lilies. She received flowers—just one bunch, freesias—when Albert had been arrested. No note. She'd thought it odd. What on earth was she supposed to do with flowers? As the petals wilted, she had denied the authorities and the journalists nothing. Not because she was charitable, like Mr. Herrera, but because she hadn't had the strength to say no. She sat in her living room as they took over her house, her lips tentatively forming but never quite releasing the words she didn't feel she deserved to say: *Get out.*

Mr. Herrera offers her a cup of coffee. She declines, wondering where Cheryl's mother is, knowing it's entirely possible that she is behind the closed bedroom door.

"That's Cherry's room, right there." Mr. Herrera gestures to another door, which is propped open. There is a nameplate on its outside, sneakers and stars scrawled in lurid felt-tip pen. Elsie swallows. She had forgotten that Cheryl was only a few years out of high school.

Beyond the doorway, the room has a time-capsule quality about it, a strange, nostalgic glow—the kind that only rooms of the deceased can have.

"You can look if you like. I'd just ask that you don't touch anything." Cheryl's father glances at his feet.

She could wait, tell him that she wouldn't want to disturb his daughter's things, that it would be improper of her to snoop around. They could just talk here, on the couch, by the lilies. Instead, she rises and crosses to the room, called in by half-used cosmetics, by the wardrobe door left open, an avalanche of clothes bulging from inside. An old Chatty Cathy doll sits slumped on the windowsill, next to a forgotten ant farm. Its soil is dry, but a few insects still beaver away, oblivious to the somberness outside their glass. On the floor, a pair of purple socks lies wrinkled. Cheryl must have slipped them off, kicked them aside when she got too hot. Elsie takes care to step around them, not to touch anything—to leave the room just as it was when Cheryl was last here.

The walls are covered in certificates, Elsie sees. Medals dangle in thick clutches, hanging from nails wedged into the wall. She moves closer to try to read some of the details.

"She was about to go to state finals."

Elsie startles.

Mr. Herrera steps into the room and takes a bunch of medals down from a nail, loops the ribbons tightly around his palm, holds the disks out for her to inspect.

"She just had *it*," he says. "She was a superstar, Daddy's little princess."

Elsie watches his face, searches for something unsaid behind the words. She has a journalist's mind, and she knows a journalist's first impulse is to try to pin down details. Sometimes it's the father. She has to consider that possibility.

"She was clearly talented." Elsie brushes her fingertips across embossed gold. "You must have been proud. Was there anyone she ran track with who—"

"She would have made it senior year," he cuts her off, "but she got mono, was laid up sick—lost ten pounds of muscle."

Elsie imagines him weighing his daughter, invested in her routine, her performance, wanting her to reach her potential. Did it anger him when she didn't?

"She was going to be homecoming queen that year, too." He hangs the medals carefully back on the wall. "She cried herself to sleep. Her mother had even made the dress, bright blue. She looked so beautiful in it. Too beautiful." His laugh is hollow. "Too grown-up. I almost didn't let her go."

Elsie flinches as a memory daggers in. Her own father, the day of her homecoming, the strike of his arm across her face, the way her mother apologized for him, said he didn't mean it. He couldn't control himself. He'd been through so much. They'd covered the bruise with makeup. The dress she wore was yellow. Albert had called her a sunflower as he grasped the silk in his fist, pulled it tight, just as Mr. Herrera had done with the ribbons.

"When she came down with mono she took it out on me. Typical teenager." He pulls at his chin as if the memory of it hurts him. "She said I was happy that she was stuck in the house. But I was never happy when she was ill. I never liked seeing Cherry like that."

"I'm sure any girl who missed out would have acted the same," Elsie consoles.

He nods, exhales. "You got kids?"

"Never happened for us." It's only half a lie. He doesn't have to know that she is relieved, every day, that she never had kids with Albert, that she never wanted them.

"The school put her in the yearbook, though," he says, ignoring her answer. "The photographer let her come in one day, in her dress, and shot her in a little crown." He taps his head.

Elsie never had this, a desire to share such details about someone as a means of holding on to them for a little while longer. There was the grief that came after Albert's arrest, sure. Grief for the future, the life she thought she had mapped out in front of her. Grief for a past self, for the privilege of ignorance. But the very worst thing, the thing Elsie found hardest of all, was how cowardly Albert had been when he was caught.

He'd admitted that the girls were dead, eventually. But rather than taking ownership of their murders, he maintained that each of them had died through some misfortune of circumstance, not his own violent acts. Elizabeth Bird: oh, she'd simply fallen down the stairs, and he'd had no choice but to dismember her, to bury her body—he'd had a job to preserve, after all, a wife to protect. August Jones: *she* was a real klutz. She'd flipped out—way overkill—when she got shocked by him there, with her, in an alley late at night. He couldn't be blamed if she grabbed the knife he was carrying for self-defense—the streets of San Francisco could be dangerous after hours. He couldn't be blamed if, in the struggle, the knife slipped and went in, there, just under her rib.

Still, Elsie never felt that she'd lost as much as Beverley and Margot. When their husbands' crimes were revealed, Beverley lost the father of her children and Margot lost financial security: a large house, status, money, power. But being a murderer's wife gifted Elsie something—a layer of armor that, until then, she'd been lacking. She'd felt out of place, being English in America, ever since her family moved over when she was just eight years old. Compared to the American proclivities for casualness, for confidence, she felt meek and underwhelming, painfully polite. But Albert's crimes, Albert's cowardly behavior post-arrest, emboldened her. What gall he had to think he could manipulate people, manipulate the truth, manipulate her. The lies, the crocodile tears in court, the pleas for Elsie to stay with him—they were pathetic. It was then that she finally *knew* she was stronger than him.

She glances around Cheryl's room again. She's not entirely sure what she is hoping to find. A diary, perhaps? Some note Cheryl wrote before she left her family's house for the final time? But who is she kidding? The cops have already been here; she's not even the first reporter to be in this room.

So she decides to ask the question again, thinking of those people dressed in running gear and sneakers outside. "Mr. Herrera, was there anyone on Cheryl's track team, or anyone else you knew of, who might have wished your daughter harm?"

His eyes snap up.

"Maybe someone she argued with? A rival on the track? Maybe even someone who had feelings for her, but those feelings weren't reciprocated?"

"Why are you asking that?" His posture stiffens. "You're saying this was Cherry's fault because she didn't want to go out with some guy?"

"No, no." She rushes to correct herself. "That's not what I meant."

"Get outta here. I already answered those questions."

His sudden anger alarms her. She takes a deep breath. It wasn't supposed to go like this.

"Mr. Herrera, I apologize. That's not what I meant."

"You're not listening, just like the cops didn't listen."

"Maybe you could just tell me—" She blinks. "What do you mean, the cops didn't listen?"

"About the bracelet. That's what I said to Roachford. They didn't want to know."

"A bracelet of Cheryl's?"

He pauses, frowns. Assessing her as if double-checking whether she can be trusted. "She wore it every day," he says eventually. "In the shower, on the track, in the pool. Three initials, *CJH*. She never took it off." He glances around the room. "Now it's gone."

She waits for him to continue, to banish her again, but he doesn't, his fury dampened.

"When we had to go identify the body"—his frustration is audible—"she didn't have it on. I asked if we could take it home with us. I figured they must have packed it away somewhere. But they said she wasn't wearing any jewelry when she was . . . when she died."

If Elsie were someone else, if she were maternal like Beverley, she would reach out for him, comfort him.

"Do you have any photographs of Cheryl wearing the bracelet?" This is what she can do to help.

"Sure."

"Then there may be something we can do."

OUTSIDE, THE EARLY-EVENING sun paints the sky a clementine orange. It will be dark soon, and Elsie can see that people are readying their candles.

As she passes them, some of the guilt she felt on arriving at the vigil lifts. If she can convince Hunter to run a story about Cheryl and the missing bracelet, if she can convince him to print the photographs, to ask the public for help, that might bring about new leads.

As she walks away from the house, she sees that the figure she saw hovering on the periphery when she arrived is still there. Something crystallizes in the air around her. She looks back toward the house. By now, everyone else has gathered in the front yard, around the tables, flames lit. She looks to the figure again. Male, she can see, purely by the height and posture. He has thin hair to his shoulders and wears a scruffy-looking jacket. Strange, she thinks, in this weather.

Not wanting to draw attention to herself, she crosses the street and heads in the direction of her car. Maybe she can wait there, watch him for a while. Every so often, as she walks, she turns her head, checking that he hasn't moved. Each time he remains in the same position, half shielded by a lamppost and watching the crowd with an uneasy intensity.

Then his head turns abruptly, and their eyes meet. Even from a hundred yards away, it sends a chill through her blood. Immediately, the man takes off.

Elsie glances at her car. She could get in, start the engine, trail him that way. It would take only seconds to get the key into the ignition, but she already knows she doesn't have seconds to spare.

She turns on her heels and begins to follow him. What was this person doing hiding, *watching*, while Cheryl's friends and family mourned?

He is tall, she notices as she follows him, and as slim as a rod. He has an unusual gait, as if his bones don't bend. But he is quick, quicker than her, and she struggles to keep him in her sights as he turns a corner at the end of the street. She hurries to catch up, rounding the corner just as he is getting into a vehicle, a utility van that he had parked out of the way, under an oak.

There is a logo on the back of his vehicle, a company advertisement of sorts, but from this distance it is blurred and indecipherable. Elsie takes the splutter of the engine as her cue, and she runs, heels pounding the sidewalk. When she is close enough, she pulls out her notepad, leafing past scrawled notes and puzzle clues, then takes a pencil and quickly sketches what she can see.

When the truck has disappeared, Elsie's ears pounding with the echoes of adrenaline, she moves her hand away from her notebook and reveals what could be their very first piece of evidence.

TEN

Roger had arrived just after nine, as Beverley was anxiously turning a whiskey sour in her hands.

She knew she couldn't ask him about Emily Roswell, the name she had heard on the radio, straightaway. She'd likely get as much information as he'd given her about Cheryl Herrera, which was next to nothing. So she'd removed his coat, hung it on the rack and allowed him to lead her upstairs.

It's the behavior of a mistress, a shameful routine she has mastered since things began, with a crappy cup of coffee at a diner off the interstate. Henry had been sentenced and was already at San Quentin. Roger had kept in touch, telling Beverley to drop him a line if she ever needed anything, anything at all. He was grateful for how she had cooperated with the police when they were looking to strengthen their case after Henry's arrest. Beverley had given them everything, whatever they wanted: free rein in the house, access to Henry's business papers, her family's calendars, photographs, water from the taps and food from the fridge. At that point, she'd have done anything to ward off the finger-pointing, the *of course she knew*s.

But there was something else. She felt she owed Roger. When Henry had been arrested, Roger was one of the only people to treat her with kindness instead of hostility and suspicion. She had been dumbstruck, entirely numb, when the police knocked on her door and told her why they were taking her husband, but Roger had placed a hand on her shoulder and gently told her to pack a bag and grab some clothes for Benjamin and the baby. "We're going to take you to a hotel and check you in under a different name, okay?" His voice was gravelly but warm. "The press won't know you're there. You're going to stay there for a few days while we search your home. Everything's going to be okay."

Those were the words she'd needed to hear, and she'd clung to them. She still does.

She was so lonely, back in the house, once the cops had eventually left, when there was no more digging and probing and the walls rang with silence. How could they expect her simply to tidy up behind them and continue with the rest of her life? She had been granted an emergency divorce from Henry; he hadn't contested it. She had money of her own, from her modeling when she was a teen, and she owned the house, not Henry, so in theory she would never need a man again. But the isolation, the shame, the endless, gnawing questions, the waking up to find the planters smashed out front, the accusations hurled from the open windows of passing cars—it all got to her after a while.

So she'd called Roger, and gratefully swallowed the kindness he extended.

"Is there anything I could have done to stop it?" she asked him as they sat across from each other, her nails picking at the flimsy checkered tablecloth. She's seen it since—survivors of tragedy will often look back and talk about the small signs of impending disaster. The minute yet seismic details that indicated that their day was about to be different, that their life was about to change. They'd smashed a glass that morning, perhaps; there was something uneasy about the quality of the air in their house; they'd burned their toast. But Beverley hadn't known, hadn't woken up feeling any differently at all on the morning Henry was arrested.

The diner smelled of frying onions and stale coffee. Hamburgers sat untouched on Beverley's and Roger's plates. Curtis Lee was on the radio, "Pretty Little Angel Eyes." She'd waited for the detective to answer. She needed him to say no. She needed him to say there was nothing she could have done differently.

"I don't know, Mrs. Lightfoot."

"It's Edwards now." She glanced nervously at her plate. Relish was oozing from the burger.

Roger sighed, reached for his food, then thought better of it, folded his arms. "It's possible he displayed some transgressive behaviors that you missed, but you can't be blamed for that."

Her eyes shot up to his, her heart quickening with gratitude. He didn't blame her. He didn't think it was all her fault.

"These guys"—he slowly leaned back in his seat, spread his legs—"they're clever. They pass by unnoticed, get away with these things for so long, because they are masters at manipulating those around them." He leaned forward again, put his large hand flat on the table, and she was sure she could see his forefinger move almost imperceptibly toward hers. "A woman like you didn't stand a chance."

Roger came around after that. She was careful to keep their trysts hidden from the children. Benjamin and Audrey were still very young—they wouldn't know what was going on—but hiding it all from them meant she could almost pretend to herself that it wasn't happening, that she hadn't become the sort of woman her mother would despise.

She rarely asked about his wife. The details she gleaned from Roger's passing comments did nothing to make her feel any better about their deception. Enid was British; she knew that, at least. Her family had moved over after the First World War and had settled in California. Enid had been a schoolteacher for a while—kindergarten—before Roger's job took over their lives. She was athletic, Beverley gathered, accomplished—golf, swimming, that sort of thing. Beverley could barely lift a tennis racket.

"There are three kinds of police officers," Roger says now as he steps under the showerhead, his hair darkening to slate in the hot water, "because there are different reasons people become cops."

She asked him why he'd joined the police. It's a habit of hers: asking questions that demand complex answers—a means to keep him here, with her. She steps into the shower and reaches for the soap behind him, then runs the bar vigorously across her nails. She resents the fact that she will never feel truly clean again, no matter how hard she scrubs in the shower.

"You've got your guys who fall into it," Roger continues. "Maybe their fathers were cops, or they didn't know what else to do, figured it would be an easy life—free coffee, paperwork at the station—the guys who do the bare minimum, wear the uniform, get fat, collect their pension."

She begins lathering his chest, comforted by the feel of his bones, his flesh, the hard reality of his body.

"Then you've got your guys with a point to prove. Now, these guys can be dangerous. They're here for a *reason*. I heard about a guy in Saratoga"—he lifts his elbows so she can soap his armpits—"who joined up because his own daughter was murdered. Smart guy, a good cop, but emotionally he wasn't fit for it, wound up shooting two innocent guys because he liked them for a kidnapping case. Obsession—that's what happens when you bring your own baggage into the job."

"And the third?" She reaches around to his back, smoothing the soap over the muscles there, once taut but now softened with age.

"The third are those who do it because they know what's *just*." He moves a strand of wet hair from her forehead. "They know there are people born bad, and that those who aren't, the people like you, need protecting—simple as that."

"I take it you're the third kind?" She smiles. She knows Roger feels overlooked in his job, always playing second fiddle to Cornwell.

"Well"—he tips his head back, allows the water to fall across his face—"if you think it fits, I'll go with that." He grins, then bends to kiss her, hard. She lets him, allowing the tension in her body to uncoil as he moves his mouth down, across her neck, to her breasts and stomach, until he is kneeling before her. When he kisses her there, the hot water easing the knots in her shoulders, she feels herself unspooling, and any thoughts of the police ebb with the steam.

When he has finished, they return to the bedroom and Roger asks her to fetch his cigarettes. She quickly obliges, pulling on a robe and descending to the hallway. She reaches for his coat and pats down the pockets—putting aside movie stubs and receipts for car repairs—to retrieve the box.

Back up in the bedroom, Roger pushes the corner of a towel into his ear and jiggles it. Beverley takes a Lucky Strike from the box and places it between his lips, slowly lighting it for him. He takes a drag and leans his head back blissfully. She uses the opportunity to ask him about Emily Roswell.

"Sure. We found a girl," he admits, blowing out a curl of smoke.

She knows Roger secretly likes that she takes an interest in his work. She knows Enid doesn't. She knows he likes it because it gives him a chance to sing his own praises.

"Where was she?"

She knows the answer—she heard it on the radio—but she wants to see if he will be honest with her this time.

"On the golf course."

She holds his gaze.

"Where on the golf course?"

Roger takes the cigarette away from his mouth, tilts his head suspiciously. "The divers found her."

"Did she drown?"

"No, she didn't drown." He flicks ash into the tray. "She was dumped there after she was killed."

"Strangled?"

"Bev."

"Was she strangled?" She repeats the question with feeling. Cheryl Herrera, the young track athlete, had been strangled.

"She had been stabbed, okay?" Roger concedes. "Multiple times."

"Damn it."

"What do you mean, *damn it*?" Ash has fallen on the bedspread. He flicks it off. "Bev?"

"Were there any unusual details?"

"What's going on here?" He studies her face.

She knows that means there must have been something. She ties her nightgown and reaches for his shirt, then holds it out to him. He plunges his arms in, one by one, like a child, then sighs.

"Her hands," he says quietly.

"Mm-hmm?" She leans into him as she fastens his buttons, taking great care not to sound too invested.

"Whoever did it to her had . . ." He's shaking his head. He takes another deep drag on the cigarette. "Whoever did it had tattooed something on her knuckles."

She fumbles the top button, forces herself to stay calm. "Tattooed?"

"He'd etched something into her hands."

She's got him in a weakened state, soft from the shower and the sex. She knows he shouldn't be telling her this. "What did the tattoos say?"

He pushes her away gently and fastens the remaining button. "*Love* and *hate*," he says reluctantly. "One on each hand."

"Like some Hells Angels thing?"

"We don't know. We're still puzzling it out."

"Why would someone do that?"

"Like I said"—he exhales through his nose—"we don't know. The motive's abnormal."

"'Abnormal'?"

"We can't explain it yet."

"So you don't think it's someone close to her, then? Isn't it usually a boyfriend?"

"Bev"—he shakes his head—"don't."

"Please," she says softly, rubs his neck.

"I don't think it's family, okay?"

"Why not?"

He sucks his teeth, but she knows he'll answer.

"Men like this, they don't kill family."

"'Men like this'?"

"I've met plenty of killers before who think they're saints because they never harmed their family."

Beverley frowns. "But it's okay to kill strangers?"

He holds his hands up as if he can't explain it.

"One guy even quoted the Bible at me. 'Behold!'" He adopts a Southern drawl. "'Children are a heritage from the Lord.'" He pauses, straightens, as if realizing he is getting carried away.

Beverley moves her hand to his knee, gently traces the skin, coaxing him.

"This isn't some domestic-violence situation"—he shifts his leg away from her—"not some jealous husband, or someone who got rejected. *Those* crimes, where victims know their killers, they're intimate, messy—facial lacerations, black eyes. It's almost like . . . with this guy, the victims don't matter. It's more about the *way* he does it."

"So, is it easy to get onto the golf course?"

"All right, no." His demeanor quickly hardens. "No more talking about this. It's not right."

"I'm just . . ." She pauses. "I'm just trying to figure something out, okay?"

She feels Roger shoot her a warning glance.

"Don't you think there's a chance that this is linked to the Herrera case?"

He seems alarmed. "Beverley!"

"You said she was a prostitute."

Roger is shaking his head, but these murders did not take place that far away from each other, and neither of them follows the rules of your "standard" killings. Roger said it himself—they don't seem like crimes of passion or relationship disputes. The arrow, the tattoos—there has to be meaning to those. This could be the same killer trying to send some sort of warped message.

"What about prints? Have you found fingerprints on anything?"

He glares, and she knows she is overstepping. Of course they checked for prints.

"Why are you doing this, Bev? What are you trying to prove?"

She pulls away from him.

He seems to weigh up the right words. "With the scrapbook, the sudden interest in these cases, is it just something you're doing to try and handle your own feelings of guilt?"

She inhales sharply, turns away.

"*Misplaced* guilt." He pulls her back by the shoulder, and she dodges his kiss. "You know what I meant."

"If they're linked, people need to know," she argues. "It could be the same killer. There could be someone dangerous out there."

"No, they don't need to know," Roger replies sternly. "It'll cause unnecessary panic."

"Is panic really unnecessary when women are being killed?"

"They're not linked, Beverley."

"Roger..."

"The methods of killing are totally different," he argues. "And that Jane Doe, Herrera—she's Hispanic. They don't even have the same skin color. But you know who *is* Hispanic? The Kings."

"Different skin color doesn't mean—"

"It's a nice story, Bev, but women go missing all the time. Women get killed."

"And that's okay with you?"

"That's a cheap shot."

She pulls her dressing gown tighter around her and smooths down her hair. He will never take her seriously, just like everybody else. She will always be just the woman who was married to Henry Lightfoot, the wife who didn't know what her husband was doing.

"Beverley"—he moves his palm to her cheek—"I wish I could stop asshole husbands and boyfriends from killing their wives and their girlfriends. I really do."

"Isn't it literally your job to try to stop that?"

Roger exhales frustratedly, moves away from her and stubs out his cigarette.

"What if, even if the chances are slim, the cases *are* linked?" she asks. "What if this is a mass killer? He could do it again."

He shakes his head. "Cornwell's plowing a lot of money into surveilling the Kings. New audio technology. Covert officers. It's his project, okay? He's being hot on this. And these guys? They are not good guys, Bev. People like you shouldn't be trying—"

"People like me?" She raises an eyebrow. "Women?"

Roger rolls his eyes. "No, Bev. Civilians."

She huffs.

"It gets in our way and, more importantly, it can be dangerous." He reaches for her. "If you'd seen the things I've seen, if you knew what people were really capable of—"

She shoots him a glance and he pauses.

"I just want you to be safe."

She softens a little. She believes him. She knows he would do anything to protect her. She also knows that, deep down, that's one reason she was so drawn to him in the first place.

"I'm not talking about hanging around in dark alleys," she counters, "but surely we can find a link between these victims."

"It's not that easy . . ."

"We won't know until we try."

"Beverley."

She flinches at his sudden change of tone.

"No," he warns, his body stiffening. "Leave it alone. You'll be interfering with an investigation. Tell me you're not going to take this any further."

She drops her eyes to the floor. "Sure, Roger," she replies evenly, shrugging off his arm and crossing to the window. "I don't know what came over me." She moves the curtain slightly to the side and gazes at the dark, neat street. Then she allows the fabric to fall. Something has its hooks in her, she knows, and she has no intention of letting it go.

ELEVEN

"DAIQUIRI, MISS?"

Margot takes a coupe from the tray, puts the glass to her lips and allows her eyes to roam the party.

She, Bev and Elsie now seem to be spending a lot of their time mulling over unsolved murders, but that doesn't mean she has to sit at home getting depressed. She can get out and put an ear to the ground, get the latest gossip from the area. That's why the three of them make such a good team. She smiles to herself at the oddness of it—clever Elsie with her brainteasers and her unfashionable clothes; Beverley with her model looks and that baby-deer way about her. It's an unusual arrangement, but together, they should not be underestimated.

Friendship was a peculiar concept for Margot before she met Bev and Elsie. Friends had always been a temporary distraction for her—glamorous, transient people who kissed cheeks in wafts of Chanel, then gossiped behind one another's backs—but Bev and Elsie had taught her that friendship *actually* meant that people were forced to listen to your thoughts and opinions and weren't allowed to judge you for them. She rather liked that. That's why, when they were together, they never had to fake the smiles, plaster over the cracks, add a little sweetness to their stories.

She casts her eyes around the party again. Yes, *this* is what she can do to help—see what makes people tick when they're relaxed, off guard. What would anyone learn about the human psyche by staying in and watching *The Danny Kaye Show* anyway? This is psychology in motion, just with pot and Vesper martinis.

Music blares around the Hollywood Hills. Cute girls in rainbow sequins and men with studio connections move their bodies to the Temptations. Above them all, the moon shines like a huge, buffed pearl. Margot can see it reflected on the surface of the pool, until someone cannonballs in and the disk shatters. She suddenly stumbles. The heel of one of her vintage Hélène Arpels feels loose. She perches on the side of a lounger and gives it a wiggle. She should never have worn them, really; they're on their last legs, but they're her only shoes that go with her gold Oleg Cassini dress.

Mark, the young actor she is seeing, is somewhere inside, trying to get a meet with Mason Clarke. Rumor has it, the movie director tends to station himself near the lavatory at parties like this, no doubt so that he doesn't have to walk far to snort his drugs off the toilet tank. She pictures a line of hard-chested, bronzed men with Elvis haircuts and space-eyed girls in silver jumpsuits hanging on his every word.

"Margot?"

She is jarred back to the terrace, the pool, her goddamn broken heel.

The girl looking down at her is smiling and chewing bubble gum. She wears go-go boots and a minidress the color of fresh milk.

Dangling mirror ball earrings hang from her lobes and she has individual lashes painted under her eyes.

"Oh my gosh, hello, you." Margot knows she knows her name but also knows she cannot for the life of her remember it. They used to party together—that must be it—but she wasn't the girlfriend of one of Stephen's colleagues. Was she an actress? A model?

"How have you been?" The girl takes a seat next to Margot on the lounger. She smells of blue raspberry and curaçao. *Diana? Delilah?* "Are you still at Arnold's?"

Margot winces inside. She knows people see her job at the department store as a fall from grace. From a politician's wife to a shopgirl. Sure, this isn't exactly how she imagined her life would turn out. It isn't convertibles gliding down the Sunset Strip; it isn't Grauman's Chinese Theatre, or a huge house in the Bird Streets with views of the canyon. But it's okay. At least she's out there, making a living. Does Diana or Delilah have a job? Probably not. She probably has some rich older guy, just like Stephen, taking care of everything.

"For my sins," Margot replies.

"I bet you get to try on all the clothes, though, right?" The woman's eyes flash hungrily.

Margot humors her with a smile.

"You here with someone?"

"Mark," Margot replies.

The girl raises an eyebrow.

"He's an actor." They share a knowing smirk. "About ten years too young for me, but he looks extremely fine in a suit." Margot gestures with her glass at the open double doors. "He's currently on the hunt for Mason Clarke."

"Ugh." The girl opens her handbag, rifles past blister packs of Enovid to pull out a rolled joint. Margot took the same birth control pills for a while but stopped when she realized she'd spent ten days straight watching *I Dream of Jeannie* with unwashed hair.

"If he finds him, tell him to keep his wits about him." She sparks up the joint, takes a toke. As she stuffs the lighter back into her bag, Margot glimpses a bunch of lipsticks in there, too. That's when she realizes who it is. Barbie Cook. A makeup artist with the studios. A woman who knows more about Gregory Peck's T-zone than his own wife.

"What do you mean?"

The girl offers her a puff, but Margot raises a hand to decline.

"Clarke. Haven't you heard the rumors? That guy's really some monster."

Margot lowers her voice. "Like, sexually?" She's heard stories of actresses buying their way onto the sets of Clarke's films with certain "favors." She knows he sometimes demands meetings with the next hot young thing, and if she doesn't comply with his demands, she disappears from the scene, blacklisted.

"Sexually, physically, psychopathically. Did you hear about the girl?"

"What girl?" A tray of glasses smashes nearby.

"Some model from Golden Point. I heard she was trying to get into acting, had been writing him letters. Then she just . . . disappeared." Barbie clicks her fingers.

"Golden Point," Margot murmurs.

"Apparently her folks are losing their minds. But Clarke will never be implicated." Another toke.

"Why?"

"Because he's famous," Barbie replies, her vocal cords strained by the pot. "And powerful, and rich." She blows out smoke.

"What's her name?" Margot asks. "Wait—let me get a pen and paper. Actually, hand me one of those lipsticks, will you?"

"What?" Barbie sighs and lets her head hang heavily backward, gazing up at the stars.

"Give me one of those lipsticks in your bag." Margot turns her left arm over, waits for Barbie to hand her a tube.

"Now, how do you spell it?"

TWELVE

THE SUN WAS sharp the day Elsie first met Margot and Beverley. She held a palm to her eyes, cowered in its shade, felt as if the rays might slice her skin. She wore a new silk blouse for the occasion, something she'd never normally choose, and the tiny buttons at the back of her neck scratched terribly, as if the outfit knew it didn't belong on her. She'd rolled the sleeves back in a vain bid to cool herself down, and her freckled forearms had already started to redden. Her English complexion would never get used to the California heat.

She glanced nervously at her shoes as she stood on the doorstep of what she knew was Beverley's house, the house Bev had described in the letters they'd been exchanging for months.

As soon as Beverley opened the door—with that wide, beautiful face, those swimming-pool eyes, that thick head of blond hair—she felt frumpy. Bev's house, too, was beautiful, filled with the sorts of products Elsie could never afford herself: a Sony TV, a pink Bell Princess telephone—the one with the light-up dial that seemed unnecessarily showy. She was led through the hallway to the kitchen, passing a living room filled with mustard furniture and that print of the beautiful Chinese woman that all fashionable people seemed to own. She practically balked when she saw the striking red-haired woman who must have been ten years older than her and Beverley leaning against the kitchen counter, a cigarette held to scarlet-painted lips. The smoke curled around her like something from those movie billboards you saw on Rodeo Drive. The woman lowered the cigarette and flashed a white smile. The kitchen clock ticked loudly above their heads. Elsie had been stunned.

This was not what she had expected the women—who had experienced exactly what she had experienced—to look like. In her mind, they were meek and apologetic. Women you wouldn't look at twice on the street. Women who could be trampled by men, conned, deceived. Women just like her.

Beverley poured Elsie a drink, and the afternoon slipped into evening in a haze of Chardonnay and vodka cocktails. Elsie was not used to drinking cocktails. She spent her evenings with Dickens and Archimedes' tangrams. So her thoughts soon felt fluid, dizzy. They ate food that Bev had prepared—a frozen Sara Lee lasagne—no one commenting on the fact that it was hugely overcooked, and they discussed their lives, their husbands, their unique and horrific shared experience. Elsie had to pinch herself on more than one occasion; things she had always concealed, things she had never dared share with anyone, were being splayed and dissected as if the women were chewing over the latest episode of *Naked City*. She was struck by the intimacy of it all. Until then, her past had been a secret stored against her skin, hidden from sight, a private responsibility. In meeting them, she would have to cut herself open, show the blood.

Margot, Elsie felt, was overloud and, if she was honest, a bit obnoxious; she certainly didn't seem as affected by her husband's crimes as the gentler Beverley, who seemed so poised, so put together, but whose childlike vulnerability slipped out now and then. Bev seemed to flinch whenever Margot derided their husbands.

"They're animals," Margot had quipped plainly, dabbing the corner of her mouth with a pinkie finger.

"Well..."

Margot widened her eyes at Beverley. "What do you mean, *well...*?"

"Henry was a good father," Beverley countered hesitantly. "He doted on Benjamin. He bought him Christmas toys, made him peanut butter and jelly sandwiches, Hawaiian punch."

"Hold on." Margot held up a palm, and Elsie marveled at the familiarity between the women, their ease, their comfort in challenging each other.

"Does tossing a ball in the yard with your son excuse you from slitting girls' throats?"

Elsie bristled, expecting Beverley to react in horror. Instead, Beverley continued calmly. "What I'm saying is that I believe he could have been both things at the same time: a dangerous man"—she opened a hand—"and a good father." She opened the other next to it, like they were balancing scales.

Margot blew a raspberry. "That's stupid."

Elsie had watched, entranced by the interaction, as Beverley had tilted her head patiently and replied, "And what did Dr. Garvey say, Margot?"

Elsie would later discover that the women had been seen by the same psychologist after their husbands were arrested.

Margot rolled her eyes and parroted, in a crisp British accent, "'You are to ban the word *stupid* from your vocabulary.'" She took a drag on the cigarette she was holding loosely between her fingers. "But sometimes it just fits. Okay, not for you, Bev, but it does for some of the wives."

The wives? Elsie was intrigued to hear women, presumably women who'd been through what they'd been through, discussed like this.

"Like that Harbinger woman. She genuinely *is* an idiot."

"Who's that?" Elsie dared to ask.

"Do you not remember?" Margot blew out smoke. "She flat-out *refused* to believe her husband was a killer. She launched an actual campaign to protest his innocence, told the press the cops had got the wrong guy."

"Well, what's so wrong with that?" Elsie glanced between them, unsure of what she'd missed. "She was being supportive."

"He ended up taking a plea deal," Margot said bluntly, "to avoid the chair. He admitted to twenty-five murders. Twenty-five! He used to make her call him on an intercom if she wanted to enter the garage."

"But if she didn't know—"

"She found a bloodstained mattress at their house!" Margot screeched.

"No, it wasn't a bloodstained mattress," Beverley countered. "It was no carpets. He'd had the carpets taken up."

"That's right"—Margot pointed at Beverley enthusiastically—"because he'd killed a load of women on their best carpet."

"Oh." Elsie felt foolish.

"That's not even a smoking gun, is it? That's a gun held to your head while someone says, *Just in case you hadn't noticed, honey, I get a kick outta killing people on your shag pile.*"

"I heard she got a letter from one of the victims' mothers, empathizing with her." Beverley seemed to know what to say to calm Margot, Elsie noticed, to distract, to steer the conversation in a different way when things got heated. "She was deceived," Bev continued. "She genuinely thought he was a good man, not a monster."

Monster. It was an interesting term. Elsie was never sure that it fit for Albert, either, although she supposed there were plenty of people who would level the term at him, and not just because he killed those girls.

It was in a high school classroom that she had first met him. He was standing beside the chalkboard; she was straight backed at her desk in the front row. She heard some of the other girls snicker. His sweater-vest had soup stains on it and his stomach slightly overhung the waistband of his trousers, but something in his eyes intrigued Elsie—the steady gaze, the expression that told her he knew the girls were laughing at him but he would never trouble himself to care.

He had taught English literature, Elsie's favorite subject, and she found herself even more attentive in his classes than she had been in others. She was excited, she realized, for him to know what she was capable of, to know that her mind was suited to the subject, that she had a way with words.

So when he tossed her first graded essay on her desk and she saw a large *C* scrawled across it, she found herself reeling from shock. *I think you can do better,* he'd written below. So she found herself with one goal: to get an A from Albert Moss. It became her sole focus; it consumed her, and she tweaked her essays every week in the hope that he'd finally be satisfied, that she would impress him.

D. See me, the next paper read.

There was no way she'd got a D. She'd never got a D in her life.

"You didn't get a D," he'd said with a wry grin when she hung back after class. "I just wanted the opportunity to talk with you properly." Elsie had glowed as if a furnace had been lit inside her.

From that day on, she always hung back after English literature.

They'd discuss Ernest Hemingway, Dylan Thomas, Zora Neale Hurston. "You see," he said one day, leaning toward her so the hairs on her arm lifted as if each one were reaching for him, "everyone else might call you odd, but forget them. This is why you're special. Your brain is remarkable, Elsie."

Remarkable. Elsie had clung to the word and rolled it around like a precious marble. She tried to ignore what he'd said about others finding her odd. She'd certainly never got that impression herself, but he must see what's going on in that classroom better than she could.

He brought her a book one day, held it out to her.

"It makes me think of you," he'd said. He seemed flustered as he stepped in closer; Elsie noticed the raggedness of his breathing. She took the paperback and turned the cover over. *Lady Chatterley's Lover.* She knew the book. Knew it had been banned. Knew just what sort of content it contained. There was a small part of her then that wanted to hand it back, to leave the room. But here was someone who saw her for who she really was, what her mind could achieve, when everyone else, she was now sure, saw her as out of place. He reached his hand toward her and brushed the skin of her cheek. "My English rose," he whispered.

"Not all women who are duped are stupid," Beverley concluded in her argument with Margot. "Think about ten years ago. Women were treated very differently then, seen and not heard."

"You think it's any different now?" Margot asked. "The way we're supposed to behave?"

"I don't know." Beverley flopped back in her chair. "But in the fifties, women weren't *supposed*"—she raised her fingers in quotation marks—"to ask what their husbands were getting up to. Therefore, they were easier to dupe."

"And now? What's their excuse?"

"I truly think some of them *choose* not to see what their husbands are capable of, even if it's a subconscious decision."

"Why would you do that, though?" Margot asked. "I just don't understand."

"To keep a family together, for one," Beverley replied. "Some women—they see their husbands' crimes as a sickness. That's what

Dr. Garvey said. They see it as something that's afflicted them, and they've got to support them through it."

"Idiots."

Elsie knew her and Margot's experiences were very different from Beverley's; they had no children to steer through post-disaster fallout. She could not imagine what it must be like to know that you'd carried a child for someone who could do these things.

"Then there's fear," Beverley continued. "Fear of confrontation, fear for their own safety, fear that they won't be believed."

"Hmm," Margot half-conceded.

"And did Dr. Garvey ever talk to you about dissociation?"

"Bev, I was just trying to get through those sessions."

Beverley shook her head disapprovingly. "She said there's a link between trauma and dissociation, that the brain can sometimes protect us from the truth, from ourselves, from others, like . . . an involuntary detachment from reality, a way of burying memories in order to survive."

"So . . . denial," Margot argued flatly.

"No, not denial. It's more complicated than that."

Elsie's head filled with a strange sound as they talked. This concept, dissociation—it wasn't something she'd ever heard of, yet it felt discomfortingly familiar. Buried memories—she knew those. She knew what it was like to remove your mind from a situation as a means to survive it. She'd had to do that so much as a child.

"Not only that, but it's difficult to extricate yourself fully from someone you've already spent half a lifetime with," Bev was saying as Elsie's attention returned to the conversation, "especially as a woman with no income and with kids to look after. You know how many women I know who don't even have a bank account?"

"Okay, but I don't think staying together for the kids is going to cut it if your husband's an axe murderer."

Elsie had never met anyone who spoke about murder the way Margot did. She was electric with it, tossing the concept around like a kitten batting at yarn.

"I'd argue that it's incredibly healthy *not* to want to have anything to do with a man who murdered people in cold blood. Wouldn't you, Bev?" Margot gibed. "Look." She'd turned to them both. "I say we make a pact, something that will be good for all of us." She looked pointedly at Beverley. "We cut them out of our lives completely."

Elsie noticed Beverley raise her eyebrows.

"No visits," she continued. "Easy for me, obviously. No correspondence, no second thoughts. They're dead to us. Again, easier for me, but you girls need to move on. This way, they're out of our lives forever. Deal?"

Margot held her hand out to them both. Slowly but firmly, Elsie shook it.

THIRTEEN

MARGOT HAS NEWS. Elsie can see it in her as soon as she steps through the doorway, joining them in Beverley's house.

"What is it?" Elsie asks, closing the door behind her friend—although she knows it's likely gossip about some actor she's never heard of disgracing himself at a party.

They make their way to the living room. The children are watching a *Flintstones* repeat; Wilma and Betty are performing lawn maintenance while Fred and Barney recline against a rock, smoking Winston cigarettes.

Margot raises her eyebrows at Bev and tilts her head toward the backyard.

"Kids, go and play outside," Bev responds. Then she calls after them, "Stay by the door!"

"Elsie"—Margot points firmly at her—"get something to drink. We're going to need it."

Reluctantly, Elsie goes to the kitchen. She casts her eyes around the space, worthy of the pages of a magazine. The refrigerator is mint green, as are the laminate countertops, the percolator and the toaster. There's a bowl of lemons arranged neatly on the breakfast bar. She's not quite sure why anyone would need that many lemons, but they look pleasing, she supposes. Mustard-colored geometric tiles climb the walls behind the stove, and a chrome Sunbeam Mixmaster has been positioned near the sink. Elsie is almost certain that Bev has never used it, just like she's never used the hostess trolley tucked into a corner of the room. Bev is a horrible cook.

Elsie moves to the refrigerator. The blare of the television being flicked over to the news winds its way into the kitchen. There are photos stuck to the fridge door with magnets: Beverley and her children; Benjamin and Audrey playing with the garden sprinkler; the kids with their grandmother, Alice; Elsie, Beverley and Margot at the beach. She raises a hand, tilts her head. The bottom of a photograph is peeking out from behind the rest. She grasps it and starts to pull it out, catching a glimpse of a wedding dress, the middle buttons of a man's best suit.

"Hello? We're dying of thirst in here!"

Elsie rolls her eyes, opens the refrigerator and takes out a jug of iced tea. Margot will complain, but it's far too early for cocktails.

In the living room, Bev has kicked off her shoes, leaving them abandoned on the tufted turquoise carpet. Margot is fanning herself dramatically with the *TV Guide*.

"So, what the hell's going on, Margot?" Bev asks as Elsie sets the jug down.

Margot bites her lip, widens her eyes, always one to drag out the drama. "I think we might have another victim," she says, eyes ricocheting between them.

"What?"

"It could be another murder!"

"Oh God."

"I was at a party last night." Margot's words streak along. "Someone told me a model had gone missing from Golden Point. Diane Howard Murray—that's her name."

Elsie reaches for her notebook, pulls a pen from the ring binding at the top. "A model? Did you get any other details? How old?"

"Well, the girl who told me wasn't really sure," says Margot, "but she thinks early twenties. So she could fit, right? With the other two women, Cheryl Herrera and this Emily Roswell you told us about, Bev."

"Hmm." Bev ponders. "If we don't know any details about the crime, or if there even *has* been a crime, it's hard. Where's Golden Point?" She reaches behind her for something and eventually pulls open a map, then spreads it across her knees.

"Golden Point... Golden Point," she murmurs, before locating it with a finger. "It's quite far away from the other crime scenes."

"Apparently she worked in Calabasas a lot," Margot offers.

Beverley's finger hovers above the map. Elsie can see she has already ringed the locations of the two other murders in red ink. Eventually Beverley taps it.

"Calabasas. That would make more sense. Look." She turns the map, holds it up and indicates three different spots. "That would be three locations, each less than an hour from Berryview, each accessed"—she runs a finger horizontally—"via the interstate, here."

"And where are we? Where's Berryview?" Elsie asks.

Beverley leans across the map and taps a central point.

"Right there, in the middle of it all."

"Bingo!" Margot yelps. "That's three bodies in, what—just over three and a half weeks?" She is enjoying this a bit too much for Elsie's liking.

They often butted heads, Margot and Elsie—not because Elsie disagreed with Margot about what she wore, or about the men she slept with, or about the way she was so comfortable with her body that it scared Elsie a little, but because Elsie thought Margot was dramatic and Margot thought Elsie was uptight. If anyone asked Margot about her husband—and they did; his case had been in the papers for months when everything happened—she batted it away with a joke. *Now, why would I want to talk about a sad little guy like that?* But people couldn't get enough of the story, a killer politician shopped to the police by his young, glamorous wife. Margot took up a lot of the news coverage. Pictures of her in tight skirts and claret lipstick splashed across the front pages. While Elsie was used to a quiet existence—James Joyce and drab roast beef sandwiches in Saran Wrap on a Monday—Margot lived her life like a comet. She was a woman who knew important people at Warner Brothers, who had been hit on by Elvis. The newspapers called Margot a "free spirit" when they reported on Stephen's crimes—their way of saying *a woman who likes a drink*, Elsie supposes. And it was as if Margot saw people's perceptions of her as a challenge, a reason to jut out her chin and dig in her heels. Elsie knows that, underneath it all, Margot is as damaged by what her husband did as she and Beverley are by the acts of theirs. She knows that Margot sleeps around because she won't allow herself to forge any sort of deeper connection with anyone, will never trust another man. But the fact that Margot won't accept that, won't let it show, even for just a second, seems to Elsie like betrayal.

"That's three girls, all very beautiful. Bit of a cliché, but whatever," Margot says. "Cheryl Herrera was a track athlete. Emily Roswell, pulled from the lake, was a cheerleader. And this Diane is a model. All killed by some freak who leaves weird calling cards on his victims?"

"'Calling cards'?" Elsie asks, confused. As far as she knows, Albert didn't leave anything at his crime scenes except bodies.

"The arrow, the tattooed knuckles. This can't be some guy going crazy with a knife or a rope. It's too intentional. He's doing these things as a taunt, a way of saying something. What if this next murder—"

"We don't know that yet, Margot," Beverley interjects, always ready to add a layer of calmness. "We don't know there's been another murder. Diane might have just skipped town."

Elsie nods. They are getting carried away. They need to be careful. She knows what desperation does, how it twists the brain into locating causalities.

"Do you really believe that?" Margot asks Bev. "You think she's just on vacation?"

Beverley's reply is cut off by the sound of the six o'clock news on the television. Their heads turn in unison as the mustachioed figure of Tom Cornwell, grasping the sides of a lectern emblazoned with the LAPD logo, fills the screen.

"I'd like to thank the press for cooperating with us in our investigation into the murder of Cheryl Herrera." He doesn't smile, his eyes fixed firmly on his notes.

"Well, look who it is," Margot drawls. "Mr. Charisma."

"We'd like to talk to anyone from the Mexican community who might know anything about Cheryl or who might have links to prolific street gang the Kings."

"Oh, he's really going for it?" Margot cries. "Straight in on the Kings?"

"It's not the Kings." Elsie sighs, Patti's words in her head.

"Aren't the Kings Puerto Rican?" Margot asks, head swiveling between Elsie and Beverley, who holds her face in her hands. "We're just lumping people all together, are we? Mexicans, Puerto Ricans . . . Three cheers for police prejudice."

"They're not going to mention Emily Roswell." Bev tuts as the conference comes to a close. "It's irresponsible." She rises from the couch and clicks off the television.

"They're making such a mess of it," Elsie grumbles, then lifts her head suddenly, eyes determined. "We've really got to do it now." She sees Bev frown but is undeterred. "We'll keep looking at these three cases, see if we can find a link." She has the detail of Cheryl Herrera's bracelet now, and the logo on the van at the vigil.

"So, what?" Bev says drily. "Just ignore the police and do our own investigation?"

Elsie nods. She is quite happy to ignore the police. She does not trust the police. She knows the LAPD chief, Tom Cornwell, is as bent as a right angle. He's been discussed at the *Signal* before, many times, but there's been little they could write about his dubious professionalism. The man is untouchable. She doesn't trust any of his officers to carry out their duties effectively or honestly, either, not with a boss like that.

"Isn't that what we've been doing for the past few weeks anyway? Why not make it official? Think about it," she levels. "The girls—Henry's victims, Stephen's victims, Albert's—if you could go back in time and stop them being harmed, wouldn't you do it?"

Bev's jaw flinches. "Well, of course. But this isn't—"

"I'm not suggesting that we can change what happened," she quickly corrects. Elsie knows they would all do that if they could. "My point is, if we can see that there might be a link, and if we *might* be able to help, in some small way, to find out who might be doing this, shouldn't we do it?"

"That's a lot of *might*s," Margot quips, but Elsie can see that she's intrigued.

The women look at one another. No words pass between them, but they feel the weight of their shared history, the downward pull of their husbands' actions.

"If they are linked, and Berryview is in the middle of this killer's operating zone"—Elsie gestures to Beverley's map, with its three red rings—"maybe it's someone close to here. Maybe we could find him, or at least work out what sort of person he might be."

"Now, that *is* something we'd be excellent at," Margot agrees.

Bev raises an eyebrow in question.

Margot looks between them. "Have these cops shared a bed with a killer? Have they baked him a pie? Have they slipped his jacket off his shoulders at the end of a long day?"

"No," Elsie obliges.

"We know what it's like to live with a dangerous man," Margot continues. "We know—with the benefit of hindsight, of course—what the signs are that he's dangerous. We may not know *why* our husbands did what they did, but I'd say we have a pretty good chance of figuring out what kind of guy this killer is."

"The police will be looking at circumstantial suspects." Elsie works hard to keep the enthusiasm from her own voice. "People who worked with the victims, laborers carrying out jobs near where they were killed. Let them do that. It's grunt work. We can get ahead of the game."

"Get into this man's head." Margot's eyes grow large.

"And on that note: I've been thinking," Elsie posits. She's already won over Margot; she just needs to ensure that Bev's fully on board. But with the scrapbook, the map, the connection Bev feels to Cheryl Herrera, Elsie knows there's no way she'll say no. "All three of our husbands were going through high pressure in their lives at the time that they were killing, right?" She'd had the thought in the car on her way home from work the other day. She'd been trying to link Albert's situation with those of Henry and Stephen. They were a teacher, an air-conditioning engineer and a politician, men who on the surface seemed so very different, but all committed abhorrent acts, expertly covering their tracks.

"'High pressure'?" Bev asks.

"Take Stephen," Elsie replies. "Didn't you say he was running for election before his crimes started, Margot?"

Margot confirms it.

"He didn't win, did he? His ego must have taken a bit of a knock..."

"He certainly had an ego."

"He might have found the loss humiliating?"

Margot nods, tongue pressed against her cheek in thought. "So, what about Albert?"

"He'd lost his job at the school," Elsie answers. "He *hated* that. He was so angry. He was forced to look for jobs that he felt were beneath him, and even those places wouldn't give him a shot. What about Henry?"

Beverley sighs.

"Any work issues?"

She shakes her head. "Not really, but . . ." Bev frowns, pauses. "There was something."

Elsie nods. "Go on."

"His brother got in touch, said their father was dying."

"So, what? Grief?" Margot asks.

"Not even grief, something different. Something more complicated."

Elsie knows Bev's husband had a difficult relationship with his father, that he was abusive, controlling.

"So you're saying that anyone experiencing a challenging life situation is more likely to kill?" Bev asks.

"No, but if someone already has the propensity or the characteristics to be able to kill, something difficult in their lives might create an environment that pushes them to do so—like a padlock." She twists her hands. "Something has to happen to make all the numbers align. Then..."

"Boom." Margot opens her hand. "Like a pressure-cooker situation."

"Exactly," says Elsie.

"So if we do this—*if*—" Bev says, "we could be looking for someone going through financial difficulty? Or facing something else challenging?"

"Bankruptcy, a struggling business, family drama..."

"How do we even go about looking for that?" Margot asks, dubious.

Before Elsie can answer, Beverley suddenly interjects, "You do know how it will look, though, right?"

They turn to her.

"Taking an interest in Cheryl's case, in Emily's, is one thing, but doing a whole investigation ourselves? You know how it looks that we aren't locking ourselves in our houses all day?" Her voice is tight. "If we go nosing around at crime scenes, what will people think?"

"Who cares how it looks?" Elsie argues. "Don't we owe the girls this? The girls our husbands took, other girls—don't we owe it to them to try to protect future victims?"

"Anyway," Margot butts in, placing her tumbler on the floor, "do I really have to say it again? God. I am not what my husband did. You are not what Henry did. Elsie is not what Albert did. People might want to see us as by-products of their actions, but I am not that. I refuse to be a footnote in his story for the rest of my life. I'm in. I say we do it."

"You keep everything in that scrapbook, Bev," Elsie encourages. She knows they have to work together to do this. "Don't you have those letters? From all the women who wrote to you whose husbands did bad things. Maybe the letters can tell us something about what kind of guy this killer could be—how they found out what their husbands were doing."

"We can build a picture of him." Margot takes the baton. "Try to track him down that way. Find out *why* he might be doing this, what motivates him." She watches Bev, hopeful. "We'll tell the police if we find anything significant, if that makes you feel better. Elsie, there must be more you can do with that logo, some digging you can do at the *Signal*?"

She nods. She still needs to convince Hunter to run a story about the bracelet. If the public knows about it, they can keep an eye out for it. Finding that bracelet, wherever it might be, could give them a clue to the killer's identity, his whereabouts.

"And can you look into this missing model?" she asks Margot in return. "Try to remember if there was anything else you heard—someone she was in touch with, a boyfriend, someone she was dating, anything."

"And you?" Margot asks Beverley. "Are you in?"

Beverley is quiet for a while, then swallows thickly. "All right." She nods eventually. "I'm in."

TWO DAYS MISSING

THE WEATHER WAS fine the day you took me. The sun—high and marbled in the sky—streamed in through the windows and fell in warm pools on the floor. I could tell there was someone close by, my animal senses alert to an intruder, and the breath caught in my throat as I waited. Time seemed to stretch out slowly then as I turned, held still, a fly trapped in amber.

I could not speak, could not breathe, first struck not by the fact that you were there but by how the light cast your face in the cold, hard contours of a statue. I had mere seconds to consider whether I had time to run, and then it hit. There was only sensation. Something blunt. A searing pain. My mind flooded with black.

FOURTEEN

THE GATES OF the San Quentin high-security prison loom above Beverley's head. The sky must have sensed her arrival, because it has mottled itself gray with sea fog—a macabre armor that makes her skin feel too heavy for her bones.

She peers at the huge concrete building far beyond the gates, barbed wire twisted around its exterior, windows barred and bolted.

It took a week or so to arrange the paperwork for the visit, but she didn't tell anyone she was coming here, not even Elsie or Margot. They want to investigate these murders, but they wouldn't agree with *this*. Elsie has never visited Albert in prison, and Margot has always seemed more than happy that Stephen is no longer around to visit. Beverley knows that if she did tell them, they would order her not to do it, that they would judge her for even being willing to sit in the same room as Henry, for breaking their pact.

She didn't tell her mother for a very different reason; she could not stomach the self-satisfied look that Alice would give her. *It's about time,* the look would say. Alice seemed to be the only person in California who thought that Henry deserved to have contact with his children, that Beverley should be grateful that she'd ever had a husband.

Her mother dated men after her father left, but it always seemed to be out of spite rather than anything else. Some were jolly and kind, smelling of wrapped candies and cigar smoke; others were deadbeats, trying to milk Alice for her money. There was one guy, Geoff, who loved to gamble. He wore a tasseled leather vest and reeked of Glen Moray. Beverley never liked being left in a room with him. He'd watch her, his eyes sliding over her legs, her breasts, drinking her in as if she were something served to him in a highball glass. One afternoon, when she'd returned from school and was changing in her bedroom, she'd felt the weight of someone at her door. She moved her face just slightly and saw, through the crack, leather tassels. She could hear his heavy breathing, the rhythmic clink of his unfastened belt as he tugged on himself. He did not notice when her mother twisted the key in the front door. He noticed only once she had approached him from behind, called out and raised an open palm to strike him, hard, across the cheek. Later, that evening, Beverley found her mother red-eyed on the couch, half a bottle of scotch, Geoff's favorite, on the table. Beverley hovered in the doorway as her mother slowly, shakily turned.

"He never would have done it if you hadn't been such a flirt," she slurred. "Get out!" The bottle smashed as Alice hurled it against the wall.

This will be the first time Beverley has seen Henry in the five years since he was arrested. She chose not to go and see him in court. Chose to ignore the letter he sent, via his lawyer, which she knew would be filled with excuses instead of accountability. She has seen photographs of him in the newspapers, of course, has carefully cut them out and fixed them into the pages of her scrapbook. When she sees them, she's reminded of their first meeting, on set for a soda commercial. Beverley, the nervous teen model possessed of the kind of clean girl-next-door beauty that unadventurous men seemed to like, chaperoned by her mother. Beverley posing with glass soda bottles wet with condensation. Henry striding in to fix the air-conditioning unit—older, cute, magnetic. The space between them crackling with charged ions. Her life never being the same again.

Will he look that way, like her husband, now? Will he still have those same eyes, that same assured, alpha way about him?

She makes her way to the guard post and gives her name, explains that she called earlier in the week, that she's here to see Henry Lightfoot. She expects the guard to look up at her, to purse his lips—Henry's crimes are notorious—but he simply ticks her name off a ledger, hands her a badge and waves her toward another uniformed figure.

She follows him across the bleak yard and toward the prison entrance, the keys hanging from his belt loudly jangling. The closer they get, the more the air seems to hum with something hostile. San Quentin has a reputation for violence—riots, escapes, prisoners killing guards, prisoners killing prisoners. She wonders, briefly, how Henry has fit into all of that. Has he had to bargain for his own safety in here, or is he one of the dangerous ones? Are people scared of him in here, too?

She follows the guard through a side door and they make their way along sterile gray corridors. The prison has a fetid feel to it, a stink of boiled cabbage and old disinfectant. Although she cannot see the men in their cells, she can hear them—quarreling, posturing, coughing with phlegmy rattles. They can sense her here; she knows it. They can smell her, a lone female, even from a distance. She keeps her head down, focusing only on her red shoes. They have black tarmac scuffs from the prison parking lot.

Eventually they reach a room and the guard opens a heavy door, waving a hand for her to enter. Inside, the room is long and a thick window runs from wall to wall. On one side of the reinforced glass are seats for visitors; on the other are stools. She hadn't realized she would have to talk to Henry like this, with people present. Thankfully, there are not many visitors today, just a young woman in a yellow twinset at the very far end of the room. She has tissues bunched to her eyes. Beverley cannot see the prisoner behind the glass. She can hear only the woman's sobs, her breathy hiccups. The walls are painted a pale salmon pink, and the smell of bleach lingers thick in the air. The guard shows her to a seat and she sits, taking out a pack of cigarettes she has brought for Henry and placing them on the shelf in front of her. The stool opposite her is empty, and that makes Beverley even more anxious. She is going to have to wait for Henry to arrive, to watch him enter.

Without thinking, she moves her hands to her hair, smooths down the stray ends. She is furious to be as nervous as she is. To want to look good for him.

She looks around her. The paint is flaking off the walls and dirt is hunkered in the room's dark corners. The weak lighting washes everything in an anemic glow. It will not do her face any favors. The circles beneath her eyes will bloat with shadow. Her jawline will look soft; she imagines her mother tapping the underside of her chin with the backs of her fingers, encouraging her to lift her head. She was so distracted this morning that she forwent the skin routine that Alice always prescribed her—a double cleanse followed by immersion in ice water, to make the pores close up tight. Whenever she held her face in that bowl and sensed the ache of the ice behind her eyes, she felt that she could scream from the pain.

She considers reaching into her handbag for her lipstick but grasps her own wrist to stop herself.

That's when the door on the other side of the partition opens and Henry is led inside.

She looks up and, just for a second, her heart stops its beating. The guard stands with Henry by the stool, unfastening a pair of handcuffs.

She cannot take in all the details—everything is blurry and unspecific—just the wash of blue overalls, a shock of black hair, those pale eyes, stony and marbled.

She stands up as if she is at a dinner table, waiting for someone important to sit down.

She cannot meet his eyes just yet, but she knows that he is looking at her. She can feel it. She remembers that first meeting in the studio, by the sandwich table when they broke for lunch. He was a foot or so taller than her, and he smelled like a man from the movies. Well, what she'd always imagined men in the movies smelled like, not of cheap drugstore aftershave or English Leather—she was sure as hell Marlon Brando didn't smell of English Leather—but of the sweat of being a man: of work, of something animalistic and intoxicating and adult. Henry's cheeks weren't smooth. He had a chicken pox scar on his forehead, a tiny crater that, in the years to come, she would press with her finger when they were in bed, when he let her. She could see the creep of tattoos peering out from his shirtsleeves. The boys in her graduating class in high school had clear, hairless skin. They didn't have smiles like his, either—small but magnetic, as if she had done something secret to amuse him.

From the flash of yellowed-white, Beverley can tell that Henry is smiling now. He is much bigger than she expected him to be, much stronger, more robust than she had envisaged. She had thought prison might have diminished him, hewn meat from his bones. Instead, it has added muscle and sinew. A glance at his forearms suggests days spent lifting weights or boxing. Henry was never into exercise before his arrest, but now he looks powerful, formidable.

"The green suits you."

A slither of ice water runs through her. His voice. She had almost forgotten his voice, hushed and gentle but with a strange force to it.

Henry never had to speak loudly to get what he wanted. She looks down at her green silk blouse, formfitting, with mother-of-pearl buttons. She spent a long time picking it out, along with a claret A-line skirt. She fiddles with the collar, working up the strength to reply. Then she raises her head, and their eyes meet.

She cannot look away from him. She never could.

"Surprised to see me in such good shape?" He flashes that lopsided smile that once drove her crazy. "Yeah, there's not a lot to do in here except pump weights."

Is that a bruise? Beneath his right eye? Or just the stain of fatigue? His body looks strong, but age has found its way into his face, scoured it out at the cheekbones, added lines.

"Can't lie. Didn't think I'd ever see you here, Bev. You dying or something?" His laugh is hollow, unsure.

She swallows, her eyes trained on him.

"Are the kids okay? Tell them Daddy loves them."

A sourness pricks at the back of her throat.

He hasn't lost that arrogance. It wafts off him. Henry was never scared of anything, except his father. He was always so comfortable being the one to speak, the one to manipulate any situation for his own gain. She won't let him do that now.

"I'm getting married," he says before she has a chance to open her mouth. "A lovely girl. Lorraine. We've been writing each other for a while. We're in love."

Her gut sways. *Love.* She never understood how some people looked at killers and saw rock stars. Sure, someone might be taken in by Henry's looks, his charisma. He always had a magnetism to him. But since his arrest? Since he had admitted killing seven women? How could someone fall in love with that?

Henry watches her intently, as if curious to see her reaction.

"Congratulations," she says, sitting a little straighter in her chair. She won't give him the satisfaction of surprise. Henry blinks, but his expression does not change.

"How are you, Beverley?" he asks after a while, with a tilt of the head, as if he pities her. She is not here to be pitied. She is here to find out *why* he did what he did.

She knows she is going to have to flatter him, to use her own weakness, her fragility, to make him think he is the one with the power. Her cheeks tremble slightly as she draws them into a smile. "I need your help." She swallows again, watches for his reaction.

"Sure," he says without hesitation, but she sees something strange flicker across his face. "Whatever you need." He clasps his hands together and places them on his knee.

How can it possibly feel as if he is toying with her when he is the one behind glass? She glances at the guard waiting in the corner of the room. He looks half asleep, linked fingers resting on his convex belly. The woman at the far end has ceased her sobbing and has moved on to apology, palm flat like a starfish against the glass.

Beverley leans in, lowers her voice. "There's someone killing women around Berryview."

Henry's fingers suddenly unlace, and his boot thuds to the floor.

"Are the kids okay?"

She won't be drawn in. "I want to try to learn about him."

Henry looks confused. "You don't know who it is, right? Or are you in here to tell me my uncle Marvin's been misbehaving?" That empty bravado again. Always with the jokes, deflections.

"I want to know about the sort of person this killer might be."

He raises his thumb and forefinger and wipes at each dry corner of his lips. Then he looks up at her and she is pinned, once again, by those eyes. "Bev, I'm not a headshrinker." He smiles.

"No, but you are a killer."

His smile becomes wider then—but there's a chill to it, as if he's resentful of being bested. He reassembles his features. He always was so conscious of how he appeared.

"Go on, then," he says, waving a hand. "Try me."

She doesn't pause for breath or to give him the opportunity to change his mind. She tells him about the girls, Cheryl, Emily and Diane. She tells him of the ways in which Cheryl and Emily were killed, the ritualistic nature of their murders, the posing, the props, the arrow, the tattooed knuckles. She tells him how she went into his study and found his road maps, how the locations of the cases all intersect at one very specific part of the interstate. The whole time, Henry watches her intently, his eyes never leaving her face.

"So, what do you need me for? Sounds like you've become some sort of detective since I got locked up." He forces another laugh, a fox-like scrape.

She leans back in her chair, tries to mirror his posture. She is sure she has read about this technique in a book somewhere. Mirror someone; it makes them trust you.

"I want to know about *you*. I want to know why you did what you did."

He doesn't tell her to stop as she had expected him to.

"How did you choose your victims?" she asks.

He smiles and does not blink, watching her for a while. His hand goes to the back of his neck, scratches. He seems reluctant, at first, to answer, and she wonders if that is because he cares about what she thinks or because he has become accustomed to lying.

"I just went for whoever was easiest," he supplies eventually, with a shrug.

"Easiest?"

"Yep. Whichever house looked easiest to get into, wherever there wasn't a man home."

Beverley looks briefly to the floor, wonders if she is strong enough for this. But then the faces of Henry's victims appear in her mind's eye, the women he killed. Some of them mothers. One girl in her teens. A housewife in her forties. All of them had tried to fight back, every single one, but given Henry's strength, they never had a chance.

"You watched them?"

"Yeah." He says it as easily as if he is talking about a ball game. "For a while. Just to check there was no boyfriend or anything."

She recalls evenings he spent out of the house, returning late, telling her he'd had a job that went on too long, or that his boss had called him into the warehouse for a meeting. Was this what he was really doing? Watching women? Checking whether they double-locked their doors at night, whether they left windows cracked in hot weather, whether their yards were easy to access?

"In the car?" she manages to ask.

"Or on foot. I'd just walk past the house at the same time every night."

"Always the same car?"

"Yeah. Just our car, Bev."

She blinks away disgust. That was the steering wheel she still touched every day, the same gearshift, the same driver's seat.

"Your guy using different types of cars?"

She nods. That was one reason Roger had given for the crimes not being linked—different vehicles had been spotted at each crime scene.

"That's easy enough," Henry says. "Anyone can access multiple cars. You just take 'em. Maybe your guy's some small-time felon taking things further, pushing boundaries."

"'Pushing boundaries'?"

"In my experience, these things start small," Henry explains, clearly relishing having authority on the matter. "Like, a killer might start off with little things—breaking and entering, stealing women's lingerie, watching people in their houses . . ."

She bristles.

"Then he might wake up one day and find that's just not cutting it, that he needs something else, something bigger, to satisfy him."

Beverley can't meet his eye. He is talking in the third person, but she knows he must be referring to himself, his own behaviors.

"So then he might move to grabbing a girl, touching her, sexual assault or whatever, and it spirals from there. It's an urge for him."

Him, not *me*.

"The itch becomes harder to scratch, the thrill harder to come by."

Through dizziness, Beverley must concede that he has a point. Their killer could be someone with a few smaller crimes under his belt. He could have a record already.

"But, Beverley." Her head snaps up. It's the first time he hasn't had a hint of a smile about him. She remembers that expression: a blankness that came upon his face whenever he spoke about his father, whenever he talked about trying to make him proud as a kid but never succeeding, whenever he recalled how his father would taunt and belittle him.

"This guy, your killer—he hates women."

"What?" Despite herself, she is stunned.

"Pretty women, successful, talented. That's what you said, right? The type of girls that were prom queens." Henry scratches his neck. "He probably feels . . . what's the word? Emaculated."

"Emasculated."

"Yeah. He feels emasculated by them—rejected, or whatever."

Did Henry hate women? Had he hated her during those few years that they'd been married? It had sometimes felt as if he had, his resentment bubbling up through the cracks, convincing her that she had done something wrong in those moments, that she'd failed as a wife, as a woman, to keep him happy.

"Did he touch 'em?"

She is jarred back to the room. "Sorry?"

"Did he have his way?" He has adopted a mock prim tone.

Her eyes dart. How can he talk about them like that?

"I don't know."

She *doesn't* know. She didn't ask if the women had been sexually assaulted. She doesn't even want to know the answer.

"He's probably some sad guy who struck out with too many women and wants to punish them for it," he says plainly.

She pauses.

"Maybe a loner," Henry continues. "Maybe never married." Henry scratches at the stubble on his neck again. "I bet he uses hookers."

Her eyes flick up to his.

"How come?"

"He'll be finding ways to feel in control." His hand rests at his neck and she wonders if it's intentional. "That'll give him a kick, making a woman do anything he wants her to do. I'd bet on it."

She considers it. That would make sense—killing is so often about control—but how might they find the sorts of men who pay for sex? She makes a mental note to discuss this with Elsie and Margot. She just won't tell them how she got the idea.

"What of the fact that there are different weapons involved," she asks, "different ways of killing? Does that suggest it's different people? Killers normally—" She pauses, feeling suddenly absurd talking to him like this. "Don't they usually stick with the same weapon?"

Henry snorts drily. It raises the hair on the back of her neck.

"Bev, there are men in here who've killed people with sharpened pencils, done things I could never harm your ears with. They don't care if they're using the same thing. They just care about the killing."

She thinks of the men in her scrapbook, what the newspapers had said—how they favored strangling or shooting. There definitely seemed to be some consistency to their actions.

"What about you?" she asks him. "Did it matter to you?" Her mouth feels dry. "How you did it."

A grin splits his face.

"Bev, I'm a lazy guy." His laugh is chilling. "I just used what was easiest—what I could find, whatever fit my mood."

She is sure she has misheard him. "Your mood?"

"Sure," he says flippantly. "If I felt angry that day, something like a bit of pipe or a wrench or a fire poker—something like that would do it. If I wanted something quicker, if I didn't want too much mess, just a rope or hands. It's more—" He pauses, and she wonders if he is finally realizing the horror of what he's saying. "It's more poetic like that," he says eventually, glancing at the ceiling as if summoning some grand idea. "Like art, or music, or whatever."

Despite herself, she has begun to shake. She tries her hardest to hide it, burying her hands under her legs, nails gripping the Formica chair.

"Wrap it up, lovebirds." The guard stands, glances at his watch.

The sobbing woman, the only other visitor, screeches her chair back so violently that it topples. Then she tears across the room and waits with clenched fists for the guard to let her out.

"But how are you really, Beverley?" Henry doesn't seem to want their meeting to end. "I worry about you, y'know?" He clearly knows he has her rattled.

Another guard has arrived at Henry's side and is replacing the handcuffs. Henry watches Beverley as he stands, keeps his eyes fixed on hers as he is led out of the room.

She does not stop shaking until he has left and she has followed the guard down the corridor, has stepped out of those barbaric-looking gates. Pressure is building at the backs of her eyes. She is so frustrated at herself, frustrated at the sheer impotence of her anger. It changes nothing. Rage becomes ridiculous when it has nowhere to go. It will not change what Henry has done, what she needs to do now. It cannot continue like this—men taking whatever they want and no one holding them accountable for the harm they cause. Henry might have thought he was manipulating her from the other side of that glass—he might have thought he had control, as he had five years ago—but really he has gifted her ammunition. If Henry's right, she has a workable lead. She just needs to figure out how to find the men who use prostitutes in the areas around the killings and determine how the victims they're investigating could possibly be linked to that.

As she crosses the parking lot, she winces. Raising her hand to her aching jaw, she realizes she has been clenching her teeth this whole time. She forces her face to slacken, shakes out her hands, tries to remind herself of her own strength. She has looked into the eyes of a killer; she has seen what's inside his head. She is in control. Still, when she's reached the car, slammed the door and locked it from the inside, she begins, loudly, wildly, to scream.

FIFTEEN

DIANE HOWARD MURRAY, the missing model whose name Margot had scrawled on her arm at the party, is found dead in an alleyway in Calabasas on a sweltering day in late July. Little is said about her, or about any of the details of her murder, in the newspapers. All she is afforded is a small paragraph, a cursory acknowledgment of a death, tucked away among advertisements for golf course developments and meatball subs. There are no mentions of any links to the previous killings, no tributes, no pleas for information from the public.

Margot knows why this is. She knows why there were no half-page photos of Diane, as there had been of the cheerleader Emily Roswell. Newspaper reporters don't write about trailer parks, and Golden Point is no exception to the rule. Named ambitiously after the color the sun turns the dirt as it sets, Golden Point is not somewhere you'll find on postcards or in holiday brochures—a mixed neighborhood, home to low-income families and those forced to watch as town planners build on land their families owned. It is not "well-kept," like the neighboring suburb of Hyder Hills, whose residents spend their lives alongside the second houses of Hollywood execs, mansions looming high on the shrub-pocked hillsides. But Margot knows that "aspirational" suburb is separated from Golden Point by only a couple of meaningless miles. She also knows that "aspirational" is just another way of saying "rich and white."

In some ways, though, Margot feels more at home in Golden Point than she ever has on the manicured streets of LA. It's not her first visit here, after all.

She drives easily through the park's gates, left wide-open and rusting, no security guard checking ID, no bolts, no padlocks. The message is clear: *If you're willing to come here, have at it.* There's a sign, its neon bulbs cracked and furred with dirt, welcoming visitors with fading cheer. Duke, from his spot on the passenger seat, thrusts his head out of the open window and barks. Margot shushes the dog and locates the lot she's looking for.

In the rearview mirror, she can see a couple of old folks in deck chairs, half eyeing her from outside their trailers.

She makes for the front door of the Airstream, its metal contracting noisily in the heat. She knocks and waits. She knows the code. Three loud knocks, followed by a pause, then four more.

The door is opened by a man whose shoulders fill the whole frame; Ray must have taken on some more security. The man blinks stone-faced at Margot, then flinches as Duke licks his hand with a wet tongue.

"Ah, ah, ah!"

Margot leans to the side and sees, behind the guard's huge bulk, Ray Roberts seated at a cramped table, waggling his finger at her.

"Get that horse out of here, Margot. He'll eat all my stock."

She glances down at the dog. "He's a Great Dane," she calls weakly, as if that's the answer to anything.

"He'll tolerate being tied up outside, thank you very much,

Margot." Ray places exaggerated horn-rimmed glasses on the bridge of his nose and bends over the table. He's weighing powders and pills, a pile of brown paper packages stacked up by his elbow.

She sighs, then retreats down the steps, searching for something that will take Duke's strength. She settles for a fence post, hopes for the best and loops the leash around the base several times.

"Now, that's better." Ray smiles when she returns. "We're not a zoo in here." He turns back to the pills and begins diligently portioning out a new pile. "Just a social visit?" He doesn't look up.

The guard has stepped away and sits thumbing his way through *Playboy*. The air smells bitter. "I'll Never Smile Again" by Doris Day is playing on the radio.

"I broke a heel," she says. "The Hélène Arpels. Taupe."

It is not just pills and powders that Ray Roberts deals in. He also does a fine line in rare designer shoes. Margot had heard rumors a while back that the studio stylists sometimes went to him if they wanted something special for one of their pictures at short notice. Marilyn had even worn a pair of his Ferragamo pumps once. Margot had had to check him out for herself.

"Okay, so we know you're not here for the Hélène Arpels."

Margot begins to protest.

Ray interrupts her with a raised finger stacked with rings. "You're a terrible liar." He removes his glasses and watches her from beneath his brow. "Try harder."

"The heel did break." Technically, it did.

"What is it that you really want, Margot? I'm busy here."

She holds his gaze, considers, momentarily, trying to lie. "Did you know Diane Howard Murray?" she asks outright.

Ray almost recoils, shakes his head in surprise. "Why is someone like you asking about a girl like that?"

"What do you mean, *someone like me*?"

"Well, Margot, forgive me for being blunt, but Diane wasn't someone who someone like *you* is normally concerned with."

"Didn't she want to be a model? I'm into fashion."

Ray raises a skeptical eyebrow.

She lets him. She is being glib.

"Girls are being harmed." Margot steps closer to the table.

The guard glances up from his magazine, then at Ray, who keeps him in place with a shake of the head.

"They're being killed. Diane was not the first, and at this rate she won't be the last. I know she lived in Golden Point. I'm just trying to find out a bit more about her, okay?"

"So . . . what?" He allows his glasses to drop to his chest on their chain. "You're working for the cops?"

She feels the energy in the room change instantly.

"No, Ray, I'm not working for the cops."

He scans her face, and she knows he sees the real meaning there, that she is working *in spite of* the cops.

"Was she in the game?" Margot thinks about Beverley's theory that the killer might be using prostitutes. Well, she knows plenty of girls around Golden Point who had to resort to that to get by. Ray does, too.

"Folks won't like you poking around." He avoids the question.

"Was she?" Margot can't help thinking of her mother blotting her lipstick in the mirror, heavy perfume in the air, the rush of the cold streaming in through the door as she stepped out into the darkness.

Ray considers for a while, stroking his glasses chain. "She may have done it on the side," he relents, "but I heard she really was making a go of the modeling."

Margot nods. She knew it. "Does she have family around here?"

"Her grandma Pearl owns the junk store on the corner," Ray says eventually. "Less of a store, more of a shack. Posters in the window. You won't miss it. But hey." He fixes Margot's eye, warns, "She's just lost her granddaughter. Go easy."

He's already chopping powder by the time the door slams shut behind her. She leaves Duke tied up outside. Ray won't mind. Duke looks like a watchdog, even if he acts like a poodle. She turns back when she is halfway down the next lot and sees the security guard bending to place a bowl of water beside the animal as he pats its head.

R**AY WAS RIGHT.** Diane's face is plastered across the windows of the junk store. She is captured in multiple iterations of the same pose, with the same wide smile, the same dark bob sharp at the chin. She was beautiful—that's clear—like someone you'd see on a TV talent show, in a sequined dress shining under studio lights.

Margot can relate to wanting to find your way out of the life, the situation, that you were born into. She herself had started out just like Diane. Her mother had tried, as best she could, to raise her well, but it was hard when she had no money, no electricity, no food. Margot had learned then that beauty, that appealing to men, was a means to better your situation. So she studied it. Studied how best to get a man's attention. How best to manipulate those around you into believing you are something you are not. She had no qualms about acknowledging her own beauty. After all, she cannot take any credit for it. She did not select the genes that gave her this face; her body was a gift from her mother. It cannot be arrogant, surely, to admire the work of others. She became a master at convincing people that she deserved to be in the room, that she had a command of herself and her body. It made them want to be near her. It's how she ended up meeting Stephen. She never would have found herself at the same party as someone like him had she not looked the way she looks, had she not held herself the way she holds herself—unapologetically on show, never doubting that women wanted to be her and men wanted to be with her. It was all an act, of course. A ruse. A lie honed from childhood. Diane, too, had been using her looks, to try to find her way out of life at Golden Point. And she was close, so very, very close, until everything was taken away from her.

JUSTICE FOR DIANE, the posters read, and Margot feels a stab of hatred for the newspaper editors, the news network producers, who have no doubt heard about Diane's murder but didn't deem it consumable for their audiences. Murder stories—or, rather, what makes a *good* murder story—so often hinge on the social standing of the victims. Like with the "Career Girls Murders," the name slapped by the media on the murders of Emily Hoffert and Janice Wylie in Manhattan a couple of years ago. Janice, who worked as a researcher for *Newsweek*, was the daughter of an influential advertising exec. Schoolteacher Emily was the daughter of a high-powered surgeon. Their faces were splashed across the newspapers, highlighted on the evening news. White Working Women were under threat! The stories ran for weeks. This crime against Diane was just as brutal, the details just as appalling, yet one dominated the headlines while the other is being swept under the carpet.

Margot pushes on the door and a crude bell signals her entrance. In a corner, an elderly woman reclines, fingers pinching the bridge of her nose. The rest of the shop, Margot can see, is full to the roof with pots, pans, kitchen gadgets, all cracked and crumbling facets of life polished up and put on sale. The posters in the window are snatching all the light, so the space is gloomy, sprinkled with spiraling motes of dust.

"Lost?" the woman levels from the corner.

Margot resists the urge to smooth down her skirt, to plaster a smile across her face.

"You must be Mrs. Howard Murray."

The woman rocks in the chair, then sighs. "I am she."

"I'm Margot Green. I wanted to ask you about Diane."

The woman's eyes snap up. Margot can see, then, the jarring resemblance—the high cheekbones, the hazel eyes, a beauty passed down by blood. She imagines Pearl decades earlier, the same age as Diane, in front of a mirror, fixing her hair, fastening a necklace around her throat.

"Diane never did nothing wrong."

Margot shakes her head quickly. "No." She steps forward. "I'm trying to find out who might be responsible for what happened to her."

"Who are you to care?" Pearl eyes Margot's dress, her shoes, her jewelry. "Newspapers don't care. Damn police don't care." She rocks back and forth in the chair.

"I grew up here," Margot says. "I know what it's like to come from a place like Golden Point."

The woman watches her, shoulders rounding guardedly.

Margot continues, determined. "I want people to know about Diane. I think it's possible she was killed by someone who has killed two other women already."

"What?"

"Both young, like Diane. Beautiful."

"You know who did this?" Pearl hauls herself from the seat, fists clenched beside her, and Margot can see the delicate bones showing through the skin.

"We don't know who yet."

The woman tuts, starts to turn away.

"But we're trying to find a link between the girls. Maybe it was someone they all knew. Maybe there's something connecting them that we're not yet seeing."

"So you're a cop." She nods, disgusted. "We already told you everything, and you did nothing."

"I'm not a cop," Margot assures her. "I'm someone who's had her life ruined by someone dangerous, too. I want you to know that people are interested in your granddaughter, in what happened. They *do* care."

The woman is silent, watching her as if weighing up whether Margot can be trusted.

"Diane was trying to make it as a model, right? Was she having any luck?"

The woman purses her lips, then reluctantly crosses the floor toward a desk pushed up against the wall.

"She was doing okay with it," Pearl says as she strains to reach for something on the desktop. "She'd had meetings with a couple agencies, was doing cleaning work to make money, get straight again. Here." She thrusts a pile of photographs toward Margot. Margot takes them and flicks through a series of headshots of Diane, a face that commands attention, one that seems as if it belongs to someone whose name you would one day know. There are some candid photographs, too: Diane in the sunshine, tongue bared as she's about to lick a Popsicle; Diane in her cleaning company's apron, a bold logo on her chest.

"I tried to show these to the police." Pearl's rheumy eyes meet Margot's. "I wanted them to know she was a person, with a family and a life. All the press printed was a paragraph, made it sound like she'd accidentally stepped into the wrong alleyway and got herself killed." Her eyes close. "It wasn't like that." Pearl's voice grows more urgent. "He'd thought about it, that bastard—whoever it was that took her."

Her tone tightens. "There were things he did to her; they had to be planned. But the papers didn't even talk about 'em."

This she hadn't expected. "Are you able to tell me about those things?" Margot feels her palms growing clammy. She thinks of Cheryl Herrera and the arrow, Emily Roswell's tattooed knuckles.

Pearl eyes Margot cagily, then spits out, "He choked her."

Margot can feel the vitriol, the scorch of anger, in the words. Another strangling.

"He dressed her. He . . . put a coat on her, some designer thing."

A coat. He dressed her. Just like he dressed Cheryl Herrera in the wig.

"He put suspenders on her. Left her body to be seen like that. Put it on show for everyone, like she was some shop mannequin." Pearl's hand goes to her mouth.

Margot's mind is reeling, searching for traction. She knows she should comfort the old woman, but she's trying to order her own thoughts. Diane was strangled, the body dressed and posed. That's more than enough to suggest that this is the work of the same killer. What else can the cops be looking for?

Pearl stands there, her body fragile, her face wracked with grief, with rage. Then Margot remembers something—something Barbie Cook mentioned at the party.

"She'd been writing letters, I heard—to a movie director, Mason Clarke."

"To who?"

"Can I borrow these pictures?" Margot asks. "I'll return them; I'll bring them right back here to you. I promise you that."

Pearl hesitates.

"I need to show someone Diane's picture," she coaxes. "I need to ask them some questions—if you'll allow it. I think it could help us find her killer." She searches Pearl's face, the hollow cheeks, the soft, crepey skin of her neck. "I know what it's like when no one will believe that what you say is true," Margot says softly. "I know what it's like to feel discarded. Please. Trust me."

The woman closes her eyes for a moment, and then opens them. When they meet Margot's, she sees something in them she recognizes—a steeliness, a warning. *You'd better find out who did this,* they say.

Pearl hands over the photos.

FIVE DAYS MISSING

THERE ARE THINGS we fear as women. Everyday, pedestrian things. Things that lift the hair on our necks, that stiffen our vertebrae, that ratchet our already heightened nervous systems to a state of alert.

Perhaps he sits an inch too close to us on a public bus. Perhaps we hear his footsteps behind us on a street that's just a little underlit.

He might be that guy from work, the one who made an advance, the one we had to rebuff—maybe it pissed him off; maybe we denied him something he felt he was owed.

Maybe it's missing the last train home. Or those several agonizing seconds it takes to get the key out of our purse on the front doorstep at night. Maybe it's smiling in the wrong way at the figure on the street corner, sensing him watch you, eyes boring into your body, as you go.

It can be coming upon an intruder in our own homes—here for the television and the jewelry but deciding that while he's here he might have something else, too.

It's locating the door in every room.

It's the sizing up of peers, of neighbors, of colleagues, of the guy behind the counter at the store, the one sitting a few seats away from you in an otherwise empty movie theater.

It is the minute-by-minute decision-making, the endless calculations, the mapping of escape routes, the constant, exhausting negotiation of egos.

These fears have become so embedded in the breath of my own life that they are as known to me as the lines on my palm.

Yet I never thought to fear this. I never allowed my mind to wander that far, to stretch itself to something so completely outlandish.

Now I am trapped, bound, and it is so very dark. My head pounds, hot and heavy, something wet and sticky congealed at the base of my skull. When I touch it, an image of split fruit flashes into my mind—nauseating—and I kick myself for having been prepared for every eventuality but this one.

There I go again.

Blaming myself. For being a woman. For allowing myself to be taken when, in reality, nothing in my power was ever going to stop you, was it?

You are the one who has done wrong, who has harmed. You are the one who has turned my life on its head and reduced it to four damp walls; one pipe; bound, bruised hands.

But the next step is on me. I am the one who is going to have to find a way to get out.

SIXTEEN

Beverley is restless, drifting into and out of sleep.

She's been seeing faces in her dreams. Henry. The dead girls. The image of Emily Roswell in her cheerleader uniform. Cheryl Herrera on the track, sneakers pummeling the crushed shale. Then she sees blood, arrows slicing through tissue, a body engorged and swollen at the bottom of a lake.

Henry may have slaughtered seven people, but she herself had seen only one dead body: her father's, in an open casket at his funeral when she was a child. She remembers waiting in line to walk past his corpse, although she wasn't quite sure why she had to queue to see her own dead father. His latest girlfriend had sat in the very front row, stinking up the pews with her cheap drugstore perfume. Beverley and her mother had huddled at the back so Alice could escape every few minutes to smoke. When she returned to the church each time, her hands trembled. Beverley was never sure if it was the nicotine that made them shake or her mother's anger that her father had now abandoned them twice.

Beverley knows Margot thinks she has "daddy issues," that she's incapable of making decisions for herself. What pains her the most is that she knows Margot is right. Things happened quickly after Beverley met Henry at the studio that day. High school graduation came and went, and the two moved in together after a small, hurried wedding. She wore broderie anglaise from Macy's. Alice wasn't overly happy about things. She thought Beverley could do better than an air-conditioning salesman—but at least she'd found a man who would take her. And what could Alice do? Bev had turned eighteen in the fall and could make decisions for herself. She had money saved from her modeling jobs, and a man who loved her. She was set.

Henry, it became clear very quickly, was a man of appetite. He couldn't get enough of her—in the bedroom after work, sometimes even in the kitchen as she was making his breakfast. She'd been bewildered by his advances the first week after she moved in—she'd had sex ed classes at school, but she'd never gone further than kissing a boy before—but this was obviously what being a wife was. She was there to see to his impulses and keep him happy, even if it meant doing things she didn't want to do. It was worth it, though, for the way he looked at her. That's what she told herself. Sometimes he clasped her hair in his hands and held it tight at the base of her skull. He'd lean her over his arm and kiss her so hard that it left her breathless. Even if he spent the rest of the evening ignoring her and she busied herself around the house desperately trying to work out what she had done to turn his mood, it was worth it. It was worth it to be desired, even if just for a moment.

She has never wanted to admit it, but there was always a part of her that enjoyed being controlled. Henry had liked to know where she was at all times, whom she was with. She had earned the bulk of their money, but Henry was in charge of the finances. He didn't want her to work anymore, didn't want men looking at her in that way, but he had no qualms about spending the money she had earned. When Beverley had learned of Henry's crimes, the shock and disgust eventually shifted to something else entirely: confusion, a sense of being adrift. Who was she if there was no man there to admire her? How was she to act when there was no one there to pull her strings?

A noise startles her and she sits bolt upright in bed, pulse quickening. She waits awhile for the noise to come again. When it does, it is familiar, that routine shuffling sound, the soft swish of a small body brushing against the wall outside her room.

Benjamin must be sleepwalking again.

She pulls the sheets away, noticing that they are damp with her sweat, and climbs out of bed. She must be careful not to alarm her son, not to wake him. That can be dangerous, the doctor said. She must simply guide him back into bed, tuck him in, hope he settles.

The corridor is dark, lit only by the moon's glow through a gap in the curtains. She can see Benjamin. He looks so small in his pajamas—his tiny hands, his bare toes, his eyes open but unseeing as he shuffles along the hallway.

Beverley feels a stab of guilt. Her mother maintains that Benjamin sleepwalks because he is disturbed by the loss of his father. Beverley has never told him, or Audrey, the truth about Henry's crimes—that's a conversation they will have when they are older—but they know he did a bad thing and is being punished for it, that it means Benjamin cannot see him, that Audrey will never meet him. They were so trusting, the kids, when she told them. They watched her wide-eyed and nodded even though she knew they must have been scared by what she was saying. Benjamin started sleepwalking as soon as he turned four. It has been a regular occurrence since then, and another reason for Beverley's mother to judge her.

She goes to Benjamin and bends, taking him softly by the shoulders. She can smell the apple shampoo on his hair, the delicious scent of sleepy children that makes her want to gather him up and squeeze him tight. But she doesn't. She leads him back to his room and steers him into his bed. She tucks him in, kisses him on the soft peach of his cheek and closes the door behind her.

She hovers outside the room for a while, eyeing the nails on the wall where photos of her and Henry once hung. Her modeling pictures had been up there, too—Beverley in spearfishing gear and neoprene for Tampax, in frothy white lace for Clairol. She remembers tearing them down, hurling them to the floor, the glass frames smashing. She has still never got around to replacing them, the sun stains a daily reminder of exactly what went wrong. Henry was never houseproud, but he was a practical, capable man, good with his hands. When he was put away, Beverley found herself as head of a household she wasn't entirely sure how to run. A fortnight after his arrest, a fuse blew upstairs, plunging Benjamin's bedroom into darkness. It was ten days before she managed to get to the library to find the right book and work out how to fix it. She was too ashamed to ask anyone else for help.

She walks to the window on the landing to pull the curtain to, glancing through the glass, up at the stars, then down to the front lawn, as manicured as ever.

Except...

There is something down there.

There is something laid out on the lawn, bulky and dark—something the size of... the size of a body.

She freezes, her blood going still in her veins before it surges and she bolts down the stairs, the sound of her breath, heavy and frantic, in the air. She pulls at the sideboard pushed up against the front door. It screeches as she drags it across the vinyl floor, but she does not care if it wakes the children; she has to get out there to see what, or who, is on her lawn. Her hands shake as she unlocks the door, and she sprints out into the still night and across to the *thing* that lies, bathed in moonlight, in the very center of the lawn. She reaches it and immediately recoils. Then she forces herself to look, horror scuttling up from the bottom of her belly.

It's a carcass. Not human, but animal. A pig. Its snout is horrifyingly soft and pink. Its eyes are open. The grass surrounding it is soaked in blood.

Beverley feels as if she might be sick.

She wheels around, her eyes roaming every bush, every crevice, every shadow of the yard, searching for someone hiding. She rushes to the fence and looks down the street, expecting to find someone fleeing. But the street is silent, the cars static.

She steps back to the carcass. She has to move it. She cannot let the neighbors see. She quickly considers what she will need—a tarpaulin, some gloves, a large spade. As she runs through the list, she can't help but think of the animal's significance. *Pigs*. A derogatory word for cops. Her mind goes to the posters she's seen in some of her neighbors' windows, the newspaper articles she's seen about marches against the police. Has someone seen Roger coming to the house? Does someone know she's sleeping with the very man who arrested her own husband? She considers, briefly, that it might even be a threat to Roger himself.

Whatever it is, she thinks as she eyes the carcass, its slit throat, she knows it's a warning.

SEVENTEEN

THE GIRLS AT the department store are rattled. They tear around the shop floor, straightening Biba jackets on their mannequins, fastening metallic buttons, smoothing their own set hair in front of their window reflections. September is only a few weeks away, and they've just learned that Broderick Arnold, *the* Broderick Arnold of Arnold's Department Stores, is on his way for his preseason inspection, and the man is more than particular when it comes to the appearance of his shop floors.

Margot stands behind the till, thumbing her way through an old *Vogue*. She glances up at the other girls, flapping like hummingbirds, and takes a breath. She'd woken soaked in sweat this morning, the embers of a nightmare she hadn't had for a long time smoldering in the muggy air of the room. Stephen had been in her dream, reaching out for her, clawing desperately at her face, screaming her name. She'd watched him fall backward, away from her, plummeting downward into spiraling darkness. It was a nightmare she'd had for months after Stephen was arrested, and after he did what he did to himself while in jail, awaiting trial. She'd never told anyone about that nightmare—just as she'd never told anyone how she'd holed up in her mother's old apartment when it had all happened, numbing herself with alcohol and pain pills. She couldn't say his name for two whole years. Whenever she tried, her throat would spasm and swallow the letters down. But no one knows that.

She straightens her shoulders. The nightmare might have returned, but she cannot allow herself to go back there. She will not allow herself to be that weak again.

She watches as a pretty sales assistant uses two hands to tug the straps of her bra upward, lifting her breasts into bullet positions. Margot could use her chest, too, she supposes, but she knows all she has to do to impress Arnold, to impress any powerful man, is to breathe and hold his eye contact. Women in subservient positions, women working in department stores owned by wealthy entrepreneurs, do not usually meet the eyes of powerful men. Margot likes to launch that challenge, to disarm, see what comes back. When she does it, she can almost see the whirring of the men's brains inside their heads. *Who is this woman?* she can see them thinking. *Who the hell does she think she is? And what does she know that I don't know?*

Twenty minutes later, Broderick Arnold steps through the revolving doors and the hummingbirds scatter. He smiles and does the rounds, greets them all—a businessman's routine—and when he passes by Margot, she fixes his eye, keeps her expression plain.

It brings him to a stop in front of her counter.

He tilts his head, a smile twitching at the corners of his mouth. She notices the cut of his suit—tailor-made. Broderick Arnold would never wear anything sold in his stores.

He raises a finger. "Remind me of your name," he orders.

She smiles, happy to play along for watching eyes. "Margot Green."

He slaps a palm on the counter. "Have a beautiful day, Ms. Green."

Minutes later, she's in a familiar position on the desk in his office, his head between her thighs.

It's not sex per se that Margot gets a kick out of. It's the tipping scales of power that sex facilitates. Broderick Arnold is one of the wealthiest men in California, with multiple businesses under his belt, including this department store, yet she can manipulate him with her body, with just the *suggestion* of her body, and she has done so on many occasions. She wonders, from time to time, when they meet like this, whether Broderick knows who she was before this life. Perhaps he does—Margot has never hidden from the press. Perhaps he even finds it titillating. The papers always made her out as some femme fatale, a seductress who used her wiles to catch her husband in the act of killing—entirely inaccurately, of course. But she didn't hate it.

She was drinking grasshoppers at home when the cops finally came to tell her that Stephen had been arrested. She wasn't surprised, but it annoyed her that the news channels had got hold of the information before she did; Stephen's face was already being plastered across TV screens statewide. As the detectives sat her down on Stephen's expensive couch to tell her that he had been arrested for the murders of eight people, the phone began to ring. It didn't stop for the next two hours, until one of the detectives convinced Margot to unplug it from the wall. Soon enough, the press arrived, cameras pushed up against the window, the door knocker rattling. Margot stood up. "I really wouldn't do that, Mrs. Green," a detective called after her. But Margot knew the only way she would survive this scrutiny was to face it head-on, so she opened the door, tucked her hair behind her ear and stood before them.

When Arnold is finished and Margot is sated, she lights a cigarette and accepts a whiskey poured from a crystal decanter.

"Do you know Mason Clarke?" she asks him as she puffs out a plume of smoke.

Arnold laughs. "Never one for the small talk, were you, Margot?"

"Do you?" She tilts her head, smiles.

Arnold takes a gulp from his glass. "Sure. I've never met him, but we helped fund some of his pictures. Why do you ask?"

"Think you could get me an intro?"

"Should I be jealous?" he teases, crushing ice between his teeth.

"You know I've only got eyes for you, Mr. Arnold."

He places the glass on the desktop, turns to her with a serious expression. "What's this about?"

"What do you mean?"

"Clarke. I've heard some stuff about him. Not pretty." He sips again.

"And?"

"You sure you want a part of that?"

"I just want to sound him out about something."

"Hmm." He smiles dubiously. "I guess I can see you on-screen—that face, those pins." He reaches for her and she lets him. "I'll get my assistant to put in a call." He runs his fingers around her ankle, traces the contour of her calf muscle. "But, Margot?"

She quirks an eyebrow.

"Be careful, okay?"

"Don't you worry, Mr. Arnold." She strokes his hand away, stands. She needs to get back out onto the shop floor. "I can take care of myself."

"Don't doubt it for a minute." He raises his glass.

EIGHTEEN

Beverley had planned to meet her friends in the bar of the Monument Hotel at two p.m. sharp. But it's two twenty-two p.m. and she's hovering across the street from the lobby doors, her collar damp with perspiration, her path blocked not by tardiness or reluctance, but by hundreds of marching protestors.

As bodies surge past, she watches, taking in their signs, their shouts, their passionate songs. The news has been filled with protests like this for as long as she can remember. A handful of her Berryview neighbors keep posters in their windows to show support. She's surprised Elsie is not out here, too, taking notes, asking questions, grabbing a placard for herself.

END POLICE BRUTALITY! one large sign reads, held by several people. Someone holds a bullhorn aloft and cries, "Stop the violence! Equal rights for all. End. Police. Brutality. Now."

A cheer goes up from the crowd and Beverley feels her face flushing hot. Can they see it on her? she wonders. Can they see the traces of her relationship with Roger?

She cannot shake the image of pink animal flesh from her mind. She thinks of the warning, the taunt. It can only have been meant for her, but she still does not know who left it, and she cannot tell Elsie and Margot about it. They have no idea about Roger. They'd never understand.

Beverley had never much considered the role of the police until the police had slammed into her life like an avalanche. When she was younger, she placed cops in the same benign category as teachers or doctors—people who operated on a benevolent plane, a force for good, the sort of people who lived according to a strict moral code—but that has changed of late. She has never known Roger, or the other officers at his precinct, to be racist or cruel, but there are so many things about his job that she will never be privy to. She is not his wife or his colleague. Roger doesn't speak in depth about the civil rights movement. They don't discuss the newspaper headlines about police corruption, about prejudice, about violence against minorities. He won't be drawn in when she asks him about yet another activist being killed, or clashes between protestors and police, heavy-handed arrests, rumors of corruption, supremacism, violence.

Her mind is tugged suddenly back to the street by something familiar in the crowd. It's a face she recognizes, one that sparks something strange inside of her. He is in front of her for only a few seconds, carrying his own placard but staying silent, gaze fixed firmly ahead. It's Christopher Appleton, the new neighbor from across the street—number forty-four. She's sure of it. She stares at the back of his head as he departs, swept up in the crowd. She would never have expected someone like him to be part of a protest like this. Her stomach twists. What else does she not know about her new neighbor?

The protest eventually thins, and she makes her way across the street to the hotel.

Inside, the air-conditioning has been cranked up to full blast, a jarring contrast to the August mugginess outside. The restaurant is decked out like some sort of space station. Sputnik lights hang from the ceiling; silver paper with a geometric pattern lines the walls. The seats and tables are sleek stainless steel. It makes her think of the NASA astronauts she saw on the news—shot up into the star-flecked unknown in little more than a fiery tin can. What must they see from up there, looking down on the swirling green-blue marbled earth; their days marked by the fluid, repeated rising and setting of the sun; the watchful moon, cratered and surreal, filling the windows, waiting for human footsteps? For a short moment, she is envious. Perhaps life would be easy up there, above the earth's gravitational pull, her weightless body reduced to its base functions: sleeping, eating, excreting. No Henry. No nightmares. Away from the burden of what has happened to her in this life.

"Hey, aren't you the girl from the half-and-half commercial?" Margot calls playfully, and Bev's attention snaps back down to terra firma. "Don't worry. We haven't started yet."

As she takes a seat, the metal unnervingly cold against her thighs, she sees that Margot and Elsie have brought notes along with them. She feels immediately redundant. They have both been off chasing leads in the murder cases. What has she contributed, beyond a few nervous questions tossed Roger's way? She cannot tell them about her visit to San Quentin. They'd be furious if they knew she'd been in contact with Henry. She cannot tell them about the carcass on her lawn. She looks like she's shown up empty-handed.

"Bloody Mary," Margot calls, and a few moments later the drink appears on the table. She leans toward Beverley, grabs her wrist and shoves the glass into her hand. "Drink." Margot has always seemed so certain of her own movements, possessed of a confidence that eludes most other women. When they first met, Beverley was shocked at how tactile Margot was, not thinking twice about grasping Beverley's knee or allowing their shoulders to brush together. Beverley's mother rarely touched her, even when Beverley was a child. She never braided her hair or held a sponge to her skin in the bath. Margot's obviously did. Others might look at her friend and see a party girl, someone flippant, shallow, but Beverley has always been in awe of her ability to make a connection, and quickly, with any sort of person, from any walk of life. Her smile wins people over, and that easy wink. People lean in for it, grasp, like iron filings rushing to a magnet.

The drink has barely touched Beverley's lips before Margot starts talking about Diane Howard Murray. Beverley struggles to imagine her glamorous friend traipsing around a trailer park in her sunglasses and her chisel-toe heels. The image almost amuses her, but as Margot continues to tell them about Diane's grandmother Pearl, what she's learned about Diane's life, Beverley cannot help but be impressed. Margot is sharp, smart, braver than Beverley could ever imagine herself to be. She takes them through the specifics of the crime scene, the way that Diane was dressed in a coat, how the killer took great care to stage the body, putting her in black suspenders and placing her on display.

Elsie tells them that Hunter has agreed to run one small story about Cheryl Herrera's missing bracelet. Patti had to take the lead to him, told him she'd had the tip-off from one of her old colleagues, Dom Roachford.

"So, then," Elsie continues, opening her notebook, "let's try to think differently. What sort of guy would commit these crimes?"

Margot swivels in her seat and begins to list as if she is answering a question on a game show. "Boyfriends. Fathers. Close male relatives. Male friends who want to be more than that—always the first port of call."

"Well, you say that, but our husbands all murdered people they didn't know," Beverley counters. "And these killings—they're not like the sort of murders you see committed by family members." She thinks of Roger, how he was convinced these weren't domestic disputes.

Margot frowns in defeat.

"Emily Roswell didn't even have a boyfriend," adds Elsie. "We know that. She wasn't seeing anyone, or at least as far as the parents knew. And the father has an alibi, confirmed by his work. Same with Cheryl's father, and her family maintains she wasn't seeing anyone, either. No recent breakups. Do we know whether Diane had a boyfriend?"

Margot shakes her head. "Okay, maybe a stranger," she concedes. "But why? And should we, for a second, consider that it might be a woman? It doesn't have to be a man."

"It does have to be a man," says Elsie plainly. "It's a man."

"No, but what about that torture-mother woman?" asks Margot. "Ugh. What's her name . . . ?"

"Gertrude Baniszewski," Beverley says quietly.

"That's the one. She tortured that girl, that teenager. Killed her. It could be a woman."

"Baniszewski was an anomaly." Elsie sounds impatient. "Women don't kill. Not like this."

"Well, maybe they do but we just don't know about it yet," Margot argues. "Maybe we're not considering that it could be a woman because we don't give women—we don't give *ourselves*—enough credit."

"*I* give myself credit," Elsie hollers suddenly, and Beverley flinches at the uncharacteristic outburst. "I give myself credit for not killing people. In fact, I find it very easy not to kill people, Margot."

The other diners are starting to stare, to crane their necks. Beverley knows she has to steer them back on course to avoid a full-blown row.

"Well, he obviously owns at least one car," she prompts, "or has access to multiple vehicles."

"Right." Elsie's frustration is thankfully subsiding. "Which would fit with the guy I saw at the vigil."

"He must be relatively fit," adds Margot eventually. "He managed to catch up to Cheryl. She's a track athlete." She takes another sip of her drink. "And he got Emily Roswell into the lake. Chances are, he took Diane, killed her elsewhere, then moved her to the alleyway. This isn't some old, frail guy. I think we're looking for someone young."

"Not necessarily young," Beverley says, "but under sixty, surely."

"Do we have any actual statistics? How old are murderers on average?" Margot asks.

"We have some books at work," Elsie replies. "They say that most mass murderers are in their mid-thirties, and more than half of their victims are younger than that, usually under the age of thirty."

They all nod, assessing one another, comparing the facts to their own experiences, the people their husbands killed, seeing if it adds up.

"Well, that fits," Beverley eventually concludes. "Especially for you, Elsie." Albert was exactly thirty-five when he was put away at San Quentin. And Henry was thirty-six.

"Maybe someone who seems trustworthy," posits Elsie. "Don't they think the Boston Strangler posed as a utility guy, a super? That's why those women let him into their apartments. Maybe our guy does the same?"

"Sicko." Margot pulls out her cigarettes.

"Do we know anything about other demographics?"

"Just that, overwhelmingly, these killers are white and male," says Elsie. "At least the ones the newspapers can be bothered to report on are."

"The world's untouchables." Margot takes a drag on her Lucky Strike. "And why do they do it?"

Beverley pictures the long pink room, the stools, the glass—Henry's gaze burning her skin.

"Did you ever ask Stephen?" Elsie asks, and Beverley is grateful that the focus is not on her.

"I did," Margot admits, "the last time I saw him before he . . ." She waves a hand. "Do you know what he said?" She looks at them both. "He said he was *bored*."

Elsie lets out a quick breath of shock.

"Can you believe that? He said he was getting bored by politics, that he needed a challenge."

Beverley scoffs disgustedly.

"He was too clever for his own good," Margot concedes. "That's why he acted so superior all the time. He thought he was better than everyone else. He thought he was owed the power that politics would give him, because people just *needed* him to tell them what to do."

"Okay," Elsie says after a while. "So, boredom. It's an odd one but it's going on the list. What other reasons are there? What else makes men commit mass murder? Why do they kill?"

"Money?" Margot blows smoke from the side of her mouth.

"Financial gain." Elsie nods, writes it down. "But these girls were college students, part-time models, barely more than children. They didn't have money. Bev, have you noticed any sort of pattern in terms of motive in the clippings you collect? Anything in the letters people have written you?"

Beverley frowns for a moment, then nods. "There is something, but I'm not sure if it will help."

Elsie holds her pen aloft, waiting.

"Well, many of them, if you look at articles on killers from here or around the world—Australia's Night Caller, the Argentine Vampire—they mostly say they did it just for the sheer enjoyment."

"Great." Margot takes another drag.

"Thrill, lust, power . . . it made them feel good."

"But this can't be just about that," Elsie argues. "If it was just for the thrill, surely he'd do it indiscriminately, kill when the chance presents itself, something knee-jerk to satisfy an urge."

"Mm-hmm," Margot agrees. "Get in and get out."

"There has to be more to this, because the details are so specific," continues Elsie. "I don't think any of our husbands thought as much about the people they were killing or the optics of it all as this guy does."

"They certainly weren't as coordinated." Bev leans in, lowers her voice. "Henry used different weapons, but I don't think that was intentional. He just used whatever he could find. I think it was more about the urge to kill for him." Her heart has picked up pace; it always does when she confronts the ugly reality of Henry's crimes.

"The fire poker." Margot nods gently.

"Albert got lazy with his, I think." Elsie tilts her head. "He must have spent a long time working out how to cover his tracks, how to get rid of everything, how not to get caught, until he . . ." She trails off. Beverley knows she's talking about the body that was found at Elsie and Albert's house, in the crawl space—Lucy Glass, one of his students. He'd followed her into an alleyway with a rope.

"So, with this guy, there's a *message* he's trying to send, along with whatever he derives from killing. Otherwise, why bother with the details? They must have taken planning—particular weapons, places, words, even clothing. But why?"

The women look at one another, stumped.

"What about famous murderers?" Margot offers. "Lee Harvey Oswald—why'd he do it?"

"Lee Harvey Oswald was a schizophrenic," says Elsie plainly.

"Was he, though?" asks Beverley. "I thought he was just an egomaniac."

"That's if JFK is even really dead." Margot holds her hands up as if confronted by evidence she can't contest. "I'm just saying . . ."

"For Christ's sake, Margot, tell me you did not just say that." Elsie turns in her seat so her body is faced away from Margot, who takes an extra-long drag on her cigarette.

"Okay," Elsie continues after a while, shifting stubbornly back to the table. "So, he's most likely a man in his mid-thirties, white, who has access to a car and is physically mobile." She looks at the notes they've made. "He may have an interest in cults or some sort of religious affinity, and his killings have a ritualistic quality, a bit like the Boston Strangler's. He's probably not killing for money, given his victims' profiles, and I'd question whether it's for pleasure or other emotional reasons, too—anger, lust. I think it's something different."

"An abnormal motive," Bev adds.

"Abnormal?" Elsie asks.

"The motive for his killing is obscure, not normal."

"Is it ever normal?" Margot drains her glass.

"All right. Abnormal motive," Elsie says. "And we have reason to believe he lives or works within striking distance of the 101."

"A white guy with a car." Margot sighs. "Aren't you supposed to be good at this stuff, Elsie?" She taps the table. "Like puzzles or whatever. Are there rules for solving them?"

"Always start with the obvious," Elsie answers flatly.

"Well, as I've said, he's *obviously* a lunatic."

"There's other stuff we should be looking for." Beverley knows they're all frustrated, but surely they can do better. "Stuff we won't find in the books or the papers, but things *we* know, like behavioral signs. Did you notice anything strange about Albert and Stephen in the run-up to their crimes? Because Henry could be . . ." Beverley falters. It's hard for her to admit, but she still feels an unsettling guilt when she talks this way about Henry—as if she's betraying him. She knows no one, not even Margot and Elsie, would ever understand what it's like to feel that they were married to two different people, to feel that they had a past with a good man—a great father, a hard worker, a friend—but that he simply went away, and in his place: an impostor who brought the world around him crashing down.

"Go on," Elsie prompts.

Beverley takes a breath. "He could be very controlling."

"I love you, Bev, but that's hardly a newsflash," Margot says gently.

"It got worse," she adds, "periodically, like in a cycle."

"What do you mean?"

"It was as if there was this pressure building inside of him. There were times when he'd seem more restless, more short-tempered, more—" She still struggles to say it. "More violent."

"Did he hurt you often?" Elsie asks quietly.

"In some ways, yes." She thinks about the scorching barbecue tongs, about hands around her throat, thumbs applying downward force during sex. "He seemed so *frustrated* sometimes, almost hungry, like he was punishing me for not being able to give him what he so badly needed."

Elsie nods calmly, encouragingly.

"Then sometimes it was like he wanted to keep me in a cage, *make* me stay home. There was one time... Well..."

"Bev, we're in this together," Margot says. "Nothing you can say will shock us."

Beverley swallows, continues reluctantly. "He told me to stay home one day. He basically ordered it. Looking back, I wonder if this was his way of trying to keep me safe—from him. But I couldn't do it. My friend Sandie was in town for her father's funeral, and I said I'd help her buy a dress. I figured Henry would understand that."

"I'm guessing you figured wrong."

"He followed us"—Beverley's fists twist beside her—"in the car.

Then, when he caught up with us"—she swallows—"he revved the engine, hard, and the car just came at us, straight up onto the sidewalk, like he'd lost control of the wheel."

"Jesus Christ."

"Were you hurt?"

"Sandie broke a leg." She shakes her head quickly. "She missed the funeral. Her own father's funeral."

"Did you go to the police?"

"Henry said it was an accident, that the gearshift stuck. He seemed really cut up about it at the time."

"Poor sweetie." Margot raises an eyebrow.

"Then, that night, he stayed out late. I figured he was drinking to calm his nerves. I was in bed when he got back. Must have been two, three o'clock in the morning. I thought I'd smell the drink on him, but all I smelled was soap. His hair was wet. He'd taken a shower."

"That'll do it." Elsie smiles tightly.

"The next day, though," Beverley continues, "he was like a different person: kissing me on the cheek, smiling, laughing. He seemed . . . lighter, satisfied, like he'd had an aching tooth that he'd finally had pulled."

"He had killed that night, right?" Margot asks.

"Carol Waterford," she answers. "She was just drinking with friends at a bar."

There's a stark silence.

"So, do you think this guy could be showing signs that he's killing?" Margot asks. "You think someone close to him might be able to tell what he's doing if they had the right information?"

"I think it's possible." Beverley nods. "A wife, a friend, a sister—they might be able to recognize these behaviors. Did you notice changes with Stephen? With Albert?" She looks between them.

"Stephen was a chameleon," Margot answers. "We were always surrounded by other people—at parties, rallies, whatever—so it was hard to spot. What about Albert?"

Elsie considers, frowning. "There was this *look*," she says, "this look he would get in his eyes from time to time. Glazed. Like his body was there but his mind was occupied with something else."

"His work?"

"No. There was other stuff." Elsie frowns. "I'd find these magazines stashed down the side of the bed."

"Ah. Here we go," Margot enthuses. "The dirty-magazine stage."

"Not just dirty, though. Shocking. Violent. I can see that now, but back then I didn't know what I was looking at. Albert was the only guy I ever . . ." She waves a hand. "I convinced myself it meant he needed more from me—you know, in the bedroom."

"We know." Margot nods.

"So I tried, but he couldn't . . . see it through. He even said at one point that he wasn't a very sexual person."

Beverley scoffs.

"What sort of nonsexual person has those magazines?!"

Margot recaps. "So, we've got this sort of violent pressure, the sexual perversions, the look they get in their eyes. Can that really help us catch this guy? What do we do, ask every woman in California whether her husband has a stack of pornos behind the toilet tank?"

"It *can* help us," Elsie argues. "I'm sure of it. But what do we actually know now? Margot, did you ask the family about the letters Diane Howard Murray had been writing to that movie guy?"

"Pearl didn't seem to know anything about them, but I pulled some strings, managed to get myself an invitation to a party he's throwing tonight. Thought I'd spritz on some Diorissimo, do a bit of undercover work."

Beverley shifts in her seat. There's something that's been ticking over in her head, something about Diane. "Pearl said Diane had been working for a cleaning company, right?" she asks. "Any idea what the name is? Where they're based?"

"Hmm." Margot turns the sides of her lips downward. "No specifics per se, but there is this." She reaches for an envelope on the table and pulls out several photographs, fanning them out.

Diane Howard Murray is a knockout. Even in a photograph, she has the sort of wide, clear eyes that seem as if they are peering into your soul.

"Let me just . . ." Margot sorts through them, then pulls one out, hands it to Beverley. "She's got a logo on those overalls, I think. I couldn't read the name."

Beverley studies it, but the logo is so small, she can't make out the name, either.

"Wait a minute."

Beverley looks up to see Elsie leaning across the table, peering intently at the photograph.

"Show me that."

She hands it over, and they watch as Elsie squints, then as her mouth falls slowly open.

"What is it?" Margot asks. Beverley leans in closer.

"The logo," Elsie replies, reaching for her notebook. "I've seen it before."

TEN DAYS MISSING

My days down here are marked by the sounds of everyday life continuing, time marching on, things turning as normal, just feet above my head.

Ten trills of the paperboy's bell.

Ten rising swells of the birds' morning chorus.

Ten barking fits from the neighbor's dog when the mailman arrives with his bag.

I've lost count of the footsteps—so close but so far away—of the occasions when I've heard a distant laugh, wondered if I could rattle this pipe loudly enough to catch their attention, if I could use the power of my mind to let them know, to let *anyone* know, that I am being kept here.

I've spent hours assessing how I might get out. What I might use as a weapon if I could free my hands. Whether I could break a window, scream loudly enough, overpower you.

What terrifies me most is not what you might do to me next. Not the cable ties around my wrists. Not the way I'm forced to go in a bucket, hunched and watched like an animal. But the sheer helplessness. The loss of any control I once knew.

If I get out of here, if I survive—no, *when* I survive—I'll never forget this feeling. When I brush my teeth, when I choose what to wear in the morning, when I take a lipstick from the vanity and spread crimson slowly across my Cupid's bow, I will remember how I didn't let you win. I will remind myself, every day, that you did not defeat me.

NINETEEN

"Huh." Patti hooks her thumbs into the pockets of her bellbottoms, bends to inspect the photograph more closely. She turns her attention to the sketch Elsie hurriedly put down on paper after Cheryl Herrera's vigil, glances up at her. "Same logo."

"Same logo." Elsie nods eagerly.

"So, what does that tell us?" Patti stands and fixes Elsie's eye as if she's setting a challenge.

"That the same guy murdered Cheryl Herrera and Diane Howard Murray?" Elsie hates the weakness in her own voice, but something about Patti pulls her vocal cords taut.

"Bit of a stretch." Patti tilts her head. "Same logo on Diane's overalls and the van at the vigil, and we've got our guy?"

"I know. I'm sorry," Elsie groans. "I just thought..."

Patti's smiling now, calmly watching her stutter. Elsie feels her ears grow hot. There's something about Patti that makes Elsie feel ridiculous—that strength of mind, that cool confidence that keeps her unruffled when others might stumble and overspeak—but Elsie also knows there's something emboldening about being with Patti, and she has recently found herself acting in ways she almost doesn't recognize.

"No, don't apologize. Pause," Patti encourages. "Slow down." Patti reaches for the pack of cigarettes on her desk. "I'm trying to get you to work it through." She taps one from the box. "Tell me what you know. Tell me the facts."

Elsie takes a deep breath, recounts everything she discussed with Beverley and Margot at the hotel the day before. "We've got to find out who owns this company," she concludes.

"Agreed." Patti nods. "So I think we need to pay my old friends Greaves and Bale a visit."

"Greaves and Bale?"

"Tweedledum and Tweedledee, I like to call them." Patti reclines, crosses her legs. "They're the detectives assigned to the homicides." She pauses, lights up. "You've got a real interest in this case," she says, cigarette clasped between her lips. It's not a question. Patti doesn't ask questions.

Elsie pauses. It's unfamiliar territory, a conversation like this, after hours at the office, with someone who has chosen to spend time with her.

"It's sort of something I'm familiar with." The words just come out.

Patti doesn't respond. Her eyes stay with Elsie's.

"Something happened, in my past, something bad—some*one* bad."

It was just a whiff at first, of something stale and animal, a smell like meat gone bad in the house. Things had been a little rocky with Albert back then. She had been trying to meet his needs ever since they married, ever since he'd suffered the ignominy of being dismissed from his teaching position at the high school. She was the reason he'd lost his job; therefore, it was her duty to give him what he wanted, whenever he wanted it, to be a good wife. But she was stymied by a constant feeling of failure.

In bed, Albert had assumed the mantle of teacher from the start. Elsie followed his instructions dutifully. She had never been with a man before, and she found Albert's soft flesh and wiry body hair off-putting at first. He didn't look like the boys she'd seen in magazines, with smooth skin and taut muscles. But she wasn't supposed to enjoy it. She was a wife. This was her job now, after all.

Albert got frustrated when his body didn't do what it was supposed to do. That was when Elsie saw him truly angry. Something would harden in his eyes and he'd push her off him, sometimes so forcefully that she'd end up out of the bed and on the floor. There was one occasion when she fell and hit her head on the wall. It left a bloody mark, in the shape of a tennis ball, that they'd never painted over. She knew she had failed when those moments came. That she wasn't enough for him. That she didn't look right. That she was doing *something* wrong.

So she tried to improve herself in other areas. She was accustomed to being a star pupil. It felt disorienting and confusing to underperform. She started cooking—properly cooking. If she could become accomplished in the kitchen, perhaps Albert would see her as appealing in the bedroom and his body would work. She began with stews and casseroles, the meat sweaty, the sauces rich. Then she moved on to pies, remembering how her mother used to make them every Sunday. She worked her way through *McCall's*, arranging pastry like fretwork, pricking the top of it with a fork, letting the heat rush out to fill their tiny kitchen.

She was a couple of months into her routine when the strange smell arrived.

She checked inside the fridge and behind the oven. Perhaps she'd missed something while cleaning. Maybe a mouse had died under the floorboards. It would go away eventually, she reasoned. She'd keep cooking to try to mask the stink until then.

But each morning when she awoke, the smell was worse. She tried everything: air freshener, potpourri, endless bottles of perfume. When she asked Albert if he could smell it, he frowned and sniffed, shook his head.

Then, one day, as she returned from the store, bags bulging, something brought her to a halt at the doorstep. The smell. It was out here, so pungent that it could not be missed. *How* could Albert claim that he didn't notice it? Unless there was something wrong with her, with her brain. Her father smelled strange smells occasionally, gas and burned flesh. At least he did when he was having one of his moments.

She sniffed again. It seemed to intensify by the entrance to the crawl space under the house. The dirt had been disturbed. A raccoon must have got in and succumbed. That would explain the god-awful stink.

Elsie glanced down the street. Albert had always told her not to go anywhere near the crawl space. There were strong chemicals down there, he'd said. She might get sick.

Regardless, she knelt in the dirt and placed the groceries beside her. She'd bought oranges and a pineapple for a fruit salad, wanted to be careful that they didn't roll out and get ruined. She removed her heels, the ones Albert liked her to wear, and placed them beside the paper bag. Then she bent to remove the access panel. The smell was something solid down there. There was very little light, and she wished she'd brought a flashlight, but she wasn't going to back her way out now and risk the chance of someone seeing her like this. She didn't want Albert to know she'd been poking around the house, either. She'd have to be quick, cover her tracks. So she crawled in farther, battling disgust as the stench flattened against her skin, crept into the folds of her clothing. She knew her skirt was getting stained at the knees, but something undefinable compelled her to keep going, to pull herself onward.

Then, there it was.

Something built of flesh, yet indiscernible, piled stiffly in a corner of the space, lit strangely, beautifully, by the light that bled in through the access panel. Elsie's breath faltered. A raccoon. It had to be. Just a dead raccoon.

But it looked too large for that.

She steeled herself and dragged her body closer, fingernails blackening with dirt. She just had to confirm that it was an animal. Then she could send Albert down here later, shove a spade into his hands. But as she moved even closer, veins slushy with dread, horrifying details began to narrow into sharpness. There was hair. Elsie inhaled quickly. Not fur, but black human hair. It was unmistakable. Then: skin—pale skin turned blue like a bruise, mottled. She saw the fabric of a dress, printed with oranges, just like the fruit in the paper bag lying only yards away. A boiling wash of horror flooded everything. Elsie's scream sent the birds in the trees shooting up into the sky.

I KNOW THAT, ELSIE," Patti responds calmly.

"You know ... what?"

"I'm a reporter. It's my job to uncover information, and you intrigued me from the start."

Elsie feels certain that she is blushing. "You know who I am?"

"I don't know who *you* are, not yet—I've only just met you—but I do know what your husband did, yes."

Elsie lets out a bark of disbelief. "You're not going to—"

"I'm not going to tell anyone."

"I'd lose my job."

Patti frowns. "You don't give yourself enough credit."

"Credit?"

"You're a strong woman."

"Okay."

"You're certainly the most interesting person in this building. Hell, you're the most interesting person in the state, probably. What you've lived through, what you've experienced, what you do here, every day..."

"I just make coffee."

"Oh, quit it, Elsie. I see you. I know you know you're more important than that. You're just diminishing yourself because you think people won't accept your brilliance because of what happened to you."

She feels suddenly as if her skin has been exposed, as if Patti has peeled back her clothing and is studying every blemish, every fold.

"So, you wanna find this shithead or not?" Patti smiles.

Elsie falters. Is she really going to do this? Let someone else see her for what she is, widen her world beyond Beverley and Margot? Is she prepared to make herself vulnerable like that?

She swallows. "I want to find this shithead."

TWENTY

IT'S A BRIGHT August Thursday when Bob Taggit, a plumber from Ventura, pulls his truck into the Safeway parking lot to pick up supplies for his daughter's birthday party. He steps out of the driver's seat into the smothering midday fug and locks the truck, scanning the trailer to check that all his equipment is secured.

Inside the store, the air-conditioning is blasting bitter air. Dusty Springfield is playing on the speakers—"You Don't Have to Say You Love Me," his wife's favorite. He takes a cart and browses the aisles, whistling along to the tune, picking up balloons, cake, candy and a six-pack of Budweiser for himself. From the deli down the street he'll get some meat for the grill. James Finnegan always complains that the steak's too tough, but he's just gloating; he thinks he can grill better than anyone else. Bob will ask the deli guy for an especially tender cut.

He dawdles for a while in the magazine aisle, making a show of picking up *Man's Life* and *Blue Book* before grabbing *Playboy* and flicking to the centerfold. He blows out air from the side of his mouth.

Back out in the lot, the heat has solidified. The sun javelins off the windshields of vehicles lined up as neatly as toys in a box. The air smells of oil, dust and the fumes from the interstate just a couple hundred yards away.

Taggit returns to his truck and hauls the shopping bags into the back, moving tools aside—wrenches, ropes and hammers, newly cleaned. He pulls a sheet of tarpaulin over them to stop the cake from melting, then returns to the driver's-side door, unlocks it and slides into his seat. He fastens his seat belt, shoves the key into the ignition and then pauses. Something has been tucked beneath one of the wiper blades. *Bastards*. It's some crappy car wash pamphlet, no doubt. He huffs, unbuckles his seat belt, opens the door and steps out to grab it. Without a glance, he crumples it in his fist, but the material is harder than paper; it resists.

He looks down and realizes it's the back of a cereal box—Lucky Charms. Then he notices the scrawled handwriting. He squints, leans back into the car to retrieve his glasses. As he slides them on, the words swim into focus.

> *To the police and to the newspapers,*
>
> *Be quicker.*
>
> *I WILL kill again.*
>
> *Why can't you guys see the big picture? Why aren't you covering my crimes more? If you do not print an article about me in the next week, you'll regret it.*
>
> *Cheryl Herrera—Almost didn't get her.*
>
> *Emily Roswell—Beautiful hands. Shame.*
>
> *Diane Howard Murray—Begged for life, made me angry, she deserved it.*
>
> *The next one will be your fault. I'll hook another girl, and you will have BLOOD on your hands.*

TWENTY-ONE

THE MANSION, SURROUNDED by hundreds of flaming tiki torches, looms high above a white-paved driveway. Margot has driven deep into the hills of Benedict Canyon to get here, the road a coiled serpent, headlights illuminating spectral branches of trees, skittish raccoons and expensive real estate. At the center of the turning circle at the end of the drive, there's a fountain lit by spotlights that cast the water in silver. She can hear the thudding of music from inside. Jagger wants everything black.

The women decided at the hotel that Elsie would investigate the logo—the one Diane Howard Murray had stitched onto her apron and that Elsie had seen on the van at Cheryl Herrera's vigil. Margot's job is to get to Clarke, see what she can find out. Is it possible that Mason Clarke, one of Hollywood's most powerful movie directors, is a killer? Margot has heard rumors, of course, about unsavory sexual behavior, unwanted advances. The man is a pest. But he is rich, and untouchable. Until now. She smiles.

She looks up at the mansion again, takes a cigarette from the case in her pocket, lights it.

Mason Clarke doesn't really fit the profile they've built: a loner who drives himself around and has a reason to resent women; in his mid-twenties to mid-forties, but most likely around thirty-five years of age; relatively fit and strong, with an ability to fly under the radar, appear trustworthy.

Mason Clarke is in his early sixties, but he has an imposing physique, so she wouldn't put it past him to be strong enough to get Emily Roswell into the lake and Diane Howard Murray into the alley.

Motive, though—what motive could a wealthy film director have to commit these crimes? She runs through a list of possibilities: lust, power, greed, sheer psychopathy. A movie director is creative, she supposes. Creative enough to "set the scene" by posing bodies after death? He certainly has access to multiple cars, although she can't really imagine him driving himself around suburban LA unnoticed. But he is influential, charming. No one says no to him, ever. That could be a very dangerous thing.

She makes her way toward the party, the acetate of her André Courrèges dress iridescent under moonlight. She reaches the vast lawn just as a window on the third floor is opened and a porcelain vase the size of a man is hurled out. It smashes into pieces on the grass below. She doesn't have to inspect the shards to know it's Ming.

Back when Stephen was alive, they hosted parties like this at their house in the Hamptons. Margot remembers one time, way back then, when she didn't know, when she had no suspicions at all. She woke to a world turned upside down. She remembers blinking five, six times in succession, confused, fighting the leaden pounding that boomed in her head. Then she realized, the room shifting into focus, that she'd passed out hanging backward off the bed. She raised herself up and groaned. She was still fully clothed. Stephen was nowhere around. The house was quiet. Looking out toward the pool, Margot could see a few bodies draped across sun loungers, still asleep, or lost on their acid trips.

She called out for him, then went to search the rest of the rooms. There were bodies everywhere, making out in the drowsy light of morning; actors whose posters adorned little girls' walls snorting amphetamines off naked, sleep-dampened skin.

But there was no Stephen.

She pushed her way farther through the house, dragging herself along the hallways, stumbling, the remnants of drugs clouding her system. Then she went to the front door and stepped out onto the driveway to check for his Rolls-Royce. Maybe he'd gone out there to sleep on the back seat. He did that sometimes, said it was peaceful, gave him time to think.

He wasn't there, but she took a lap around the vehicle anyway. The car looked clean—too clean, almost, as if someone had polished it just that morning, before the sun came up. Her head pulsed. She needed coffee and Tylenol stat. So she turned to make her way back into the house, but as she did, she noticed something on the concrete near the trunk of the car. She stepped closer to it, peered down and gasped. She looked again. It was blood, dried crimson in the shape of a boot sole. A sour taste crawled up through her throat. Had something happened to Stephen? Or . . . no. She stopped herself. She couldn't really be thinking that, could she? But something compelled her to go inside, to their bedroom. It made her open the closet doors and pull out one of his boots from the rack of assembled pairs. With the boot in hand, she marched back outside, to the car. She crouched over the print, then rested the boot on top of it. She looked at the house, thinking of all the times Stephen had left her in the middle of the night to sleep in his car. Then she looked back down to the bloody footprint, and Stephen's boot, exactly the same size, atop it.

Margot steps over the Ming tragedy now and passes the pool, the heat from the tiki torches caressing her bare limbs. The Stones make way for Cher on the sound system.

Bang, bang...

The haunting words spiral out into the night air.

Bang, bang...

A bunch of men she recognizes from *Billboard* magazine are gathered by the loungers, shirtless and guzzling beer, trousers so tight around the thighs that they look as if they have been sprayed on.

Bang, bang...

The men holler at Margot as she passes.

She flashes them a smile, then realizes they are watching something in the water.

She pauses, scans the surface and sees the flash of an armored tail, and the hefty bulk of a crocodile floating in the spotlit pool. One of the guys has a leash around his wrist, the end of it attached to a collar on the animal. A fucking crocodile. It seems surprisingly docile, and she wonders, with a beat of concern, what they've fed it.

The mansion doors are ajar.

My baby shot me down...

Margot slips inside.

TWENTY-TWO

THE BAR'S EXTERIOR is neon lit, bright as a fairground ride—a deceiving illumination given that, when Elsie and Patti push through the door, the light inside is so low that it takes a while for their eyes to adjust.

Patti knew where the detectives drank their whiskey. She'd accrued this knowledge while working with hard drinkers at the *Times* who often ended their evenings propped up against sticky bars, cajoling off-duty officers into revealing their leads.

Elsie assesses the room. There are green glass lamps hanging low on chains from the ceiling. Out-of-the-way booths are cushioned with battered mustard-colored leather. Men in loose ties take bleary shots at a pool table.

There's a song on the jukebox, something Elsie thinks she has heard on the radio before—a man's voice quavering with false emotion—but she doesn't follow popular music. The air is thick with smoke and burned grease from the kitchen.

"Do you see them?"

Patti scans the booths. Men recline, shoulders claiming the backs of seats, arms stretched wide, French fries decorating silver platters. Patti lifts her chin, and Elsie sees two gray-haired men hunched over a table, deep in conversation.

"What are we going to say?" Elsie feels slightly alarmed that they haven't rehearsed their roles, haven't worked out how they are going to play this. She and Patti know the grisly details of the killings. They also know the police received a note purportedly from the killer, scrawled on a Lucky Charms box. Cornwell had gifted the details to Paul Hunter, quid pro quo for running a story about an awards ceremony Cornwell was being honored at. Elsie had overheard the phone conversation while she was filing papers in Hunter's office. And now she and Patti have nailed down a suspect. But she's not quite sure how they're going to approach this conversation.

Patti doesn't seem fazed. "We've got the evidence right here." She taps her bag. "We don't need lines."

Patti leads the way, snaking past waitresses carrying shrimp and burgers aloft, waists nipped in, hair done nice, just how their customers like it. Patti draws attention as she moves, with that wild hair, that lackadaisical way; there's something masculine and intoxicating about her. Eventually they reach the back table, and Elsie realizes the detectives are hunched over not because they're conversing but because they are busy dissecting limbs. A lobster gawps with beady black eyes from the table, its shell being slowly disassembled with silver crackers. Bottles of beer stand together at the officers' elbows, condensation dripping from the glass.

Patti heaves an audible sigh and tilts her head, waiting.

"Two more," one of them barks without sparing her and Elsie a glance.

"We're not here to serve you beer, Roger," Patti deadpans.

The man glances up and his eyebrows rise in recognition. He has the type of weathered, handsome face you might expect to see on a poster for a Western movie. His harsh blue eyes make his hair look argent.

"We're here to find out why you're not doing your job." Patti flashes a sarcastic smile, then slides next to him in the booth.

The officer opposite spits a triangle of orange lobster shell into his palm. That must be Detective Bale, making the guy with the icicle eyes Detective Roger Greaves.

"Bale," Greaves murmurs reluctantly, "this is Patti Fowler from the *Times*."

"I'm at the *Signal* now, actually." Patti gestures at Elsie to take a seat. "This is my colleague Elsie Moss. We just wanted to ask you gentlemen a couple of questions."

"Nah." Bale bunches a napkin and tosses it at the tabletop. "We're not talking to the press tonight."

"Are you planning on talking to the press at all about the recent murders in the area?" Patti asks.

"Look, let me stop you there." Bale holds up a large palm. "If you're trying to *scoop* us on the Berryview girl, we're not playing this game again."

Elsie frowns. Berryview? None of the murders so far have taken place in Berryview.

"Because this is how it goes, okay?" He cocks his head in a way that men do only when they're talking to women they feel are beneath them. "Girl goes missing, people call *the cops*—not some reporter."

"Berryview," Patti repeats, not missing a beat. "Nice area. What are you going to do to make sure people are safe there?"

Elsie is astonished by the woman's bravado, how she doesn't worry that she shouldn't say these things to men, let alone men in uniform. It's kind of infectious.

"Just leave it to us, okay?" Bale draws his fingers down his mustache, eyes Patti, then Elsie, takes a swig of his beer.

"Will you be calling a conference before you arrest Sean Wilson?" Elsie finds herself asking, emboldened by Patti's confidence. It makes her head feel dizzy.

She clocks the detectives sharing a glance.

"I'm sure you'll appreciate we're not obliged to share details of open cases with members of the public," Greaves answers calmly. "That includes the press."

"You are planning on arresting Sean Wilson, though." Patti says it as a statement.

Greaves looks at her for a second too long and Elsie realizes, with a sting of surprise, that they don't know about Sean Wilson. She reaches into her bag and pulls out the two facsimile copies of the photographs. She pushes the lobster plate to the side, lays the sheets flat on the table.

The detectives study the images. Elsie searches for a change in their expressions, a widening of the eyes, a softening of muscles, but they are not giving anything away.

"Let us enlighten you." Patti grabs a bottle and takes a swig of beer, wipes her lips with the back of her hand. It's so brazen that Elsie has to stifle a laugh. "This is Diane Howard Murray." She taps one image. "You already know that, I sincerely hope."

Bale lets out a hostile snort.

"Notice the logo on her apron, there. That's the cleaning company she worked for when she wasn't modeling."

"That cleaning company is owned by Sean Wilson," Elsie continues, placing her palm briefly on the other image. It's a candid shot, taken on the street, of a man with thin hair to his shoulders, climbing out of a utility van—the van that Elsie saw parked around the corner from Cheryl Herrera's vigil. "This is him. He employs over sixty people and cleans all around the local area."

"Commercial work, mainly." Patti takes over again. "Office buildings, restaurants. But they also do college sports stadiums, athletics tracks, that sort of thing, cleaning up after game days and races."

The men are trying their hardest not to look confused. It's not working. Elsie can tell, with a flash of gratification, that she and Patti have them intrigued.

"Sean Wilson is often on-site for these events, overseeing his cleaning staff. Those events include race days at Central College's athletics track, where Cheryl Herrera trained and competed."

The men sit back in their seats. Bale raises his chin and scratches his neck.

Elsie bristles. They think it's not enough, that it could be just a coincidence. But she *knows* it's not a coincidence.

"He was at Cheryl's vigil," she urges. "I saw him. He was standing there, just watching."

Greaves leans forward as if he's about to ask a question, then appears to change his mind, picks up the Sean Wilson photo instead, studies it.

Over his shoulder, Elsie notices someone entering the bar—battered leather jacket, unkempt hair. A stab of recognition scythes in. It's Robert Heston. That chancer must have followed her and Patti here from the office. She looks away. They can't risk having him come over. He'd tell Hunter what she's been digging into; she'd lose her job.

"What if he'd been watching Cheryl at these events for a while?" She needs to make her case quickly. "What if he specifically targeted her, just as he targeted Diane, a young girl—beautiful, promising? Surely this is at least enough to make an arrest?"

Bale takes a cocktail stick and begins picking his teeth. "It's circumstantial." He pulls the stick out, inspects it. "It's not enough for an arrest."

Elsie feels her shoulders sag. Across the bar, Heston is ordering a drink, scanning the room, eyes darting.

"But we'll look into it," Greaves reassures them, more evenly.

"My gut's saying *coincidence*." Bale twirls the stick in his fingers. "The MO is too different. The victims . . ." He tilts his head this way and that.

"If he killed Cheryl and Diane, he could have killed Emily Roswell, too." Elsie needs them to see. It's so clear that the cases are linked. Why won't they see?

"All right, stop." Bale fixes her eye, but she won't be deterred.

"You're failing women, you know, by not taking these links seriously." She has no choice but to push it. "It's the same guy."

Bale's whole demeanor changes then, as if a frost constricts the muscles in his shoulders. He leaps up, slams a palm on the table. "*We* decide if there's a link. Us." He looks crazed. "We don't need some hack to tell us what to do."

Elsie looks past him, terrified that the raised voice will draw attention. But Heston hasn't noticed Bale's outburst. Heston stands, leaves his untouched drink at the bar and crosses the room toward the pay phone, then picks up the receiver and pushes a coin into the slot.

"All right, Bale." Greaves reaches across the table, attempts to pull his partner back down into his seat.

"If you ladies go any further with this line of inquiry," Bale warns, "if you continue to interfere in an active police investigation, I will personally see to it that you never publish a single word again." Spittle has collected in the corners of his mouth.

Elsie looks to Patti, unsure of how to proceed, but her face is motionless. She always remains so calm. Eventually she turns slightly, indicating to Elsie that it's time for them to leave, and they both stand.

Bale watches them, his eyes charged, as they slide out of the booth. Elsie scans the bar as she moves. There's no sign of Heston. His drink is still on the counter, full to the brim, and the exit door is slowly swinging shut.

"Hey," Greaves calls out to them as they leave, and they both turn. "You want a story. Why aren't you looking into Cornwell?"

Elsie's brows knit together. "Cornwell?"

"Maybe you might want to take a look at this surveillance op he's running." Greaves holds her gaze.

"On the Kings?"

"Uh-huh. Maybe you might want to take a look at, I don't know, who's making the audio equipment for that op. But"—he takes a sip of his beer—"just a thought."

Cornwell. Why would Roger Greaves give them a story about the chief of police, his boss? She knows some officers feed stories to the press, but it's usually to stroke their own egos or to appeal to the public for help with an investigation. This she hasn't come across before. Despite herself, she feels a dim beat of respect for Greaves for having the mettle to speak out against authority. She's heard plenty of stories about Cornwell; she knows he's not exactly a saint.

"Order us a couple more on your way out, won't you, ladies?" Bale waggles his bottle in the air. Patti raises her middle finger defiantly as they depart.

TWENTY-THREE

MARGOT'S WORLD BURSTS into color.

The mansion writhes with slowly pulsing bodies; they move en masse to the music—the Byrds, "Eight Miles High"—heads lolled back, necks bare, arms to the ceiling. They fill every inch of space, draped and knotted around a huge open staircase. Its wide red carpet climbs up to an enormous chandelier glittering with a thousand tiny lights like a colossal flaming planet above.

People are in costume, doe-eyed women with angel wings strapped to their shoulders, men with devil horns or sly, insidious masks. She spots the actress from Kubrick's latest picture, a plucky brunette, and a young starlet in a butter-colored silk dress who was recently disgraced in the papers because her husband had an affair with MGM's leading man.

Margot can't push herself three feet through the party without bumping into an actor or singer she recognizes from television. Long cigarette holders, dirty martinis and slicked-back hair. It's intoxicating, really, to be among them. She has already clocked multiple men eyeing her legs and the curve of her bust. It feels like victory. She's just as appealing to them as the models in diamond-encrusted corsets and tight shorts serving microscopic portions of food. A blond who must be barely out of his teens, his chest shimmering with oil, thrusts a plate of crescent rolls in her direction. She waves him away and makes for the staircase.

She has managed to ask enough questions to know that Clarke spends his own parties locked away upstairs.

As she climbs the steps she wonders, briefly, if she should be scared. If her theory is correct—well, if Barbie Cook's theory is correct—and nothing comes of Elsie's vigil guy, Clarke may have killed Diane Howard Murray. He may have strangled her, posed her body, dressed her. There's nothing to suggest that he couldn't be responsible for the other killings, too.

The stairs widen out into an open landing, off which streams a wide corridor with several doors lining it. She glances briefly back down at the party: a sea of reveling heads, the music segueing into "Wild Thing" by the Troggs. She doesn't pause for long before she strikes out across the landing. If someone confronts her, she'll tell them she's looking for the bathroom.

She holds her ear to the first large door. Nothing, just dead air inside. She turns, continues down the corridor. Expensive paintings line the walls. She knows they're expensive because they are ridiculous, and because Clarke could probably acquire the entire contents of the Whitney should he so choose. Although she notes that he still has that insipid Tretchikoff *Chinese Girl* print that she's seen on the wall of every unadventurous suburban living room over the past decade—including Beverley's. If Margot could afford it, she'd get a Warhol—not those tacky soup cans, but a Marilyn diptych—pair it with a daring Gae Aulenti piece. She sucks her teeth. Why is it that those with money never have any taste?

Suddenly there's a creak from a little farther down the hallway. Her head snaps around. Thin coils of cigar smoke spill out from a cracked doorway. Margot's first impulse is to shrink into the walls, to hide herself, but something inside of her *knows* this is where Clarke has buried himself away, and she knows she cannot turn back now.

She steps toward the door and slowly pushes it open.

The room is dark, paneled with mahogany and swarming with smoke. There is a large projector screen at the far end, upon which a black-and-white movie is being cast. The film reel gives off a static sound that makes the room feel as if it is suspended in time.

In front of the screen is a plum velvet sofa that claims almost the entire width of the room. On it, with his arms outstretched, the muscles in the back of his neck piled up like a bulldog's, is Mason Clarke.

She can tell that he's sensed her presence, but he does not turn to look at her. Instead, he takes a puff of his cigar and calls out into the gloom, his voice entirely monotone, "Chadwick."

From the shadows, a boulder of a man peels off the wall and makes for Margot.

She almost laughs. She hadn't seen him there, and it strikes her as exactly the sort of thing you would see in one of Clarke's own crummy movies—the "bad guy" emerging from the shadows, ready to manhandle a woman. She'd always thought his pictures were full of clichés.

"I'm not an actress."

The words stop Chadwick in his tracks. He must be used to warding off aspiring starlets.

"Not a model, either. And I think your movies are kind of dull, Mr. Clarke."

With this, Clarke turns on the couch, his arms still stretched wide, and he scours her up and down, his eyes lingering on her breasts, her hips. His eyes are small, lost in a meaty face, and the sides of his mouth tilt downward. His head is bald; he must wear a toupee when he goes out. His hands are the size of plates, his fingers long and thick. She imagines them gripping the handle of a hammer, ready to bludgeon.

She swallows but keeps her eyes on him. She knows the worst thing you can do while in the sights of a predator is to show your fear. She tries to make out whether he has any tattoos, *LOVE* and *HATE* looming large in her mind.

All of a sudden, Clarke's shoulders begin to shake, and she wonders if he might have a burst aneurysm. She looks to Chadwick, who is watching Clarke, until a breathy, wheezing sound fills the air, and she realizes it is laughter.

"Dull," he wheezes. "Is that right, sugarplum? Come. Tell me how you'd do it differently."

This is how it starts, she supposes, this sort of meeting. He drops his shoulder from the back of the couch and pats the cushion next to him.

She glances at Chadwick again, his face blank, then makes her way around the side of the couch toward the director. His legs are spread wide, thick as a butcher's hams. He taps the cushion beside him once more, as if she is a dog.

"Chadwick, you can go," he calls behind him. His eyes return and linger on her bare thighs. Her skin suddenly feels very cold, and she wishes she'd worn the faux fur jacket she'd left in her closet.

"It's okay. He can stay."

Chadwick hovers, unsure of what to do, but Clarke waves him off until he closes the door behind him.

Margot feels as if the shadows have suddenly grown around her. She is trapped, the pearlescent acetate of her dress held in the beam of light from the projector.

"Sit." She can tell it's an order.

She takes a seat on the armchair next to the sofa.

"No, no no," he scolds. *"Sit."* He taps the sofa cushion more forcefully. She cannot afford to anger him. She crosses to the couch, does as she's told.

She is aware of his hands, just inches from her neck. She can feel them like heat.

"So..."

"Cindy," she replies.

"Cindy." He laughs again. "I like that. It suits you. Let's go with *Cindy*. So, if you're not an actress or a model, what do you do?"

"I work in fashion."

"Ah yes, I can see that." He shifts his hips so that he sinks down deeper into the sofa. "So, you think my movies are dull, huh?" He scoffs, a rattling sound, as if his lungs are full of liquid.

On the projector screen, Jimmy Stewart raises a pair of binoculars; Grace Kelly preens prettily in front of a mirror.

Margot lowers her chin. She's sure she's seen this on some nature show before. A lesser animal must appear submissive, acknowledge its impotence, so as not to raise hell.

"There are some different stories I would tell," she says, as sweetly as she can.

"And what would those stories be?" He drops his elbow and lets his hand slide down the couch until his fingers are just millimeters from her thighs.

"There's someone killing women around Berryview." She watches his face intently as she says it.

He nods eagerly and waits for her to go on, slipping the wet tongue from his mouth and moving it across his top lip.

"He's targeting pretty, popular girls," she continues. "Talented. Athletic."

He tilts his head from side to side as if this part of the story is perhaps not to his taste.

"The killings are ritualistic and theatrical."

His eyebrows leap up. "How so?" She senses his fingers twitching beside her legs.

"The women are posed after death." She scrutinizes him, anticipating when the realization that he has been foiled might land. "They're dressed in certain clothes, defiled in certain ways, as if the killer is sending a message."

"Well, I've seen films like that, Miss Cindy." He moves his hand back up on the couch, grazing her leg as he goes. It makes her skin flood with terror. Every inch of her wants to attack, to throttle him, to grab a lamp from the table, but she needs to push him further.

"Diane Howard Murray was strangled and dressed in suspender stockings."

"Diane Howard Murray ... Is she one of MGM's?"

Margot blinks. He holds her gaze, his expression blank. The sweat of him is turning the air sour.

It dawns on her, a horrible, creeping realization that Mason Clarke is an extremely accomplished actor.

"Girls are all so similar these days. What happened to the Marlenes and the Gretas?" He reaches forward for another cigar from the box on the coffee table, bites the end off, spits it away and then uses it to punctuate the air as he talks. "Range—that's what they had. Not all these airhead blondes. You want a little limoncello? I just got back from doing a picture in Capri. Let's have a little limoncello."

"Diane Howard Murray was a model," she says as Clarke hauls himself up off the couch. She is surprised at just how tall he is, how imposing. He flexes his hands.

"She disappeared two weeks ago, but they found her on Wednesday, dumped in an alleyway in Calabasas. Whoever killed her had dressed her in a designer coat and suspenders."

"Howard Murray, Howard Murray ... Denise, you said?"

"Diane."

He mumbles as he takes two glasses from a cabinet and pours the drinks. Then he returns to the sofa and inches even closer to her. She can tell this is not the first time he has done this, that he is used to having women on his couch, making them feel compelled to stay.

"Like I said, she was a model. See—this is her." She bends, takes the photo from her purse and holds it out to him. He leans in. Margot watches his every move, won't take her eyes off him.

"She wants to be an actress in this picture you're talking about?" Clarke asks as he reclines again.

He's trying to wrong-foot her. Stephen used to do that. He was so slick at making it seem as if she was the one who was crazy. Clarke is just as manipulative and even more powerful. He is used to making people think what he wants them to think, used to weaving stories.

"You knew her, Mr. Clarke."

He frowns, but it's not convincing.

"She wrote you letters. I'm sure she even sat here, on this couch."

He stares at her, his expression blank, then tilts his head, reaches a hand forward, trails a finger down the side of her cheek.

She stands suddenly, in recoil, sways on her feet. Her eyes whip around the room. She needs to put some distance between herself and Clarke.

She crosses to the cocktail cabinet, studies the bottles in false interest, buying herself time to think. "Capri." She takes the limoncello bottle by the neck, ignoring the tremor in her hands. "Beautiful place." She and Stephen honeymooned in Capri. She can still remember the dry heat of the sun; salty skin, gripping Stephen's hips with her legs as they moved together in the sea. She blinks it away.

"Busy," says Clarke. He tips his glass back and destroys the liquid in one. "Beautiful girls."

"When did you get back?" she asks, trying to sound as offhand as possible.

He pauses, suspicious now. "Thursday."

She freezes, something horrifying solidifying in her stomach.

"Uh-huh. How long were you out there?"

He looks at her strangely but answers. "Six weeks."

"You got a plane ticket to account for those dates?"

"What the hell is this?" Clarke's jaw is flexing angrily.

Shit.

If he's telling the truth, and he was in Italy until Thursday, was out of the country for the past six weeks, then he cannot be responsible for Diane Howard Murray's murder. He cannot be responsible for Cheryl's murder, either, or Emily's.

She places the bottle back in the cabinet, swallows drily. Clarke raises his weight from the sofa and stalks toward her.

"You have a lot of questions."

"I should really get going."

He grabs her wrist, holds her in place.

"Stay awhile," he says smoothly, as if what he's asking, expecting, is entirely reasonable. "We've got a bottle to get through." His grip tightens and she feels the small bones in her wrist click. "You can tell me more about why you hate my movies." That almost silent husky laugh again. She tries to twist away. He pulls her toward him. "C'mon. I let you up here, didn't I? Let you ask questions. Not many people get to see this room. Do a little something for me, baby."

With horror she sees that he is reaching for the fly of his pants, that he is slowly unzipping it, holding her gaze like a test.

This is how it feels, she realizes, to know that you are really in trouble, that you are certain to be overpowered. No matter how hard you fight or how gently you try to reason, to coax, it feels like falling. And there's no way to stop it.

Clarke pulls at his belt buckle, then freezes as a loud knock comes at the door.

Margot wants to sprint over, yank it open, but Clarke still has her by the wrist.

He says nothing, waiting for the visitor to retreat, but the knocking comes again, more urgently.

"Mason!" a voice calls frantically from the other side of the door.

Clarke drops Margot's wrist, turns angrily. "I'm busy in here," he growls.

"It's the fucking crocodile," the voice strains. "It's got someone."

TWO WEEKS MISSING

I ONCE HEARD SOMEONE say that women's greatest fears in life are sexual assault and death. Men? The thing that keeps them up at night is the idea of being rejected and humiliated by a romantic prospect.

How pathetic is that?

How free you must feel out there, living life as normal. How incredibly light, your existence, to wander anywhere you like without fear, knowing that you are untouchable, that the worst thing that could happen to you is that cute girl you like saying no.

I've begun to wonder about the newspapers that must land on your doorstep. What stories do they contain? Am I in there? Which picture did they use?

If not me, there will be tales of other women, certainly, of women taken, women harmed. Again and again. And so it goes.

No doubt the details of these women's lives will be scant. There might be a cursory acknowledgment of her father's vocation, a few words on her appearance if she's beautiful.

The next day, there'll be a different story. A different girl. Another victim, soon forgotten, a smiling picture to be folded in half, tossed in the trash with the bread crusts from breakfast.

But you don't have to think about that, do you? Becoming a victim doesn't ever have to trouble your thoughts.

I'll make you see, though, that there are more things in life to fear than not getting what you want.

TWENTY-FOUR

Benjamin is screaming.

His face is puce, tears flowing so readily that they drip from his chin. The sound causes a bulb of panic to rise in Beverley's throat.

She doesn't know how to calm him when he gets like this—his rage so acute, erupting from nowhere, so wild and untethered. She's tried everything: hugging him tightly, whispering reassuring words in his ear, stepping back to let it all play out, like a bucking horse, until his energy depletes. But every time he explodes, Beverley feels more alarmed and more certain, with a horrified sense of impending catastrophe, that he is turning into his father.

Benjamin cries out again, then, with a roar of frustration, knocks a whole row of cans from the grocery store shelf. They clatter to the floor, where some lie dented, others rolling under the wheels of passing carts.

Shoppers click their tongues or raise silent eyebrows at Beverley. She glares back, straightens her jacket. *You try and do this,* she wants to challenge them. *You try and deal with this after everything that's happened.*

A psychopath is prone to impulsive outbursts of aggression.

She read the line in a book, just that morning, and the words tap insistently on her shoulder now. She'd picked up the book by chance at the public library. She'd spent the morning researching satanism while the kids ran amok in the aisles. She'd been considering Emily Roswell's tattooed knuckles and what they might say about the man who killed her, but when she'd come across a section on the criminal mind, she couldn't help but reach for one of the titles, quietly tuck it under her arm. As the kids tormented the librarian, she'd taken a seat on a nearby chair and flipped through the pages.

"He reacts to frustration with hostility and fury." Her fingers had traced the words, her eyes closing in guilt.

Could she really be thinking this about her own child? Could her once sweet, gentle baby, now a boy of seven, really be dangerous? She knew she was failing as a mother by even considering this, but Benjamin—once placid and thoughtful—had turned into someone whose outbursts, although it killed her to admit it, had started to scare her.

She'd continued reading, noting what the book said about upbringing. Psychopaths, it said, can be the products of difficult childhoods. Foster homes. Absent fathers. Abuse. Lack of nurture and care. *Those to whom evil is done do evil in return.* She recalled Elsie saying something along those lines when they were discussing the killer's behavior, the words of some famous English poet or something—Beverley couldn't remember who. But that was exactly why she tried so hard to give the kids everything they needed—a loving home, plenty of affection, a safe environment to grow up in. She wanted them to know that they would always be loved and protected. It was hard for Benjamin, who had idolized Henry, to have his father discussed on the school playground as some sort of monster. For Benjamin, Henry was his father, the center of his universe, the man who used to tuck him in at night and lift him onto his shoulders in the yard, spinning round and round and round. But he was a "bad man"—that's what the other children said. He was a bad man who got what he deserved. How can Beverley compete with that?

The thought that some behaviors and traits could simply be genetic had troubled Beverley. Could it be, despite everything she'd tried to do, that Benjamin had inherited the very same rotten core that lay in Henry?

She'd tried to put that thought in the back of her mind as she closed the book and added it to her pile. Not wanting anyone to see the cover, she'd quickly taken another book, a title on new satanism, and placed it on top. Then she crossed to the counter.

The occult was not something Beverley—housewife, mother—ever thought she'd be investigating. But the *LOVE* and *HATE* that had been carved into Emily's hands—it was hard not to read into that. She'd considered the Richard Speck case. Every woman her age has heard of Richard Speck, will be forever haunted by what he did. The papers teemed with stories when it all happened last month. Speck had broken into a dormitory on the south side of Chicago and murdered eight student nurses, rounding them up at gunpoint before strangling, torturing and stabbing them to death. Women everywhere had been rocked by the horror of it, the violation of his acts, the white-hot fear they induced.

He'd had a tattoo on his arm, Beverley recalled. *Born to raise hell.* It's how he'd got caught. One of the surviving nurses told the cops that she'd seen the tattoo on his forearm during the attack. The press ran with that detail. A few days later, Speck slashed his own wrists, winding up in the hospital. There, a doctor caught a glimpse of the tattoo on his arm. He was toast.

Given the message on Emily Roswell's hands, should they be considering that their killer might have distinctive tattoos, too?

"You're at number twenty-eight."

She spins around in surprise. Christopher Appleton, from number forty-four, bends to retrieve some of the cans on the floor. Images of emaciated plants and a sun-crisp lawn suddenly flash into her mind. She sees placards, closed curtains, hears the blare of the television, feels her skin growing hot.

"Yes," she says quickly, flustered. She's learned by now that gut instinct can be a powerful thing, and hers is screaming. "Yes," she says again as she blinks. "Beverley Edwards. And this is Benjamin, and Audrey."

"As in Hepburn?" he asks, then shakes his head oddly.

"I guess so," she replies, and shifts her feet as an awkward silence follows. "Are you settling in okay?" She forces the words out. "It's a friendly neighborhood once you give it a chance," she lies.

"Well enough, thank you. I don't really get out a lot to meet people."

She remembers the rally, seeing him there—she was so sure it was him. Thoughts of the pig carcass fill her head again, the old-meat smell of it. She'd had to wrap it in a tarpaulin, lift it into the trunk of her car and drive a couple of miles out of town to dispose of it after dark. She'd felt absurd, embarrassed to be sneaking around, guilty at leaving the kids asleep at home. It was only when she'd dragged the body out and stashed it in the foliage at the side of the road that she'd stopped to wonder if her husband had ever found himself in the same position while concealing his morbid crimes.

Christopher Appleton's eyes, which dart, struggling to meet hers, are small behind thick glasses. He wears a turtleneck with a sweater-vest pulled over the top, even in this heat. He is of average height and slight build, but his hands, Beverley notices, are half-clenched and the fingers are slightly crooked. This man couldn't really be the person who left the dead body of a pig on her front lawn, could he? She thinks of those twitching curtains, the times she's seen him watching her. Has he seen Roger leaving her house late at night?

Her gaze cuts to the contents of his cart, and in just a fraction of a second she feels as if the air has been snatched from her lungs. Lined up neatly, as if she has placed them in there herself, are six boxes of cereal. Their red cardboard is as distinctive as the gaudy illustrations, the cartoonish yellow lettering, the leprechaun cartoon. Lucky Charms. Elsie told her about the note that the killer had written on the back of a cereal box, a box of Lucky Charms, and stashed it behind windshield wipers, waited for it to be found.

He clocks her looking, winces. "I'm not so good at taking care of myself anymore," he begins to explain, but Beverley is already backing away, terror a siren in her head. She mutters an apology. She must get back home. No time to stay and talk. She doesn't even pay for her groceries, just abandons her cart at the store's entrance, grabs her children by their hands and flees.

TWENTY-FIVE

"So, Sarah Gunn." Patti reaches for a photograph on the desk. "If she's dead, that makes four girls now in just under eight weeks." She raises an eyebrow and lets out a guarded breath. "She's a majorette. Twenty-one years old. Her family lives in Berryview. Wealthy parents."

Both Elsie and Patti were shocked by Detective Bale's slipup at the bar, but it meant another girl was missing. The police, they have since learned, are labeling her a runaway for now, but as far as Elsie is concerned, there's no way Sarah is a runaway. She sees the pattern, even if the cops refuse to. She knows another girl is in danger.

"Her college roommates got worried when she didn't return after her waitressing shift," Patti continues. "She hasn't been seen since."

"Four girls." Elsie shakes her head. "How many will it take before the police catch this guy?"

There's something clichéd about the victims this killer is selecting, Elsie has realized. A constant given of the universe—only the pretty, non-average get picked, even for death. Elsie was an average adult and had been an average teenager, with acne, lank hair, a flat chest—

nothing remarkable to look at—but the attention Albert lavished upon her had made her feel special, as if there was something within her, something that had nothing to do with her outward appearance, that he found utterly magnetic. To be told she was different, unique, *clever*—that was more powerful to Elsie than being told she was beautiful. She flinches at the memory, wrestling with the familiar sting of regret. Recently she has been feeling further and further away from that naïve, powerless young girl. She has been looking back with pity at how moldable, dupable, *meek* she'd been when she was with Albert. There's guilt, of course, such profound, excoriating guilt that it makes her fingers tremble. But something's changed of late, something that leaves her incredulous at her own lack of awareness.

"The cops seem to be distracted by other things." Patti leans back in her seat, linking her fingers across her stomach. "Maybe that's why they're dragging their heels."

"What do you mean?" Elsie is pleased to move away from thoughts of the past.

"Thanks to our chat with Laurel and Hardy the other night, I did some digging on Cornwell's surveillance op."

Patti must have followed Greaves' lead and looked into the audio technology Cornwell was using to surveil the Kings.

"Guess who owns the company providing all the technology for that op," Patti says, "and who is getting paid handsomely to do so."

Elsie cocks her head.

"Broderick Arnold," Patti responds, eyes wide with satisfaction.

"The department store guy?" Elsie's heard of him before. In fact, she's pretty sure he owns the store that Margot works in.

"And guess what Broderick Arnold is," Patti continues.

"Incredibly wealthy?" Elsie quips.

Patti snorts. "He's also Tom Cornwell's brother-in-law."

Elsie gawps.

"Uh-huh."

"So, that means—"

"Cornwell's pushing the Kings as suspects to justify throwing so much money at his brother-in-law's company." Patti fills in the gaps. "Meaning he's *literally* looking the other way while someone else is out there killing these girls."

Elsie groans with frustration. Yet again, a man in a position of significant power has proved himself to be utterly lacking in integrity. Yet again, women have been let down. She takes the photo of Sarah and inspects it: an attractive young woman, clear eyes lined with kohl, hair slashed into an Edie Sedgwick crop. She is wearing a college sweater emblazoned with large letters.

"Berryview," Elsie mutters as she places the photo back on the table. "I've got a friend in Berryview. Do you think she's in danger there?"

She knows she has to tell Bev that another girl has gone missing, and this one was right on her doorstep.

"She's a woman," Patti deadpans. "What do you think?"

TWENTY-SIX

"MISSING? NOT KILLED?" Margot asks, browsing the skirts on the rail.

"Well," Elsie replies, "we don't know." Elsie is standing, arms folded, several feet away from Margot and Beverley, as if she could never lower herself to engage in a hobby so banal as shopping. "There's no body yet, so . . ."

"If he hasn't killed her already, he must be keeping her somewhere." Margot pulls out a Mary Quant mini and holds it to her waist. "Maybe we're looking for someone with an outbuilding or a basement? It has to be close. We know Berryview's in the middle of his operating zone."

"Bev," Elsie urges, "I just want you to be safe. Are you keeping your doors locked?"

Beverley knows the whole of Berryview has been keeping their doors locked. Recently, she has felt a blanket of terror descend over the suburb. Mothers beckon their children in as soon as the sun starts to dip; husbands lift dumbbells in open-doored garages, arming themselves with the means to protect their families.

"Do you think we need to get creative?" Margot asks with relish. "Pose as housing researchers or whatever, find out who's got a creepy basement?"

"Actually, I've been thinking about sex more than architecture," Elsie counters. Margot's relish morphs into delighted astonishment. She turns to Beverley, mouth wide.

Elsie tuts at the reaction. "I don't think we've explored the sexual motive enough," she explains. "It seems to me like all our husbands had certain sexual proclivities. They were obsessive to some degree, like they had this *need* for something that we couldn't quite fulfill, right?"

Beverley watches Margot consider it. She's sure Margot and Stephen had a great sex life. She's always been too ashamed to tell them about her and Henry's, about the times he put his hands around her throat when they were in bed.

"We don't know yet if the girls were sexually assaulted, but we do know Diane Howard Murray probably spent some time working as a prostitute," Elsie continues. "So perhaps there is a sexual element to these crimes that we're missing. Bev, you had a theory that our guy probably uses prostitutes regularly..."

"Sure." She nods. They don't need to know that it's Henry's theory, not hers.

"I think you could be right, and that's how Diane Howard Murray crossed his path. But the thing is, I've been thinking maybe we're approaching this in the wrong way."

Margot turns, knotting a malachite-colored headscarf under her chin. "What do you mean, the wrong way?"

"Surely the people we should be speaking to about this are those women, the ones being visited by these men."

"Well, how do we go about doing that?" Bev asks.

"I heard about a group of women in Calabasas who run a café for girls like Diane—somewhere for them to get warm, get a cup of coffee, somewhere safe for them to rest. Maybe we pay them a visit?"

Beverley nods eagerly. Margot raises an interested eyebrow.

"Given that Diane probably picked up guys around there, I figure we go to this café, ask around, see if they've come across anyone acting strangely, see if anyone has been particularly violent recently, any guys with weird quirks."

"Anyone with *the look*," Margot adds, widening her eyes.

"Well, you might joke, but yes," Elsie replies. "Women are intuitive. We can sense when someone is dangerous, even if it takes us a while." She looks between Beverley and Margot. "What do you think? We could go tonight. I'm sure I can track down the address."

Beverley sighs. "My mom can't take the kids tonight. She has bridge."

"Looks like it's you and me, Margot," Elsie says, with a pursed smile.

"It's a date."

TWENTY-SEVEN

THE LAST TIME Margot visited church, she managed all of five minutes. The maudlin wood of the pews, the mustiness of the air, all that stained glass—it gave her the creeps. She sat at the back, wearing one of her mother's old dresses, thought about some sort of reflection to mark the five years since Stephen had been arrested, then thought better of it, glanced at the ceiling in a makeshift prayer and hotfooted it to a nearby hotel bar to hide.

This place is a little different. She's not really sure you could even call it a church. There are no pews, no prayer books. Instead, beanbags and cushions have been carefully scattered across the floor. The windows are draped with jewel-toned scarves, and there's a distinct smell of incense sticks and stale coffee. A few cross-legged women chat in small groups. Others lean against the walls, drinking from Solo cups with the tired, glazed eyes of those who know they no longer have to be on high alert.

Margot glances at Elsie, who has her attention fixed on a group of women clustered around a table at the front of the room.

"That must be Betty," she murmurs. Margot follows her gaze to a woman who would not look out of place on the arm of a Rolling Stone. She has a tight fuchsia turtleneck and bell-bottomed jeans on, and there's a lanyard strung around her neck. Her hair is styled in the type of glossy Supremes bob you see on magazine covers.

Margot swallows guiltily. Why did she expect paisley and tofu? She's too quick to judge sometimes; she knows that. She gets it from her mother.

She follows as Elsie makes her way to the front of the room. Margot was surprised when Elsie had allowed her to come along, but Margot is aware of her own ability to put people at ease. She got that from her mother, too, an uncanny ability to shape-shift socially, to switch up her demeanor, her way of talking, to blend into any situation she might find herself in. She watched her mother do it at parties, in the grocery store, on the odd, awful occasion when she and her brother caught a glimpse of her with one of the men. She seemed at home wherever she found herself. Margot knew it was all an act, though, and was amazed at such strength of will, such clever manipulation of the people and the circumstances around her. So she studied it until she'd perfected the very same skills herself.

She looks to Elsie, whose expression is determined. They've never spent much one-on-one time together, but, to Margot's surprise, she actually enjoyed the car ride over here. They spent it discussing the ways in which their husbands had covered up their crimes. If they could find commonalities between them, patterns of behavior, perhaps it wasn't unreasonable to think that another woman, another wife, was recognizing the very same things in her own husband right now. There were the unsurprising things: stammered explanations for their absences, receipts for mystery purchases, endless stretches of time spent out of the house. Then there were the less obvious ones. Stephen took showers, Margot explained, so many showers—whenever he returned home, whether it was four p.m. or four a.m. She didn't question it at first; then, after a few weeks, she put it down to extramarital affairs—the man was hardly subtle. But with hindsight she can see that on the occasions when he wasn't washing off blood and hair and skin, he was scrubbing away guilt.

Elsie's experience with Albert was more complicated. She talked about masks, describing how he had seemed to wear different faces constantly, slipping seamlessly between them most of the time. But sometimes a mask would catch, and he'd be caught between the duality of two personalities: a calm, patient teacher who'd suddenly snap at passing children; a voracious reader who'd inexplicably spend a whole distracted afternoon gazing silently out the window. What Elsie saw when those masks misaligned scared her. It's only now that she knows just how hard he fought to keep the true Albert buried beneath them.

Could whoever is killing women around Berryview have a family at home? A wife he lies to? A nice house? A shower he stands under at the end of the day, dried blood draining off with the dirty water?

At the church café, Betty raises her head as they approach, smiling quizzically. She must know most of the women who come here, spent after long nights out working, some of them reeling from the experience, others of them merely weary, looking for somewhere to rest, to lower their guard. Margot and Elsie must present an unusual sight—Elsie with her endless sincerity, Margot with her Prada.

"Ladies, welcome. You here for coffee?" Betty doesn't miss a beat, fixing their eyes as if they belong there when it is abundantly clear that they do not. Margot is impressed.

Elsie launches straight in. "I'm a friend of Patti Fowler's. She said you might be able to help us out with something."

Margot notices Betty's mouth tightening almost imperceptibly before she relaxes into a smile once again. She glances quickly around the room, keeps that smile fixed in place. "Why don't you ladies join me out back?"

In the hallway, a single light flickers overhead. Margot brushes against the wall, and her jacket comes away damp. There are boxes stacked atop one another, marked in red felt-tip. Underwear. Warm clothing. Toiletries.

"I'd rather the ladies didn't hear us talking," Betty explains, more relaxed now. "This is a safe space for them, and I assume you're not here for the hospitality."

A safe space. Margot considers, briefly, whether her mother had a place like this to come to when she was working. She was a strong woman, capable of handling herself, a woman who would most definitely have screamed and kicked and fought if she ever found herself in a situation that meant she might not see her children again. Even when she was so diminished by illness, when it had torn out her hair and shut off the light behind her eyes, Margot's mother was the strongest person in any room.

Margot traveled to be with her in those last days, leaving the grand house she shared with Stephen to sit in her mother's cramped living room, to curl up with her on the couch, to stroke her head as if Margot had been the parent and her mother the child. She had just one week with her before she died—the very same week, she later discovered, that Stephen began his awful spree.

"We want to ask you about a young woman," Elsie says.

"Diane Howard Murray," Margot says, pulling the photograph from her pocket. She hands it over to Betty.

Betty studies the photo, nods slowly. "She came here a few times," she confirms. Margot watches as Betty runs a thumb slowly over the girl's face, an almost protective gesture. "I remember thinking how young she looked. Wasn't much of a talker."

"She was killed."

Margot is taken aback by Elsie's forthrightness, her focus on the facts.

"Her body was found in an alleyway in Calabasas, dressed in a coat and suspenders."

Betty's eyes close for a moment, and Margot knows she's processing dread. Then they flick open. "What do you need from me?"

"Did you know any of her clients? Anyone who might have acted aggressively toward her, might have been possessive, fixated?"

"There are plenty of men like that. These girls are always coming back with horror stories."

"Did she, or any of the other girls, mention someone who might have had weird sexual inclinations?"

Betty exhales drily. "Define *weird*."

"Well, maybe there's a guy who likes the girls to dress up. Maybe there's someone who . . ." Elsie falters. "Maybe there's someone who likes to hurt them."

"Have you spoken to the cops about this?" Betty asks, looking between Elsie and Margot.

"We're sort of doing our own thing," Margot explains. "And let's just say the cops aren't really on our side."

"Understood." Betty smiles tightly. "Look, if the girls come across someone unusually violent, he'll be in the book."

"'The book'?"

"The Beware Book," Betty explains. "At least that's what the girls call it. The cops were forced to use it when all those students went missing in 'sixty-one."

Margot's heart picks up speed.

"It has details of each encounter—where it happened, a description of the guy and sometimes a number plate, if the girl's had a chance and the wherewithal to note it. There are a lot of bad guys in that book."

"Any idea how we can get hold of it?" Elsie asks.

Betty glances behind them, down the hallway. "Wait here."

When she returns, she has in her hand a bunch of papers fastened with a large clip. She holds it out to Elsie. "This is precious information. It keeps the girls safe. I'll need it all back later today, okay?"

Elsie takes it, holds it to her chest.

Margot nods. "You have our word."

TWENTY-EIGHT

Beverley scratches the inside of her elbow and shifts on the hard red couch. Her legs are tightly crossed, her back unnaturally straight. She wishes she had a glass of water at hand.

She was forced to do this. Another girl was missing, a girl from Berryview. The victims were stacking up, and Beverley has received her own warning now, too. She can't put this off any longer. She knows she has to do whatever it takes to get the word out there.

The television studio is vast. The lights are pointed directly at her, hot enough to melt makeup. Someone smelling of hair spray approaches and brushes her cheeks with heavy powder. She asks Beverley to purse her lips so that she can reapply, holds out a sheet of paper, orders her to blot.

Beside Beverley, on a smaller couch, is a man in a gray suit, his trousers having lifted to show apricot-colored socks. Staff busy about behind the cameras, adjusting the lighting, speaking in strange code she doesn't understand. Behind her head, on a huge screen, is a bright, innocuously artificial sunrise. It makes Bev's eyes ache.

She knew from the moment she learned of the Jane Doe, of Cheryl Herrera, that it might come to this. The thought, the number stashed away in the kitchen drawer, lingered like an unattended itch at the back of her mind. Now three girls are dead and another has gone missing. The women of California are in danger, and that includes Margot and Elsie; it includes her mother and every other woman who locks her door at night hoping it's enough to keep her safe.

She was powerless to do anything about it—until now.

So Beverley walked to her kitchen and found the slip of paper she'd hidden away along with a bunch of business cards and scrawled notes. On it was a telephone number and three words: *The California Day*.

It was five years since Henry was imprisoned for the murders he committed. If she has to talk about *that* with host Charles Marston to get her own message across, then so be it.

The producer seemed surprised when she called him back after all this time, after so many ignored messages and phone calls. "Anything I can do to stop it from happening again . . ." she said. He booked her for the next available slot.

But that does not mean she isn't nervous. It does not mean she doesn't want to tear off her own skin. She barely slept last night, turning in a tangle of bedsheets, doubting her decision. The police gala was excruciating enough, and that was only a few hundred people. *The California Day* is broadcast across the entire state. There are likely to be millions of viewers. Charles Marston is a well-known TV personality who appears on billboards next to the highway and in television commercials for golf clubs and weight-loss pills. But that's exactly what she needs, isn't it? She needs to reach as many women as possible. She needs to ask them a question.

"So, Mrs. Lightfoot . . ." A runner with a clipboard and a headset bends in front of her and speaks quickly. "Charles is going to do a brief introduction, touching on your story, your husband, the date, et cetera, et cetera. Then he'll ask you a few questions, nothing too taxing. You can make your apology, and ta-da! Home by lunchtime." He stands and claps her on the shoulder before she has time to ask any questions. Her cheeks redden at her own foolishness. *An apology.* Of course that's what they expect of her; that's all anyone expects of her. She has spent years apologizing for Henry's actions.

When it all happened, she felt a fuzzy, consuming need to beg for forgiveness. She wrote to the mothers, cousins and siblings of Henry's victims. Only one replied, the sister of Annie Milton, who was not much older than Beverley when Henry killed her. Following a string of unanswered messages, the woman eventually agreed to meet for coffee.

Beverley waited at the café for four hours, draining cup after cup, not even leaving the table to use the restroom, desperate to cling to the idea that Annie's sister would eventually walk through the door and listen to Beverley's apology. She never showed, and when the server stopped by with the boiling coffeepot once more, Beverley wanted to snatch it from her and hold the scalding metal to her own skin.

She turned to her mother for comfort then, showing up in tears on her doorstep. Alice let her in, put a blanket around her shoulders, sat her down.

"But, darling," Alice cooed, and Beverley waited for the moment she'd always yearned for—a mother making everything better, kisses and Band-Aids. "You can't simply expect people to forgive you. Maybe this is the universe's way of telling you that that is not what you deserve."

"Okay, Charles. Ready for you in thirty." The radio bleeps with static.

Charles shifts forward on the couch.

Beverley rearranges her skirt yet again. Is she really going to do this? On live television?

"*And that's ten...*"

She used to be good at this, flashing a Vaseline smile and gazing into the camera, feeling as if it were where she belonged.

"*...nine, eight, seven...*"

They could fill her slot with news about something else—Labor Day telethons, that new *Star Trek* show, nuclear tests in Kazakhstan...

"*...three, two...*" The camera operator holds up one silent finger, and Charles Marston erupts into life.

"Welcome back to *The California Day* on this bright, sunny September morning. Jeez, it's hot out there, isn't it, folks? Hot enough to fry an egg. Hot *enough*"—he pauses briefly—"for the Heatwave Killer to strike."

There is a loud ringing in Beverley's skull.

"If that moniker sounds familiar, that's because it was the nickname given to Henry Lightfoot, the Bay Area air-conditioning salesman turned killer who snuck into young women's houses through open windows and back doors."

It sounds as if he is talking about a stranger, the plot of a movie. That is not life; that is surely not Beverley's life.

"Five years ago, after taking the lives of seven victims, he was captured by police." She thinks of the pink visiting room, the reek of bleach, Henry's crocodile smile. *I'm getting married.*

Beverley senses eyes on her—not just those in the room, but a million pairs of eyes watching her from kitchens and living room sofas. What must the audience think of her? That she's crass? Pitiful? Evil? Stiffly, she smooths down her skirt again and tugs at the hem. She wants to cover every inch of her skin, to disappear into the seat cushions, pretend she never agreed to do this.

"And with us today, marking the anniversary of her husband's conviction, is Beverley Lightfoot, the wife of Henry Lightfoot, the Heatwave Killer. Beverley, thank you so much for joining us in the studio. I know this can't be an easy thing to talk about."

"Ex-wife," Beverley says quickly. "Thank you for having me." *It's a privilege? An honor?* "It's a pleasure to be here." *Shit. No, not pleasure. Anything but pleasure.*

Charles raises his eyebrows, continues. "Tell us, how did you feel when you first discovered that your husband, Henry Lightfoot, was the Heatwave Killer?"

Like she wanted to hack off her own ears so she wouldn't have to hear what he had done. Like she could grab a knife from the kitchen counter and slice his neck open. "Well, I felt shock," she says quietly. "Horror. Disbelief."

"You had no inkling at all that he was out there at night, murdering young women in their homes?" She recognizes his tone, the undercurrent of judgment.

She takes a deep breath and lets it out. "None at all."

"He never showed signs of it in the house? Never harmed you?"

She feels a sticky heat creep up to her chin.

"What about the children? You had children together, right?" He checks his notes. "Benjamin and . . ."

"Audrey. Henry *never* harmed the children."

"Don't you worry that they might turn out like him? Little Benjamin in particular?"

The space is stifling. This isn't what she had agreed to talk about—not the kids. She wanted to protect them from things like this.

"I never really . . ."

"Do you think there was something in the home that caused him to do what he did, to flip?"

"Flip?"

"With these guys, there must be something that makes them just... explode." He opens his fingers like a detonating bomb. Beverley remembers Margot doing just the same. "Can you explain that for our viewers, the role that family, surrounding loved ones, can play in enabling these crimes?"

She looks around the studio. A dozen cameras are on her, blurred faces muttering to one another, making notes, choosing the best frames. No one is telling Charles that what he's saying, what he's suggesting, might be wrong.

"I don't really know about that," she manages to stammer out. "We were all shocked by what happened."

His right eyebrow folds. She realizes she has not given a satisfactory answer, and she scrambles to rectify it. "But I'm just so incredibly sorry. I'm so sorry for the families of the victims who have to live with the consequences of Henry's actions." She resents her own weakness.

"You feel responsible, in a way."

He doesn't give her a chance to answer.

"What was Henry's upbringing like?"

The police had asked her this; briefly, she is back there. Coffee stains on the table. Stale air. Rolled shirtsleeves and cigarettes.

"It was relatively normal," she says, blinking.

"'Relatively'?" Charles pushes.

She remembers suddenly that there are cameras pointing at her, and she straightens her back with a jolt. "His father was... overbearing. He expected a lot of his children."

"Children. That means Henry has siblings. What do they think about the fact that their brother is a murderer?"

She mustn't get rattled; she knows how that would look. She glances quickly at the camera and forces a smile, immediately wincing at how wrong it feels.

Henry's brother, James, was hounded, just as she was, when the news broke. He was forced to stand by as his own personal life was plundered and splashed across the papers. He'd been imprisoned for grand theft auto several years prior, and the headlines made the most of Henry's "criminal family past." James had a family of his own, two young children and a wife, who found themselves targeted by journalists after the murders. The last thing Beverley knew was that James' wife had divorced him and taken the kids to live in New Zealand.

"I can't talk about that, I'm afraid."

Charles tugs at his tie and clasps his hands over his knee. "Well, okay, what would you like *your* children to know about their father?"

She holds his gaze for a second. His eyes are green, his cleanly shaven face tan and healthy; he looks like a man who plays a lot of golf. There is the faintest hint of a smile lifting the corner of his mouth. She recognizes the expression. It means he does not respect her. It means he thinks he is better than her.

"I want—" she starts to say.

"No, no." He waves his finger at her. "Say it to the camera."

Her tongue brushes the front of her teeth, and the girl is there, the one in the advertisements, the one who did this all so easily so many years ago. She smiles, turns to face the lens. "I want them to know that he loved them very much."

Charles raises his eyebrows again and shuffles his notes. "I'm sure the victims' families will be very happy to hear that," he says drily. "Well, thank you, Beverley, for coming in."

No. It can't end like that.

Charles shifts on the sofa, turning away from her and back to the cameras.

That can't be it. She didn't get to say anything she wanted to say. What about the investigation? The killer who is out there. What about Cheryl, Emily, Diane and Sarah? She can't believe she squandered the opportunity, that she let herself get so flustered by his questions.

"Now, if you've ever wondered if a mongoose can surf," Charles quips to the camera, "take a look at this." Someone with a clipboard is shuffling toward Beverley, hunching over, reaching for the microphone on the lapel of her jacket.

No. Her head swivels from left to right. She can't let that be it.

"Wait!"

Charles freezes midway through the text on his teleprompter and turns his head to her, his eyes wide in silent warning.

"Sorry, folks." He turns back to the camera. "I think we're just having some technical difficulties here."

"I wasn't finished." The cameras swing back toward her. "There's something else I need to say."

Charles raises a hand to his neck and makes a subtle *cut* gesture to the camera, but he is ignored. He clears his throat, turns back to her. "Of course, Mrs. Lightfoot." She can tell by the quivering muscles in his cheek that he is furious. "It's not often that we have people like yourself on the show. What is it you would like to add?"

She has the attention of everyone in the room now. They have stepped out from behind their cameras, lowered their clipboards to watch her intently.

She looks into the largest camera, trained on her face. She can see its lens expanding and zooming in. Closer, closer. She feels as if she could get lost in it, as if it might swallow her up entirely. She stares directly ahead and makes her voice as clear as possible.

"I have a message for the women of California." This is what she practiced in the mirror. "The wives and the sisters and the girlfriends."

Charles shifts on the couch. The producers share nervous glances.

"Be aware of who is out there on the streets."

Charles nods, relieved, begins to turn back to the camera to start his mongoose segment again.

"And in your homes."

Charles stiffens.

"Women are getting hurt." Roger will be enraged if she reveals specific details of the case, but she cannot get into trouble for saying what has always been true, that women are not safe.

"Keep your doors locked and bolted," she continues, staring straight down the lens. "Shut your windows at night, no matter how hot it gets outside. And keep an eye on the men in your life."

Charles clears his throat beside her, but the camera does not move; it stays trained on her face.

"Watch your husbands, brothers and sons," she continues. "Even if he seems like an honorable man, is he acting differently? Is he cold, detached, prone to volatile mood swings or outbursts? Is he spending more time out of the house than normal? Have you found evidence of sexual digressions, perversions? Do you catch him making excuses? Is he tired, injured, secretive?"

"Hold on one moment there, Mrs. Lightfoot," Charles finally interrupts her. "Are you saying women need to be afraid of *all* men?" He barks out a laugh. "Because that doesn't really seem fair. Am I right?" He opens his arms and makes a show of looking around the studio for backup.

"Of course not," Beverley stammers. "I just mean—"

"Santa Claus?" he taunts. "He's a man. Should we fear *God* because he is male? The Easter Bunny—anyone have tabs on him?"

The camera moves from Beverley back to Charles, and she knows she's blown it.

She wants to grab the lens and jolt it back to her, to tell California that there *is* someone out there on a spree, killing women. She wants to tell them about the arrow, the tattooed knuckles, the designer coat and suspender stockings—all the shocking, strange details. But she has ruined her chance.

She is numb as staff swarm around her, removing her microphone and leading her through dark corridors and eventually out into the blinding California sun.

"Good luck, Mrs. Lightfoot," a runner calls grimly as he turns and closes the studio doors, leaving Beverley alone on the stark, bright street.

FOUR WEEKS MISSING

I **WILL DANCE TO** the Beatles on the radio.
    I will eat an apple, the skin removed in one single curl, like my father taught me.
    I will wear comfortable slippers, stretch my toes out inside them.
    I will browse the aisles at the grocery store, leave with only a bunch of grapes, a copy of *Vogue* and a bottle of cold champagne.
    I will pet a dog.
    I will take a vacation.
    I will swim in the ocean, submerge my head, blow bubbles under the water, splutter from the salt.
    I will smell a baby's head.
    I will brush my hair in front of the mirror.
    I will bake a cake, run my fingers around the bottom of the bowl, lick off the frosting.
    I will wear fresh underwear.
    I will move my body freely, feel the sun on my face.
    I will wash the smell of you from my clothes, my skin.
    I will breathe fresh air again.

TWENTY-NINE

In the days that follow her appearance on television, Beverley receives hate mail in the post. She is not used to receiving letters anymore. Her former friends, mostly preppy onetime teen models she met in waiting rooms, find her situation unpalatable. But they do send bland, perfunctory cards at Christmastime, with updates on their husbands' promotions at work, their Aspen ski vacations, little Robert's grades at school. They don't ask after her small, tragic life, as if ignoring it will scrub away the stain of blood.

But this is a deluge. Beverley opens each letter, far away from the children, early in the morning, torturing herself as the sun blares out through the treetops. She reads every single line, holding each one to her throat like a knife.

The letters tell her she's a man-hater, a hypochondriac. They tell her she's a bitch pushing an agenda against men, that she deserves to die a brutal death, just as her husband's victims did.

It's just like her mother said. Punishment. It's only what she deserves. How can she ever have expected anything else?

Alice herself stops by to tell Beverley she is endangering her children by spouting controversial opinions so publicly. Beverley questions how the opinion that male violence is a danger to women can be controversial. Her mother simply mutters in response, tells her she really must read less.

September drags on, a gluey, endless stretching of time. Beverley studies herself in the mirror and finds only the shell of someone she once knew. She used to be elegant, used to look so much like someone whose face could sell peanut butter or kitchen cleaner. She had a ballerina's posture once, shaped by years in front of the camera. Where is that girl now? This thing in front of the mirror is hunched and diminished.

Elsie and Margot have both called to tell her it wasn't too bad. That Marston was an ass. That she did a good job of getting the word out there. Even if she was vilified. Even if it didn't give them any leads, anywhere else to turn. She did her best.

Desperate, she called Roger to tell him about the incident in the supermarket—Mr. Appleton with his cartful of Lucky Charms, the way it made her skin crawl just to be near him.

"Maybe the man just really likes cereal," he deadpanned down the crackling line.

She held the handset away from her ear and clenched her teeth. She resented being mocked, especially when people's lives were at stake.

"Look, no guy over fifty would murder young, athletic women with his bare hands," Roger continued, growing tired of her suspicions. "You've got to stop this, Bev."

She was silent.

"Honey," he sighed, "I can't just stake out a guy because he has a hankering for Lucky Charms, okay?" He told her that the police were pursuing their own leads, that they now agreed that the murders could be linked, that they had their eyes on a few different suspects, each with his own history of violence and threatening behavior toward women.

She hung up frustrated and unsatisfied.

Sean Wilson, she now knows, has been alibied by his wife. But that does not explain why he was at Cheryl's vigil in the first place. "Heston did more digging," Elsie later told her. "He came away with the opinion that Wilson was obsessed with Cheryl and a couple of the other girls at her club, would watch them train, hang around at their meets, called himself a fan."

"So he's a creep even if he isn't a killer," Margot sneered.

Elsie promised her that she'd do more investigating at the *Signal*, that they'd get a break eventually—they just had to keep going. But all Beverley wanted to do was sit, the doors and windows closed, the heat bulging at the glass, the houseplants parched and abandoned, and ruminate on her punishment. Her actions—her "stunt," as her mother called it—had let the murdered women down, and Beverley had made a laughingstock of herself. How could she have done such a poor job of sticking up for those she was supposed to protect?

IT'S BEEN ALMOST ten days, and Beverley is cleaning the kitchen, hair unwashed, radio on full blast, when she realizes she has not yet checked the mail. In her robe and slippers, no longer caring what the neighbors think, she trudges out into the blinding sunlight and pulls open the mailbox. There is just one letter tucked inside, and she is relieved that the number has finally started to dwindle. She looks from left to right and across the street. No gawping neighbors, no Mrs. Akerman walking her dachshund. Just Mr. Appleton doddering up his front path, returning home from a rare outing. She peels the envelope open and gingerly unfolds the letter, bracing herself for the sting of the words she knows she deserves.

Dear Beverley Lightfoot, the letter reads, *I am writing about my husband.*

THIRTY

FIVE DAYS LATER

B EVERLEY CHECKS HER watch. Five past eleven. They were supposed to be meeting inside the diner on the hour, but she can't seem to leave her car. She considers driving off and saving herself the humiliation of being stood up, of exposing herself to a setup, but the image of Diane Howard Murray in her cleaning apron flashes into her mind, then the image of Sarah Gunn twirling her majorette batons. She pushes open the car door, steps out into the sweltering heat and makes her way across the lot.

She takes a table at the very back of the room so she can watch the door. It's close to the bathroom, in case she needs to hide. There's an old song playing on the jukebox—"Dream Lover" by Bobby Darin. It makes Bev pause, bristle. Henry used to whistle it around the house, catching her with his arm as she passed by in the hall, swaying her into a playful dance. She puts the palms of her hands to her ears to try to block out the sound.

The waitress stops by and Beverley orders a coffee, then calls her back to order another. She doesn't want to be seen as rude.

The woman signed off with a name, Sharon Farrer, although whether that was a pseudonym, Beverley couldn't be sure.

She spent the evening poring over the letter, searching every line, looking for the ruse, the trap. But there was something in Sharon's words that made Beverley certain that she wasn't lying.

The waitress brings the coffees and a jug of half-and-half. Beverley puts too much in hers and the liquid spills over. She dips her mouth to the rim of the mug to sip at it like a cat.

"You look just like you did on TV."

Beverley's eyes dart up.

"I'm Sharon."

The woman standing over her has a face full of makeup. Her aqua eye shadow and candy-pink cheeks give her the appearance of a doll, an effect heightened by her head of blond corkscrew curls. She has a pair of white roller skates slung over her shoulders and wears a fifties-style pink skirt and matching sweater.

"I'm sorry," the woman says breathily. Beverley notices she has a thick East Coast accent. "I had to come straight from work. This is the only break I get." She takes a seat opposite Beverley in the booth. "These things make it a bit easier to get around, but I swear, one of these days I'm gonna break my neck." Sharon grabs a napkin and starts mopping up the spilled coffee.

Beverley can't take her eyes off the skates. She's never seen a grown woman with a pair of roller skates before. Sharon catches her staring.

"I work at the drive-in on the corner of Mace and William." She blushes slightly. "I'm a carhop. We have to wear these dumb outfits and wigs." She tugs at the blond curls and pulls them cleanly from her head. Her hair underneath is squashed and mousy at the roots, the ends fried to a crisp by peroxide. She teases it out with her fingers, tries to make herself presentable. "But a job's a job, right? Mind if I smoke?"

The woman's words unfurl too quickly. She seems nervous. Beverley has that same habit, her words tripping from her tongue when she doesn't know what else to do.

"That was an incredible thing you did, going on television like that." Sharon lights her cigarette and takes a drag, scratching at her scalp with artificial nails. She is clearly older than Beverley, but something about her seems girlish, her eyes darting around the room as she talks, her skin lined, her pale pink lipstick faded to a chalky outline.

"Can I get a fresh coffee?" Sharon calls out to the waitress, then turns back to Beverley. "I'm sorry—I'm talking too much. I do that when I get nervous."

"Thank you for your letter," Beverley replies calmly. If what Sharon wrote is true, then she is likely scared, and desperate for answers. It must have taken courage for her to come here.

Sharon tilts her head. "What you said on the show just really made sense, y'know?" The waitress places a pot of coffee on the table. "I was watching you, and something just hit me." Sharon slaps her forehead. "It clicked. I knew I had to speak to you."

"So, your husband . . ."

"Hank."

"He's been acting strange for a while? Tell me more about that."

Sharon glances around them, checks that no one is listening in. "Everything you said." She blows on her coffee. "The staying late at work, the secrecy, the defensiveness. Then there's these sudden *explosions*. He makes out like *I'm* crazy when I ask where he's been or why he's coming home at two o'clock in the morning."

"Mm-hmm." Beverley forces a nod, but none of that makes him a killer. Perhaps he's having an affair. Perhaps he really is staying at work late. "And that's all out of character for him?"

"Not really," says Sharon glumly, flicking ash into the tray. "He's a mechanic, so he does work strange hours sometimes. He drinks. He's always been . . . aggressive." Her voice quiets. "He's not a nice guy, really. Took me a while to realize it, but it's true."

"Can you elaborate?"

"He says things about women—how they should be good wives; they should be quiet, stay at home, out of the way; how they should look after the kids, make sure the house is in order."

Beverley nods again, but this is nothing new. Plenty of men have outdated views.

"He doesn't like that I work. He hates this." She gestures to her pink outfit, the makeup, the roller skates. "Lately, he's been making me scrub my face when I get home—like, *really* scrub."

Beverley leans in a little.

"He stands there and watches me in the mirror." Sharon's voice falters slightly. "He'll tell me to use more soap, to scrub until every bit of mascara is off and my face is just this red, hot mess."

I'm sorry. A memory flicks into Beverley's head. She was shaving Henry in front of the mirror. She'd carefully used the brush to apply cream all over his neck. They'd laughed as he stuck out his chin and pouted. She'd taken a clean blade and put it to his cheek with care, pulling it upward in short motions, wiping it off on the towel next to the sink. Then she'd moved to his neck, but he twitched, then winced, sucked a sharp breath in, and she pulled the blade away. They both watched in the mirror as a blurt of red spread like an opening flower.

I'm sorry. I'm so sorry.

She didn't even see it coming, didn't see him raise his arm, and before she had a chance to turn, he dealt an almighty blow to the side of her head. The room rang with a hundred chimes, and then everything went silent.

"Do you think he's dangerous? Your husband," she asks Sharon. She wants to help her, but violent men hurt their wives and their girlfriends all the time. It's wrong, and they should never get away with it, but it does not make them killers. That does not help her here.

"He's been like that with me for a long time," Sharon eventually answers, staring into her coffee cup, "but this is the first time I've thought he might be a danger to other people. What you said on the television—it made me see him in a different light."

"If he hurts you, you should go to the police." She's a hypocrite. She never went to the police, even though she knew what Henry did to her was wrong.

"He threatens me." Sharon blinks a few times quickly; it makes her seem even more childlike. "After we argue, after he . . . hurts me, he says that if I go to the police, he'll harm the children, that he'll have nothing left, that he won't have any choice."

Beverley's breath catches at the mention of children.

"And—" Sharon's eyes flick across Beverley's face, then down to her collarless jacket, Pierre Cardin, and she appears to change her mind. "It doesn't matter."

"Go on." Beverley reaches out and puts her hand on Sharon's. She is surprised when Sharon grasps her fingers quickly—such an intimate gesture—before removing them and picking up her coffee cup.

"The police deal with people like me in a certain way," Sharon says evenly. Beverley feels the prick of guilt against her sternum. She thinks of her expensive bag, her watch, her house in Berryview, with a nice garden and a pool that birds come and drink from when it's hot. She looks at Sharon's chipped nails, her hands that spend each evening ferrying burgers and fries to teenagers in cars.

"They're not interested," Sharon continues. "They just see me as a cheap wife who gets knocked around."

"I'm sure if you told them what he—"

"Beverley? Please." The plea is cut through with desperation. "Would you take a look at him? See what you think."

"I don't know, Sharon. I'm not sure if—"

"There's something else."

Beverley pauses, searches Sharon's face.

"There's something I found." Sharon reaches into her handbag and starts to rummage. "I saw an article in the *Signal*." Beverley is not quite sure why, but she can hear her own heartbeat growing louder in her ears. When Sharon withdraws her hand and opens her palm to reveal a shining thing, Beverley cannot help but cry out in shock.

They're going to have to look into Hank Farrer after all.

THIRTY-ONE

There hasn't been a single browser in the men's fashion department for three hours. Margot doesn't blame anyone for staying away. It's too damn hot to shop. No one wants Dougie Millings when they've got pit stains like a hobo.

Her boss excused himself two hours ago. "Just stepping out"—something he had a habit of doing when the shop was quiet. Margot knows "stepping out" involves a bag of golf clubs and several jugs of Long Island iced tea. Still, it means she has the place to herself.

She moves behind the counter and takes a seat on the stool, humming along to the Lovin' Spoonful on the speakers. Back here there's a stash of *Look* magazines that she keeps for quiet days just like this. She idly picks one out and thumps it on the counter. It's a few years old. Jackie Kennedy is wearing white gloves, a pink coat and a stunning black headscarf. Jacqueline Kennedy Inspires the New International Look. Margot runs her fingers across the cover line, down to the picture, as if she is feeling her way back through the years, along the threads that link them together: the politician's wife, the Hamptons socialite, the widow.

Margot was a dedicated wife to Stephen when they'd first got married, blindly accompanying him to rallies and dinners and galas, where he'd speak from the stage for what seemed like hours. Margot would wait stageside, cigarette in hand, and pretend to listen intently. If he returned late from an event, with a headache, a thirst for Johnnie Walker and an axe to grind for a fellow candidate, she'd pour him a drink, rub his shoulders, make the right noises. She was accomplished at keeping quiet, but she could be a songbird, too—always the centerpiece at their parties, the convivial hostess, the woman who danced on tables, hollered for more.

It wasn't long into their marriage when Margot began to suspect that Stephen was having an affair. It was hardly unlikely. He was a handsome politician—what did she expect? He'd become shifty, secretive and cold. When he returned from a late night at the office and slid into their bed in the small hours of the morning, he no longer wanted to talk, her head resting on his chest, or to make love as the sun came up. Instead, he'd withdraw, mumble that he needed to shower, pull himself out of their tangled sheets. She'd roll over, confused, reaching an arm into that empty space. Eventually she would doze off. By the time she opened her eyes again, he'd already have gone, leaving behind nothing but the scent of shower soap and dirty clothes in the wash basket.

This routine had been playing out for a while when she found the bloody footprint by his car. Now, *that* she had not expected. Lipstick on his collar, a pair of panties in the back of his Rolls-Royce, a whiff of some other woman's perfume? Sure. But not this. Not blood.

She toyed with asking him about the footprint, the one the exact size of his boot. Instead, she resolved to watch him. She needed to see what he was really doing when he stayed out of their house until four in the morning. She needed to trail him. It's what any self-respecting woman would do.

A few evenings after Margot found the footprint, Stephen announced that he had a late meeting with his campaign manager. She kept her face still, kissed him goodbye, watched from the window as he got into his car and steered it smoothly out of the driveway. Then she sprinted out behind him and slid into her Porsche.

On the main roads, she was careful to stay a couple of cars back. She usually took great pains to make herself distinctive, but this was one occasion when she wanted to blend in, to be lost in a blaze of reflections.

When Stephen pulled his car off the main road, she turned her steering wheel hard and followed from a distance. After a while, the road grew narrower and was flanked on either side by an ever-thickening layer of trees. There were no other cars, the night outside the Porsche still and quiet.

Someone else might have been surprised that Stephen was driving in the opposite direction of the downtown area where his alleged meeting was taking place, but Margot was no fool. She'd known for a while that Stephen was lying to her. Now she just needed to find out what it was that he was covering up.

The forest around them was expanding, growing denser and darker, and Margot began to see glimpses of water between the trees. It was black and opalescent, the light of the low-slung moon glancing off its surface in diamond fractals. As the road was otherwise empty, Margot made the decision to switch off her headlights. She wanted to know what Stephen would be doing if no one was watching, why he really came out this way in the dark. She could still see his taillights some distance ahead, and she watched as he took a right-hand turn, the car swallowed up by the trees.

She decreased her speed, hung back, so he would not notice

another car pulling in behind him. When she finally reached the turn-off, she saw that it was marked with a sign—SILVER LAKE LOOKOUT. She'd heard of the beauty spot before, but she couldn't quite place the context. It was certainly not somewhere Stephen had ever mentioned. He had never taken her here. Goddamn it, she would have his balls if this was where he was meeting his mistress, like some horny teenager.

She turned the wheel and pulled the car off the road, joining a gravel path that stretched toward the lake, a pool of oil in the distance. She could no longer see Stephen's car, but she kept driving anyway, gravel crunching under the tires, until the path opened out into a space the size of a football field. There, she could just make out the Rolls-Royce parked up at the far side. She could not see Stephen walking around, so she assumed he was still in the driver's seat, watching the water.

Margot slammed on the brakes and switched off the engine. She still had no lights on, so she was hidden from Stephen's sight. But from here she could watch his car and any other vehicle coming down the path.

The night was hot, so she cracked a window and lit a cigarette, the low queries of hidden owls sailing in from the pines. She turned in her seat and checked the back footwell for the baseball bat she always kept stashed in the car.

Then she waited.

Stephen did not leave his car.

Margot grew increasingly frustrated by his lack of action, by the fact that no other cars arrived.

So she got out.

The velvet night took her in its embrace. She crouched low to the ground and crossed the gravel track covertly. Her heart was a noisy accompaniment, its thudding audible to her above the rustle of the trees and the soft water sounds of the lake. As she neared the Rolls-

Royce, its black paint job slick and gleaming under moonlight, she got on her hands and knees and crept closer.

She knew what she was doing was ridiculous—if he saw her, how would she explain it?—but Margot was not a woman to be dissuaded by ridicule. So she approached the back of the car and peered in through the rear window.

Stephen was in the driver's seat, reclined. His eyes were shut, and to her horror, she saw that his trousers had been pulled down around his thighs. She paused at the window, unsure if what she was seeing was correct. Stephen was touching himself, his hand moving rhythmically in the stillness of the car.

Margot ducked, her mind spinning. Why the hell had her husband driven miles out of town to sit in a parking lot and jerk off?

She stood slowly and squinted through the glass. In that instant, Stephen froze, and then he suddenly shot up in his seat.

She turned and ran as fast as she could, hoping the darkness would shield her. She couldn't look back, couldn't risk it, waiting for an inevitable hand to seize her shoulder. When she made it to the Porsche, she pulled the driver's door open and jumped inside. Panicking, she turned the key in the ignition and drove, steering wheel jammed to the left, pulling the car wildly off the path and into the space between two trees. She made it just in time before Stephen's car sped past. She half expected it to stop some yards up the track and then reverse with a slow crunch of gravel, but it didn't. His car continued until the two taillights were out of sight and Margot felt safe enough to make her way slowly out of the forest.

Stephen never came home that night.

When Margot arrived back at their house, shaken, their bed was empty and his car was not in the driveway. It was only when she had crawled into bed, taut nerves dulled with scotch and her brain sifting through every memory she could locate, that she realized where she had heard of Silver Lake Lookout before. It was last year. There were headlines on the news. She remembered the images, the faces, she saw as she flicked through the channels on the television. Two teenagers, high school sweethearts, had been killed while parked up at Silver Lake Lookout. The boyfriend had been shot in the kneecaps and then his throat had been slashed, some distance from the car, as he'd tried to escape. The girl was found tied up on the back seat, where she had been strangled before her throat was slit, too. The killer had never been found, and the police could find no motive.

Why, Margot thought, her body crushed by dread, was Stephen visiting the site of a double murder? Why was he jerking off in his car at that lake? It would be another two weeks before she found her smoking gun.

The sound of the store's revolving doors shakes Margot from her stupor. She quickly closes the magazine and springs to attention, flashing a megawatt smile at whoever is dumb enough to shop when the sidewalks are melting.

A man glances up, barely acknowledging her, but as their eyes briefly meet Margot feels something scratching at her skin. The man is disheveled—his hair an unkempt mess, his skin lined, his eyes underscored by those dark pools that only the hardest of drinkers collect—but, although Margot can't really explain why, he also looks smart, like he could catch you off guard if he wanted to.

She watches him from under lowered eyelids as he makes his way to the very back of the store and thumbs through the leather jackets. *Leather? In this heat?* She clears her throat quietly as he approaches the till, a George Harrison bomber slung under his arm.

He places it on the counter. The man reeks of whiskey.

She takes the jacket, folds it and runs the numbers through the till.

"Not too hot for leather?" she risks.

"Ah, I only come out at night," he deadpans.

Margot scoffs drily, and the man's eyes travel up to hers. He pulls his mouth into a tight, sarcastic smile.

Margot grabs a bag, stuffs the jacket in. She can feel him watching her, the familiar sensation of a man trailing his eyes down her body.

"My usual one got ruined," he says on a bored exhale. "So . . ." He shrugs, gestures toward the bag.

Margot represses a smirk. *His usual.* Only the most uninteresting men feel the need to cultivate a "thing" by dressing like the Beatles.

The customer hands over his American Express card, and Margot reasons that he can't be a bum if he uses a credit card. Her eyes flick to the name. R HESTON. She's sure she recognizes it. She swipes the card through the imprinter, hands over the carbon receipt. He takes it, and she notices that his hands are covered in fading scars. Maybe he's a manual worker, then, Margot hazards. Whatever. He's certainly someone in need of a shower.

"Have a good day." He nods as he turns and exits the store. Margot watches him leave, allowing herself to relax only when he's slipped out through the double doors and back on the street.

THIRTY-TWO

THE FARRERS' FRONT yard is sparse. There's a broken swing seat and a sad, rusted grill that makes Elsie's throat feel strangely dry. But the front door, which she is currently sizing up, is painted a classy robin's-egg blue, and there's a cheerful pair of olive bushes in terracotta pots on either side of the porch.

The house doesn't look like somewhere a killer would live.

But had Elsie's house looked like somewhere a killer would live? Who even knows what that looks like?

When Beverley came to Margot and Elsie with the first concrete lead they had since they'd started looking into the string of recent murders, Elsie was loath to believe it.

"Just because a man beats up his wife doesn't make him a killer," she argued. "She could be anyone, Bev."

"That's what I thought, too." Beverley reached into her purse. "Then she gave me this." Beverley opened her hand, and it took Elsie a few seconds to realize what she was looking at.

"That's not . . ." Elsie bent to inspect the delicate bracelet in Beverley's palm, the small silver letters attached to a fine chain. The initials *CJH. Cheryl Jean Herrera.*

"Why would this man have Cheryl Herrera's bracelet in his truck?"

Elsie paused, found she could not answer.

"Sharon said she found it by the brake pedal," Beverley continued. "Maybe it ended up there during a struggle? We *have* to take a look at him."

"You don't think we should be handing this to the police?" Elsie asked dubiously. But Bev told her that Sharon had begged her not to, that Hank had threatened to hurt her and the kids if she ever spoke to the cops about him.

Bev knocks, and a woman in a robe the color of baby powder answers. She looks tired, and Elsie thinks she can see the beginnings of a black eye forming above her cheekbone. Mascara has collected in the corners of her eyes, and her hair is dry, frizzy. Margot physically bristles beside her, and Elsie knows she is dying to brush out the woman's hair, to pat some concealer on the bruise.

"Oh, ladies, thank you for coming." Sharon's voice is strangely childlike, and Elsie is reminded of a breathy Marilyn Monroe. "I can't believe I look such a mess. I'm sorry. There just wasn't time, and Hank would've got suspicious if I started dolling myself up before he left for work." Her fingers flutter to her face, and Margot steps forward, onto the doormat. She always seems to find others' vulnerability an embarrassment, something to be ignored, like a drunk in public.

Sharon steps aside to let them in.

The house is your average low-to-mid-income suburban three-bedroom, filled with the castoffs of everyday family life—dirty dishes in the sink, baseball mitts near the door, shoes scattered in the hallway. A magazine, open to the advice columns, is spread across the kitchen table.

Dear Wendy, Elsie imagines a letter saying, *what should I do if I suspect my husband has murdered four women?*

At the center of the table, a camera sits with a bunch of pack film gathered beside it.

"Peter's latest hobby," Sharon explains. "He's got his heart set on film school." Elsie eyes the camera curiously. It's a Polaroid Automatic 100. She's seen it in all the magazines—shiny, new, modern. She imagines Sharon and Hank working overtime at their jobs to gift their son such a thing. She feels guilt pass through her body like cramps. She had simply assumed Hank and Sharon couldn't afford gifts.

Sharon apologizes for the state of the place as she shows them around, toying with the cord of her nightgown, pointing out parts of the walls that they haven't got around to painting yet. She shows them the bedroom, and Elsie eyes the vanity, crammed with makeup. Wigs hang from the mirror; magazines are stacked up next to the bed—*Reader's Digest, Better Homes and Gardens.*

They make their way back down the corridor, and Sharon indicates the two children's bedrooms, on either side of the hall. "This is Jessica's." She pushes the door wide open. A young girl, maybe eight or nine years old, is sitting cross-legged on the floor, chin in her hands, an assortment of rainbow-haired troll dolls arranged in front of her.

"Jessie, say hi to the ladies," Sharon orders sweetly.

The girl flashes them a smile worthy of a dentist's commercial before returning to her plastic lineup.

They step across the corridor. Elsie is not quite sure why they have to meet the children—they're here to talk about Sharon's husband, not her kids—but people with children always like to wave them at strangers like trophies.

Sharon puts her ear to another door and knocks softly. "Peter?" She pushes it open and the light from the corridor spills into the room. The curtains are drawn, and there's a boy, one of those almost-men Elsie knew in high school, stretched out on the bed. A distinctive smell has burrowed its way into the soft furnishings: old gym clothes and adolescence. Elsie resists the urge to pinch her nose. The walls are papered in movie posters—a suave Sean Connery and a bikini-clad Ursula Andress for *Dr. No*, neon-smeared blood drops across the face of *Dracula*, Lolita in her heart-shaped sunglasses. There are more baseball mitts and sneakers piled up by the closet. Sharon rushes over, quickly stashes them away. The thought of picking up after children has never appealed to Elsie. Cleaning a teenager's room is about as tempting as a needle in the retina.

Peter huffs and turns over on the bed. "Mom, can you just get out?"

Nice to see he's not doing anything to bust the teenage stereotypes, Elsie thinks. Peter raises a hand against the glare of the light from the hall. His palm is bandaged, Elsie notices, and she makes a mental note to ask Sharon about it later. Could Hank be harming his own children, too?

"Sorry, sweetheart. I just wanted the girls to see how handsome you are," Sharon coos, in that way that only mothers can. She ushers them backward out of the room and closes the door.

Back in the kitchen, Sharon sets about making coffee. "Peter's girlfriend broke up with him," she explains as she fills the percolator. "It's been months now, but he's still spending a lot of time in bed. You girls know what it's like, heartbreak."

"Is Hank ever violent with the kids?" Elsie asks straight-out. Perhaps she should be more subtle, but it's an important question, given the bandage on Peter's hand. If Sharon's suspicions are correct, and Hank's aggression has escalated into murder, every member of this household is in danger.

"Peter can be protective of me." Sharon's eyes drop to the floor. "Boys of his age want to look after their moms, don't they?" Elsie imagines the son squaring up to his father. Did they exchange blows? Has Peter been hurt in other ways?

"What about Jessica?" Margot asks.

Sharon shakes her head profusely. "He would *never* harm her. She's his little princess."

Little princess. That's what Mr. Herrera had called Cheryl.

Sharon takes a seat with Elsie and Margot at the table. "Hank's a good father." She says it as if she's trying to convince herself. "He is—most of the time. It's just . . ." Sharon swallows. "He gets this sort of red mist that descends. That's when we all know to keep out of his way."

"And you said you'd noticed him being more distant than usual?" asks Beverley, fingers drumming on the tabletop. "Spending more time out of the house?"

"He took on a big job a while back"—Sharon leans to pour the coffee, and it fills the room with a rich caramel scent—"restoring a whole lot of cop cars. The business has been struggling lately, financially, so he was happy to have that gig. They've had some thefts, too—equipment, gas. He's barely here, trying to keep everything afloat."

Elsie notices Bev glancing at her. She recalls their conversation about pressure-cooker situations, how things such as impending bankruptcy, family rifts and other struggles can put a choke hold on those who are already predisposed to violence.

"So it's just that he's not here much?" Margot asks, her tone dubious.

"No. Something's changed," Sharon says, slowly but emphatically.

Elsie tenses. She knows what it's like to feel that something significant has shifted in a person but not be able to identify exactly what that is. "I'm sorry," she says quietly, apologizing for Margot's brusqueness. "It's just . . . we need to be sure." She turns more pointedly to Sharon. "So, how did Hank know Cheryl Herrera?" she asks.

Sharon pauses, taps the side of her mug with a candy-colored fingernail. "Beverley told me about her, but I'd never heard the name before I read it in the *Signal*. Hank certainly never mentioned it. I can't imagine how their paths ever would have crossed. Wasn't she some athlete?"

"What about cleaning?" Elsie continues. "Do you know if Hank uses a cleaning company at the garage? Do you know if he's ever met a girl called Diane Howard Murray?"

Sharon shakes her head. "I've never heard of any of the girls who were in the papers. But Hank does like . . ." There's a horrible pause. "He does like younger girls. I mean, don't all guys like them?"

So Hank likes them young. Is that why Sharon speaks in that childlike voice?

"Do you know if he's ever visited prostitutes?" Beverley asks. An awkward pause follows. Sharon's eyes drop to the floor. She sighs. "I think . . ." She trails off, takes a beat. "I think yes." Her eyes drop again. "He's never admitted to it, but I found a stack of receipts in the pocket of his work overalls one day, for this pay-per-hour motel."

Margot purses her lips.

"He said he likes to use their sauna after work, that it helps relax his muscles." She puts fingers to her forehead, covers her eyes, embarrassed. "I may not have finished high school, but even I'm not *that* stupid."

"Okay." Margot takes the reins. "We can go see where he works, right, ladies?"

"Promise me you'll be careful," Sharon says, reaching to the counter for a flyer for the garage and handing it over. Elsie watches as Beverley takes it from her and frowns.

"One last thing," Elsie says. "Do you know his license plate number?"

THIRTY-THREE

ELSIE TAKES THE stairs two at a time, passing Mrs. Borowski, the old lady from the apartment below, with just a breathless, hurried greeting. She bursts through her front door and clambers over the piles of books that are stacked up in the living room, sending them spilling into the kitchen.

She feels the vertigo of being close to a revelation, something she's felt before, and the memory of the crawl space, the day she knew her own husband was a killer, flashes into her mind. She crawled backward on her palms and knees as quickly as she could to get out of there—away from matted hair, from the scraps of clothing, that stench. Albert was out, so she paced the house; then, when she'd paced every inch of it, she pushed open the door and strode out into the street.

She just kept walking—not looking back, not stopping for anything. Her shoes ate up the sidewalk, and soon enough her feet began to sweat and the patent leather began to rub. She did not stop for traffic when crossing the road. She did not stop when an older woman placed a concerned palm on the small of her back, asked if she was quite all right. Blisters swelled. The skin of her feet grew hot and wet. Never stopping, she walked for another hour before she saw the car. Parked up at the corner of the street. Its distinctive red and blue light.

She glanced down at her feet. The blood was oozing out of the open toes of her shoes. She thought of fresh oranges, of cooking smells. She crossed to the other side of the street and made her way toward the police car.

She had never expected her life to be so filled with bodies. But now, especially since she, Bev and Margot have started investigating these crimes, bodies are all she can think about.

Her father warned her years ago, when Albert's crimes had come to light, of exactly what was to come. It was the last time they communicated before he died, his words having arrived in a single handwritten page delivered by the mailman. There was no personal message, no preamble, no apology, just a quote from one of his favorite Shakespeare plays.

> *So shall you hear of carnal, bloody and unnatural acts,*
> *Of accidental judgments, casual slaughters,*
> *Of deaths put on by cunning and forced cause.*

At the time, Elsie thought it cowardly of her father, after everything he had put his family through, to offer someone else's words for comfort. Now she can see that it was his way of apologizing. After what he had endured—mud-drenched battles, bayonets, shells and burned flesh—he was dealing with his very own bodies, too.

SHE FINDS THE copied pages on the coffee table, right where she left them, next to the half-completed Escher jigsaw puzzle. The pile is thick; she knows it will take a while to find his name. And he probably used a false one when he picked up girls, when he did what he did to them. But the license plate: that won't be a lie.

She whips the notebook from her purse and hastily flips it to the correct page, finds the details she took down in the Farrers' kitchen. Then she turns the pages, one by one, running her finger slowly down the correct column.

When it happens, something slots together inside Elsie, as if the bones of her spine have been out of alignment but suddenly click back into place.

There it is. Hank Farrer's license plate number.

Her eyes dart to the neighboring column, where the specifics of each interaction have been jotted down, the chilling details of each violent incident. As she takes in the words, her stomach drops. Fingertips buzzing, she reaches for the phone.

THIRTY-FOUR

B EVERLEY TAKES ANOTHER gulp of her whiskey sour and collapses on the couch. Margot and Elsie have just left, and the walls still ring with their chatter.

Elsie found it in the Beware Book: Hank's license plate number. He'd used a different name, unsurprisingly, but from the physical description, it was indisputably him. What was most alarming, however, was the description of the encounter. "Erotic asphyxiation," the book said. When she told the women what it meant—the act of choking someone for sexual pleasure—and when she told them she'd seen photos of the very same act in the magazines Albert stuffed between the bed slats, a sense of horrific certainty descended on them all.

Sharon seemed so very terrified, so on edge, and how else could they explain the bracelet in Hank's car? Things were starting to add up. They were close; she could feel it. They were identifying a dangerous predator, but they had no concrete evidence to prove irrefutably that Hank Farrer was their man.

Now Beverley's head is muddled, thoughts of the murders eddying around her brain. They make her infuriatingly alert, even though her bones are exhausted. She sighs, her eyes restlessly roaming the room until they land on a familiar spot on the bookshelves. She hesitates. She knows she shouldn't, but fatigue has chipped away at her resolve. She stands, moves to the shelf and picks out a well-worn title. She thumbs to the binding at the middle, pulls out a card. She returns to the couch and opens it, warmth weaving through her blood at the sight of the handwriting.

My life was only complete when I met you.

She shoves the card back in the book, tosses it away. She has wondered, often, why she keeps these things—mementos of someone who has done so much harm. This card is not a card from a killer. It's a card from the man she loved, the man she married—not the man Henry became, the man she didn't know at all.

Her head throbs, eyelids heavy. She knows what she'll have to do to get some rest: the same thing she does night after night when thoughts of Henry threaten to take over. The kids are upstairs. They're safe. If she can sleep, the facts will order themselves, everything will slot together and she'll wake up with answers.

She shifts in her seat, plunges her arm under the couch cushion and rummages until she finds what she has stashed in there, hidden from the children. Her fingers meet foil and she pulls it out, pushes a few pills from the blister pack, places them in her mouth and washes them down with whiskey.

Then she waits for the numbness, the warm absolution of sleep.

When she wakes, sometime later, the room is dark. There is a crick in her neck—she has been slumped at an awkward angle—and the skin of her cheek is pulled tight by the remnants of drool. The hangover has already kicked in, and her head thuds. She needs water. Her eyes roam the room. Everything seems to be in its correct place, but she can't help feeling that there's something uneasy about the way the air fills the room.

A sound comes from the hallway, and Beverley flinches.

A banging.

She stiffens, alarmed. It comes again. She looks in horror at the vase on the table—the vase she usually remembers to place atop a pile of books, atop the sideboard that she usually remembers to push up against the door. But she was too depleted, too distracted, to complete her nightly routine.

She jumps from the couch and rushes to the hallway. The banging comes again, and with a wash of terror she locates its source. The front door is open, knocking on its hinges.

Alarm seizes every centimeter of her skin. She sprints up the stairs, her lungs screaming, her head pounding from the drink. She can see, once she reaches the landing, that Benjamin's bedroom door is open. She knows, as she hurls herself toward it, that she will find his bed empty.

In a panic, she runs to Audrey's room, pulls the bedsheets back and is relieved to find her daughter sleeping soundly. She whisks the girl, who complains groggily, into her arms and rushes back down the stairs.

Out on the street, she scans the road, ignoring the scratch of the pavement on her bare feet, ignoring Audrey's sleepy whines in her ear. Benjamin has to have been sleepwalking, and if he has been sleepwalking, he can't have got far. He's just a boy.

She will not allow herself to consider the other possibility, that Benjamin did not leave the house of his own accord. She will not, cannot, allow her mind to go there.

The downstairs curtains twitch across the street. Of course Christopher Appleton is awake. His television is always on, the stark light of it roving across the windows at all hours. She hears his front door open, sees him step out. He calls out to her, asking if she's okay.

"My son!" she yells accusingly at the old man. "Do you have my son?"

"What?" Mr. Appleton shakes his head, eyes wide with alarm.

"He's so small," she cries desperately.

Audrey begins to whimper.

Beverley takes off at a run, frantic, her daughter heavy in her arms. She cannot waste any time.

She does not know how long she runs for, does not know quite how her lungs, her heart, her bones, persist, but she endures—losing track of where she is, how far she is from her house; the names of the streets pass by in a blur. She is getting all turned around. The streets all look the same. Her vision is growing hazy—a smeared procession of houses, of white fences, of expensive cars.

She can no longer tell her left from her right. She cannot feel herself breathing. She cannot feel the road beneath her bare feet until she turns a corner and, with relief that folds her in half, she sees him. Benjamin is standing in the very center of the road, facing a house, studying it intently. She calls out to him, but he does not turn to her. She shifts Audrey's weight and starts running again, toward her son, to grab her baby, to keep him safe. She almost falls to her knees when she reaches him. Instead, she takes him in one arm and pulls him tightly to her. But Benjamin does not soften. She turns her own head, follows his gaze toward a porch just like hers—with a white picket fence, a tended garden, a neatly painted front door—and there, swaying slowly in the breeze, at the end of a hook, is a body.

THIRTY-FIVE

While waiting for the police to arrive at the Gunn household, Beverley sat on Sarah's parents' couch, trembling, her two children wrapped in blankets held tight at her side, and she realized that this changed everything.

She'd stumbled to the porch, screaming for help, and banged on the door to wake Sarah's parents inside. When Sarah's father answered and saw what was out there, just yards from where he'd been sleeping, he let out a sound so horrifically inhuman that Beverley wanted to smash her head into the wall. He rushed to Sarah's body, swinging lifelessly, dressed in a trench coat—just like Diane Howard Murray's—its collar fastened to a hook. He tried frantically, wracked with sobs, to lift her off, but Beverley, through the disorienting blur of it all, convinced him to leave her. Sarah's body was evidence. Sarah's body held clues the police would need. Sarah's body would help them catch their guy.

The cops cannot deny the link now: another body dressed in a coat; another body staged after death. Elsie told her about the note, too, the one found on that plumber's car in Ventura—an awful finishing piece to the puzzle. *I'll hook another girl,* it said. Beverley hadn't thought much of the language used—until now.

All the papers will pick up the story; it will go nationwide, worldwide. She, Elsie and Margot will no longer be so alone in their search to identify the killer.

When Roger and his partner, Bale, eventually show at the Gunns' house, it is easy for Beverley and Roger not to talk, not to give away their relationship. Usually, when Beverley sees him, she finds it hard not to touch him, not to fold herself into his chest and wrap his arms around her, but as Roger gives his condolences to Sarah's parents, Beverley patiently observes.

Sharon had begged her not to tell the police about Hank, and Beverley *knows* that fear. But she knows, too, that the evidence against him is too much to deny.

She needs to get Roger on his own, to tell him what she knows.

When their eyes eventually meet, it takes only a tilt of her head for Roger to excuse himself and step outside. Beverley follows, stepping out onto the porch behind him.

"We know who it is."

Roger turns, blinks incredulously, as if he's misheard her. "What?"

"I've got a name for you. He's violent, he uses prostitutes, his wife thinks—"

"Beverley, what the hell are you talking about?"

"I've got a name for you," she repeats slowly. "Just take it and do what you want with it, but I'd be putting more women in danger by not handing it over to you."

"Putting women in danger? Bev, you are putting *yourself* in danger like this"—his voice is rising—"at a crime scene in the middle of the night! You need to be staying at home."

Henry used to tell her to stay at home, and look how that turned out. She will not be staying at home and keeping quiet. They have their fingertips on the guy doing this. She will not lose her grasp.

"I'm sorry if I'm more invested in catching this guy than the police are," she levels.

Roger's jaw drops; he's stunned. "Bev..."

"You're not trying. It's almost as if you guys don't want to catch him. Is this all because of that op that Cornwell's throwing money at?"

"You think I don't want to catch him?" Roger's tone is jarring. He seems genuinely hurt.

Bev swallows, hesitates, just for a moment.

"Bev," he says gravely, "I have to wake up every day and wonder if he's taken another girl."

Her neck grows hot.

"I have to consider, when I'm brushing my teeth, whether he's destroyed another family overnight, whether I could have stopped him. That's on me."

Her mouth is dry.

"But with my job, with the way things work, I have to march to Cornwell's beat. He'll be in charge of choosing the new chief when he retires."

The shame withdraws like a wave. "Your *job*?" she barks. "You won't challenge Cornwell because you want to protect your job?"

"That's not what I said, Bev." Roger shakes his head firmly. "There are just certain protocols to follow."

"Hank Farrer," Beverley says. "F-A-R-R-E-R. There. I've told you now, so it *is* on you." She turns back to the door, pulls it open. She knows she is in danger now. The killer has struck just blocks from her house, the same killer who may have left a carcass, bloodied and bold, on her lawn to let her know she might be next. But she will not sit around and wait for harm to come to her. Tomorrow she'll continue. If the police won't act quickly on this, then she will. She has to. She has to see for herself, to keep her promise, to stop a killer.

THIRTY-SIX

THE FOLLOWING EVENING, Margot wiggles the key in the sticky lock and pushes open the door to her apartment. She flicks the light switch, and the cramped hallway illuminates with a yellow glow. It reveals patches of damp on the ceiling; peeling paint on the baseboards; a bucket on the floor, catching drops from the leak in the pipes in the apartment above. She sighs, steps over the bucket and makes her way to the small kitchen at the end of the hall. She turns on the radio and the room fills with James Brown's gravelly voice. *"This is a man's world."* She cannot help but laugh.

The tap drips loudly. Her stomach rumbles. The super still hasn't fixed the old rusting stove, so she opens the cupboard and pulls out the only item in it—saltines, on which she spreads the remaining butter from the fridge.

She knows she probably hasn't lost as much emotionally as Beverley and Elsie, that she's good at bravado, that she can keep up the act, but her tumble from politician's wife to someone eating crackers alone in her shitty apartment on a Friday night is a hard pill to swallow. She knows she looks put together. She can keep up appearances by using her discount at work—thank God for that—but she can never *ever* let anyone see this pathetic apartment. If she did, she'd have to admit to herself how very much she's lost.

She scoops the last cracker crumbs up with her fingers and throws the empty carton into the trash. Then she walks the few yards to her bedroom and takes down her hair. Does she really have the energy to go on a date tonight? It's already after ten p.m., and she's supposed to be meeting Mark at the wrap party of a crappy play he'd got some role in. She'd rather just crash and watch *The Beverly Hillbillies*. She surveys herself in the mirror, and her mother blinks back. She is there, fixing her makeup in the hallway, Margot and her little brother on the couch, feet not touching the ground. They watch as their mother pulls on a raggedy coat, clips old earrings in place.

Women have been molding themselves to fit men's desires for centuries. Her mother was no different. The women Margot knows now are no different. And it enrages her that men—fun for the most part, often base, sometimes stupid, occasionally extremely dangerous—have such a hold over them.

But Margot has never been one to do what men want her to do.

Stephen gave himself away, eventually. He was not careful enough. He let his desire for notoriety, for brilliance—brilliance he had never been able to achieve on the political scene—foil him.

They'd just had breakfast. Margot had burned the eggs, and Stephen joked that he'd let her off because she looked beautiful in that yellow dress. She'd wanted to spit into his yolk. She knew what sort of man he was—she'd seen the bloody footprint; she'd caught him jerking off at the site of a horrific slaying. She just couldn't prove it. Yet.

He told her he needed to head into town to run some errands.

Well, that was ridiculous. He was getting sloppy. He didn't even look back as she got into her car and followed him, not to Southampton, the nearest town, but an hour away, to Riverhead.

She parked the car and began to trail him on foot. He was wearing a scarf, for Christ's sake. She wondered, briefly, if it was one of hers; the thought of him rummaging through her stuff made her want to hiss.

She had to duck into a few shops, hover at a few corners, to stay hidden from him, but Stephen continued to walk, and even though he appeared to have no real destination, she knew he must have come here for a reason.

After a while, he turned down a side street and made his way toward a phone booth. There was little passing traffic, so Margot hung back, watching, as he opened the door, pulled a dime from his pocket and tugged the scarf over his face. She watched as he dialed a number, then spoke into the receiver, scarf pulled tight across his mouth. Then he replaced the handset, pushed open the door and looked up and down the street before exiting.

What was a politician doing using a public phone booth?

Margot waited, then followed him, tugging her own headscarf from her pocket and tying it around her hair and adjusting her oversize sunglasses—she couldn't run the risk of being spotted. Eventually, Stephen stopped at a mailbox, then opened his jacket to pull out an envelope. He glanced around again before depositing the letter in the slot.

She waited for him to leave, then sprinted over to the mailbox and pulled down the gate. *Damn it*. The box was designed so that you couldn't fit a hand in. Margot began to grow hot. She cast her eyes around. She *had* to see what the letter said. She had to know if it was linked to the phone call he had just made, if it was linked to Silver Lake Lookout.

She took off again at a run, clutching the scarf to the back of her head, not caring who saw her, whom she banged into. She ran all the way back to her car, opened the passenger door and retrieved the baseball bat from the footwell. Then she rushed back to the mailbox, losing a shoe on the way, the headscarf tearing free of her hair and billowing in a blaze of yellow behind her. She started swinging before she even reached the box, the bat meeting nothing but air. She kept going until she was striking the steel as hard as she could, bringing the bat up and down with force. People stared, mouths agape, as she pounded the mailbox again and again, making nothing more than the smallest dents in the steel. Some passersby smothered laughter, hurried their children away, but Margot continued her fusillade, not stopping even though her arms ached. Pounding the box, she released a guttural yell.

"Someone call the police," a voice ordered from behind her.

Sure, Margot thought. *Call the cops. Maybe they can get that letter out for me.*

With a scream, she brought the bat down once more. She knew she looked like a madwoman, but she simply did not care. She was making progress. She had begun to dent the steel more deeply now, and the drop gate was becoming warped, opening a gap through which Margot was sure she could squeeze a hand. She gave a few more blows, then allowed the bat to topple to the ground. She was panting heavily, her hair tugged out of its chignon. She wiped the back of her palm across her mouth, smearing red lipstick.

She reached her hand into the mailbox and tried to grasp the letters inside, straining with the effort.

Not quite.

She plunged her arm in, up to the shoulder, and leaned in as far as she could.

There.

Her fingers touched paper. She grabbed a fistful and hauled it out, tossing letters on the sidewalk in front of her.

"What are you looking for, honey?" An old woman who had stopped to watch peered down at her.

"My husband's handwriting," Margot answered breathlessly, scouring the envelopes for Stephen's familiar scrawl. When she could not find it, she reached in again for more letters. She scattered them before her, turned them over, then immediately scrambled for one, small and manila. The hand was vaguely recognizable to her, not exactly like Stephen's handwriting, but there was something in the flick on the *T*s that gave her pause.

She picked it up and held it to her face, allowing her back to rest on the battered mailbox. The letter was addressed to the editor at the *New York Times*. Margot tore it open and found the page she would later hand over to the police. She read the words quickly, with a horror no less pronounced because she knew it was coming. Her eyes clung to the words: *Silver Lake Lookout . . . a slashed throat . . . bullets to the kneecaps.* Then another confession: a slaughtered family, more slashed throats. But of course, he had not signed his name. The letter was a taunt, a gibe to the police, who had not yet tracked him down. But to Margot it was the truth she had been searching for.

So, yes, men have power, but Margot Green is used to besting men. As is Elsie, as is Beverley, and no one is going to stop them from solving these murders.

Margot takes her purse from the stand and reaches for her coat.

THIRTY-SEVEN

THE NIGHT IS clear, the moon full and round, sprinkling the roofs of the surrounding buildings in glitter. Beverley and Elsie sit across the street from the garage, shoulders hunched, trying to appear as small as possible in Elsie's tough vinyl seats. They've stationed the car—a hardly inconspicuous pink Buick—in the relative darkness of shadow, and it is partially obscured by the trunk of a large date palm. Every so often, Beverley allows herself to crane her neck to peer across to the garage. Rusting signs for Kendall Motor Oil sit out front, and two huge metal doors have been pulled up, revealing cars on lifts, as well as gadgets and heavy tools hanging on the walls. It makes Beverley think of the hook, of Sarah Gunn's body silently swinging.

Hank has been lumbering around inside. Even from a distance, they can hear the rhythmic thump of his steel-toed work boots, sense the energy radiating from his body, something hostile and electric, like what Beverley had once felt at the big-cat enclosure at the zoo. It's late, and they didn't expect him to stay at the garage for so long. But Sharon had mentioned that he needed all the work he could get. That fits; they'd theorized that their killer could be going through financial difficulties.

A sudden flash behind them makes them flinch. The rear window pools with white light and a car draws up slowly behind them.

"What the hell?" Beverley whispers as Elsie eyes the rear window uneasily. It is already closing in on midnight, and they didn't tell anyone they were coming here. It crosses Beverley's mind briefly that it could be the cops arriving. Maybe they've finally started looking into Hank, too.

After finding Sarah's body, Beverley couldn't sleep, so she spent hours poring over the letters she'd been sent in the years since Henry's arrest, letters from women whose husbands were in jail for violent offenses, for murder. They all had different stories—the elementary school teacher whose husband had taken his hunting rifle and shot up a grocery store, the stay-at-home wife whose husband kidnapped a young girl and drove her out to a cabin in the woods, where he kept her tied up for two months. The ways in which the wives learned of their husbands' indiscretions stretched from the mundane to the horrifying: an emptied bank account, men disappearing for hours during the working day, one woman catching her husband watching the neighbors have sex through a hole in their attic.

All the women wanted to know one thing from Beverley: *Did you see it coming?*

There were patterns in the stories, sure. Beverley had marked them all in a notebook—men with histories of violence in the home, men who worked late or were evasive when asked about the particulars of their routines. But there were also anomalies—the loving fathers, the wealthy businessmen, the prizewinning academics. Plenty of the women had asked for help but had been ignored because of where they lived, the color of their skin, the figures in their bank accounts. Plenty of them were forced to take their children from their homes and plant them in different towns, different states, so they would be accepted.

These women would never again feel safe, because they had been lied to since they were small girls playing with dolls and songs and their own naïve aspirations. *You will be loved,* they had been told. *If you only behave correctly, look the right way, keep your waist slim and your voice quiet, you will be loved. You will be safe.*

Beverley studies the garage again. Hank Farrer fits their checklist: secretive, hostile, unpredictable, physically strong, someone who uses prostitutes, someone with access to multiple cars. On top of that, the Farrers' house is right in the middle of the range that the killer is operating in. Then there is the bracelet. They have to watch Hank but maintain a safe distance from him.

As the car draws closer behind them, its distinctive yellow paint becomes clear. A cab. The door opens, and out steps a heeled foot and a bare leg. A woman makes her way over to Elsie's car, and Beverley immediately recognizes the shimmy, the bright red dress. The back door opens and Margot eases herself in. The space immediately fills with a waft of Diorissimo.

"I thought you had a date," Beverley hisses, turning in her seat.

"I couldn't miss this," Margot whispers. "Seen him kill anyone yet?"

Elsie tuts loudly.

"No activity so far," says Beverley. "We've been here since nightfall, and all we've seen is Peter Farrer driving out."

"What? The son? What's he doing here?"

"Looks like he works here, too."

"Old Peroxide didn't tell us everything, then."

"For God's sake, Margot..." Elsie fumes.

"She has used peroxide on her hair," Margot replies evenly. "It's ruined the integrity of the shafts."

Beverley tunes them out and watches as Hank kneels to change a tire, the muscles in his arms flexing. There's no doubt that this man is strong. She imagines him easily lifting a woman onto a hook, carting a body across a golf course, chasing down a terrified girl fleeing for her life. When she tunes back in, Margot is begging for the radio to be switched on.

"Don't be ridiculous!" Elsie scolds. "We're trying to stay out of sight. That man over there is a killer, and you want us to blast the Beach Boys?"

Margot whistles through her teeth and slumps back in her seat.

They sit in silence for the next hour or so, the thick night dragging like tar. Beverley resists the urge to yawn. Elsie's eyes, she can see, are fixed unflinchingly on the garage.

"We sure we've got the right guy?" Margot eventually whispers. She's never been comfortable with long periods of stillness. "He seems to be doing what a mechanic does"—she gestures to the garage—"not hanging women from hooks."

Beverley winces at the crassness.

"Do we have anything to link him to the murders other than Sharon's hunch and the bracelet?" Margot asks, not unreasonably.

"Henry said it would be someone who hated women," Beverley replies, "who wanted to see them punished—mommy issues, sexual dysfunction..."

There is a cold silence in the car, and Beverley realizes, with a wheeling sense of panic, that her exhaustion has caused her to slip. She wants to backpedal, to unsay the words. She wants to push open the door and flee the car.

"You've been speaking to Henry?" Elsie blinks in disbelief.

Beverley's mouth gapes wordlessly.

"No, she hasn't," Margot snaps. "Tell her you haven't, Bev."

Beverley turns to face her and watches Margot's expression shift as she realizes she has been lied to.

"How could you do that?" Margot hollers, incredulous. "How could you be in the same room as him?"

"I thought he could help us," Beverley replies hurriedly, glancing at Elsie's uncomfortable posture. "With what's at stake, I thought it would give us an insight into how these sorts of people think..." Her head swivels between them as she waits for them to soften, to realize that she was right to visit him at San Quentin.

Margot scoffs. "When are you going to get a backbone, Bev?"

"We all agreed," Elsie says quietly, "that the only way to move on is to not see them. We made a pact."

Beverley feels guilt slice through her stomach. She has betrayed her friends, but she has a right to visit her ex-husband if she wants to, doesn't she? It's *her* choice. They don't need to know that she regrets it, that she has had nightmares about it ever since. All she has to do is blink and her vision is scarred with the empty line of chairs, the long glass windows, the arrogance seeping from Henry's skin.

"How could you see him?" Margot won't let it go. "Even from prison, he's still controlling you, Bev. It's pathetic."

"He's still the children's father," she says weakly. "Just because you don't have kids—"

"Don't use that against us!"

Elsie's eruption shocks Beverley.

"Don't use the fact that we don't want children as evidence that we don't know what it's like to be a woman."

"That's not what I meant." Beverley shakes her head, her thoughts clunky with panic.

"I can't believe you could even look at him," Margot spits, "after what he did."

"I thought it would help us narrow down who the killer is, okay?" She's growing frustrated at her friends' judgment. She was only doing what she thought would help them track down the killer. "Not everyone's perfect like you, Margot."

It's cheap and Beverley knows it.

Elsie stiffens in her seat.

"Oh, here come the accusations," Margot jabs.

"You think you're better than the rest of us because you're not affected by anything that's happened to you," Beverley replies. She's a cornered rat. She'll have to bite her way out. "You don't give a shit that your husband killed himself in prison because of you."

"Beverley!" Elsie's eyes are wide.

But Beverley is on a roll. Panic has taken over; she no longer really knows what she's saying. "You think I'm weak because I have worries and feelings and fears."

Margot's face has hardened.

"But you're the one who's in denial, with your parties and your jokes."

"Denial?" Margot's voice is shrill. And loud. Too loud. "Are we really going to talk about denial? You still wear your wedding ring."

"I need people to respect me."

"Respect? You can't move on from a guy who killed *seven women*. How's anyone going to respect you? You still have his goddamn photograph on your fridge."

"What?"

"Elsie told me. She saw it. It's sick, Beverley. He's a murderer."

Elsie swings around in her seat. "I didn't mean to gossip. I just—"

"Well, at least I don't have to fuck anything that moves to keep my mind off my ex-husband." Beverley's words land the punch. "We all know what you get up to at those parties. If you weren't such a—"

With a sharp intake of breath, Margo suddenly pushes open the door.

"Wait!" Elsie hisses, but Margot has already slammed it behind her and is tottering down the road.

There's a movement from inside the garage, and Beverley turns to see Hank at the open doorway, silhouetted by light from inside, wiping his powerful hands on a rag. She watches as his eyes fall on the car. He looks furious to realize he is being watched.

"Shit." Beverley ducks down in her seat and prays that he cannot see them. "Elsie! Get her back in the car."

Elsie winds down her window and calls out to Margot. They have to be quick. But Margot, even in her heels, is already too far away to hear her.

A glance at the garage tells Beverley that Hank has disappeared back inside. She's likely got only seconds, but she opens the passenger-side door and calls out after Margot. The next time she looks at the garage, Hank has reappeared and is striding down the driveway, his right arm held out in front of him.

"If you fuckers think you can steal anything else from my garage," he calls out, "you better be feeling lucky!"

"Jesus!" Beverley hisses.

"Shall we hold up our hands or something?" Elsie begins to raise her palms.

As Hank nears, Beverley can see that he is holding a gun.

"Just go!" Beverley cries, and Elsie reaches for the ignition. But her shaking hands struggle to turn the key.

"Drive, Elsie! He's got a gun!"

"I can see that!" Elsie wrenches the key once more, and on the third turn the engine splutters. The radio clicks on, "California Girls" blasting into the night.

Hank is only a few feet away and holding the weapon aloft. He must be able to see them this close. Beverley prays that he cannot make out the details of their faces, that he won't jot down Elsie's license plate number, won't come after them.

The wheels screech as Elsie jolts the car forward, making a direct line for Margot as Beverley leans back to open the car door.

"Get in the damn car!" Beverley screams through the open window as they pull alongside her. Margot glances behind them, seeing what Beverley can see reflected in the rearview mirror: the towering Hank in the center of the road, the gun pointed directly at them. Margot ducks and barrels into the back seat. She doesn't even have time to close the door before Elsie screeches off, leaving Hank Farrer behind them, suspicious, furious and more dangerous than ever before.

THIRTY-EIGHT

"STABBED IN HER own bathroom." Paul Hunter plucks the cigar from his mouth and sighs out a huge plume of smoke. "What a way to go."

The *Signal*'s meeting room reeks of stale coffee and all-nighters. The news team is gathered around Hunter's desk, having been called into an early meeting, and are hanging on his every word, their notebooks open.

Elsie is standing flush to the wall at the very back of the room. Her ears are ringing with what she has just heard. She is as bone weary as any of the reporters officially assigned to the murders—not least because she spent last night staking out one of the main suspects.

Right now she is struggling to accept that, even given Hank's behavior and the evidence she and her friends have found, Hank might not be the man they are after. If this girl Hunter's just told them about, killed as she showered at home, is a victim of the same man who killed Sarah, Emily, Cheryl and Diane, and the murder happened last night, it cannot be Hank who is responsible. He did not leave the garage last night. He did not speak to anyone. Yet this murder occurred just an hour from his workplace.

Unless...

"What time did the murder take place?"

The whole room turns to Elsie. Hunter raises his eyebrows but checks his notes.

"Chief said the call came in just after midnight."

Shit.

Midnight. She was at the garage at midnight. Hank was most definitely there, which means he cannot have been responsible for this murder.

"And we're sure this is the same killer?" Elsie asks, frustrated.

"The coffee machine has a lot of opinions today," Heston quips over his shoulder, his eyes bloodshot.

Elsie snaps. "You spend the night on the street, Heston?" The room takes a quick breath. Heston turns in his seat and glares.

"Elsie," Hunter warns, incredulous, "that's not appropriate. Heston's your senior."

"And I don't have to justify myself to secretaries."

"Heston," Hunter snaps, "no assholes in my office."

The assembled group chuckles quietly.

"Chief's pretty sure it's the same guy," Hunter continues, moving on from the fuss. "We'll take his lead. Heston, do some digging."

The reporter slowly scrapes his seat back and slopes out.

As everyone else gathers up their belongings, Elsie hangs back. Hunter already has his head in some copy and is striking sentences through with a red pen.

"You want to tell me what all that was about?" He doesn't look up from his work.

Elsie clenches her jaw. "Heston has scratches all over his arms. I just wondered where he got them." There's no point in skirting the truth. She first saw the marks on his hands several weeks ago. Then, when she and Patti were in the bar questioning Greaves and Bale, he'd appeared, ordered a drink, then left immediately. It had struck Elsie as odd. Was he trying to create an alibi for himself? Since then, he's been disheveled, avoidant. What's to say the scratches aren't defensive wounds? Plus, he knows everything about the murder cases. He's always late to the office—suggesting he's been out all night. *Doing what?*

"Is that any of your business, Elsie? He's a grown man."

She sighs, begins to leave, then thinks better of it.

"What was her name?" she asks him.

Hunter glances up, looking very much as if his patience is being tested.

"The girl. Do we know anything else about her?"

"She's number five."

She growls despite herself. "These women are real people." Elsie knows it's bold, but she has to say it. "They're not just props. We should be writing more about them, looking into their lives. They deserve that." She knows she's right. Whoever is doing this may have taken their lives, but he is superfluous to their stories. She can't let the killer be the person everyone remembers. These girls deserve to be known, but she is aware that sort of sentiment won't tempt Hunter. She straightens, adds as a sweetener, "And it might help us catch this killer."

"Elsie"—Hunter removes his glasses—"it is not our job to catch the killer." He pinches the bridge of his nose. "It's our job to gather the facts and to report on them in a compelling way for the general public to consume."

"I just thought . . ." She falters. "I thought it might provide an interesting insight for readers if we looked at these women in more detail."

He glares at her wordlessly before his eyes move pointedly to the door. She knows what that means.

"Five hundred words," he calls after her as she leaves, stopping her in her tracks. "Give me half a page on the girls, and we'll run it in the domestic column."

A grin spreads across her face, but she won't let him see it. She clears her throat.

"I'll get on it right away."

"And, Elsie..."

She turns.

"Heston's wife got a cat. It hates him. Just like the rest of us."

Later, at Beverley's, Elsie tells her about the article. The most recent victim, Kate McKenzie, was a talented young horse rider and musician. She had so much life in her, so much to give, and it had all been snuffed out, just like that. Elsie cannot imagine the horror of being targeted in your own home, in your own shower, by a stranger. Her mind reels with the thought of it. She knows that writing this article is important, that it will give these lost girls a voice, reclaim some of their power.

"That's fantastic." Beverley's words are flat. Elsie can tell she is distracted.

Bev has taken the realization that Hank may not be responsible for the killings very badly.

"We were there from ten until two," Elsie explained. "Kate's murder happened sometime just before midnight. It just can't have been Hank who killed her."

Beverley tried to argue the toss. "This could have been a blip," she suggested weakly, "a separate case entirely. Maybe Hank was decompressing, getting ready to kill again." But Elsie could see that she wasn't even convincing herself.

Now she looks crestfallen. The case has taken it out of all of them, but Bev looks more harried and wrung out than Elsie has ever seen her.

"It's not your fault, the Hank stuff," she says gently.

Beverley's eyes close briefly. She shakes her head, looks away.

"It's not your fault, or *our* fault, that someone else got killed, Bev."

"We were looking in the wrong direction," Beverley argues. "Someone else got killed because we got it wrong."

"The police got it wrong!"

"*We* should be able to find this guy."

Elsie can see that Beverley is shaking.

"I thought that if we examined all the pieces and put them together, we would find the guy, and that would be it. I was so sure. Sharon was so sure."

"He's just another useless husband," Elsie counters.

"We should have stopped this from happening." Beverley's cheeks are wet, and she clenches her fists in frustration. Then she seems to come to, half stands as if about to spring into action. "We should be considering more options. Maybe we need to look at Sean Wilson again, Chris Appleton, that guy across the street. I've been trying to convince Detective Greaves—" Her words are rushed.

"I know why you're saying this." Elsie pulls Bev back down onto the couch. "But you couldn't have stopped Henry, and you can't stop this guy. It's not your job to do that. Stop punishing yourself."

"I could have stopped Henry."

"No, you couldn't. None of us could have stopped what they did."

"No, Elsie. I could have." Beverley is holding her gaze. "I could have stopped Henry. I had a chance—there was one time—and I didn't do it."

Elsie shifts awkwardly on the couch. Beverley is just agitated, upset after everything: the argument with Margot, another murder, finding Sarah's body, this whole mess.

"It was when I was pregnant with Audrey." Elsie wants to interrupt, to stop her friend from harming herself in this way, but she lets

Beverley speak. "I was having a rough time. I was constantly nauseous, and I mean *all* the time. I spent all day hanging over the kitchen sink or with my head in the toilet. I couldn't keep food down, couldn't look after Benjamin. It was just a blur."

Elsie swallows. She can feel brittle fingers grazing the back of her neck.

"Henry was never there," Beverley continues. "He was always working late or on jobs out of town. Then, when he was here, he'd leave early in the morning. He'd be out of the house before Benjamin and I were up. He said he was working hard to get overtime, to save money for when the baby came. I couldn't be mad at him. He was doing it for us, to give us a better life."

There's always something oddly tender in the way Beverley speaks about Henry, even when she's trashing what he did. Elsie knows Beverley is no longer in love with him, that she knows what he did was monstrous, but it is as if she has separated him into two men: a father and husband—a protector, a breadwinner, a hard worker—and the killer who came after him. As if the real Henry died somewhere in between.

Elsie was not as shocked as Margot to discover that Beverley had been to visit him at San Quentin. She always thought it was simply a matter of time before she would. Elsie has no desire ever to breathe the same air as Albert, but Beverley is different. Henry had a hold over Beverley that Albert had never had over her.

"What happened?" Elsie prompts softly. Beverley is inspecting a couch cushion.

"It was one night," she continues. "I was sick as a dog. I'd been in bed, a washcloth on my forehead, vomiting every twenty minutes. Henry was out. He'd been out for the past few nights. It had got to the point where I didn't even ask where he'd been. He got so tetchy when I did, so I'd stopped mentioning it. I remember checking the clock and it was ten past three in the morning. I went to the kitchen to get a glass of water. I didn't switch on the light. The moon was out, and I didn't want to wake Benjamin. So I went to the sink, poured myself a glass."

Elsie shifts her tongue in her mouth. She feels as if she is there in the kitchen with Bev, gulping down the cool water.

"That's when I saw headlights, and a car pulled into the driveway—Henry's car, our car. I ducked—I still don't know why I didn't want him to see me there in the window—but I peered just over the counter, through the glass, watched as he parked. I could have flicked on the light, greeted him at the door, but I didn't. I just watched as he got out and stood there in the driveway. Just . . . staring at his hands." She lifts her own palms to her face. "He was turning them over, this way and that, inspecting the nails. Then he looked around him, like he was checking to see if anyone was watching him, and he just pulled off his shirt, right there, in the driveway. Then he unbuttoned his belt and took his pants off, too. It crossed my mind that he must have been with another woman, that he smelled of her and he wanted to hide it. I remember gripping the edge of the sink. I felt even more sick at the thought of him with someone else. Isn't that pathetic? Then he crossed the street in his underwear and work boots and tossed his clothes in the trash can outside our neighbor's house."

"What did you say to him when he came in?"

"I didn't." Beverley shakes her head, her fingers flickering at her temples. "I hid. I held my belly and I ran up the stairs and slid into bed, waiting for his key in the lock. About a half hour later he crawled under the sheets. I rolled over, pretended to be asleep, and he draped his arm over me. I was sure that I could smell something—someone—on him."

"You still thought he was having an affair . . ."

"I reasoned that I could cope with an affair," Beverley scoffs. "When I felt so awful every day, with the baby coming and with a two-year-old to look after, I told myself that an affair was manageable, understandable, even. He'd get over it. He'd stop sneaking around at some point, and we'd settle into being a family again."

"But there was no other woman?"

"I went out first thing in the morning to check the trash can." Beverley bites her lip, nods. "It was barely light, but it was already hot. I remember, there was a coyote halfway down the street, watching me. No one else was awake. Henry was still in bed, and the clothes were still there, right at the top of the trash can, not even hidden. I pulled out Henry's shirt and his pants and—"

She pauses.

"There was... blood. All over them. I dropped them and threw the lid back on. He must have got into a fight. That's what I thought at first. He must have got into a fight at a bar and been too drunk or too embarrassed to tell me. He always had a rotten temper. It wouldn't have been the first time. The blood could have been from the other guy. I've seen people smashed in the face with glass—y'know, on TV? Maybe that's what happened, a really, really bad fight."

"You convinced yourself of it, huh?" Elsie feels leaden. She knows what it's like when your brain tries to convince you of something your body knows is untrue.

"I was pregnant. I had a young child. I couldn't let my mind go anywhere else," Beverley says. "So I let myself believe that. I didn't even ask him about it. I never brought it up. But if I'd thought—if I'd *really* thought—about it, about everything else he'd been doing, the way he was behaving, I could have stopped him."

Elsie starts to shake her head.

"He killed two more women after that, Elsie." Beverley's eyes are wide with panic. "I could have saved them. If I hadn't *wanted* to think that it was an affair, or late-night drinking, or fights, because that was easier for *me* to deal with, I could have stopped him. So actually it was my fault. Just like this. Just like now. It *is* my fault."

"Beverley? No." Elsie's voice hardens. "You have to stop this, for Christ's sake."

Bev crumples. She looks wounded, so completely exhausted.

Elsie moves closer to her, softens her tone. "Look." She touches Bev on the shoulder. "We have to make our peace with being a little bit in agony for the rest of our lives. That's what's going to happen, okay? And we need to get used to that."

Beverley lets out a slow, defeated sigh.

"We're never going to get answers to our questions. *Why did he do it? What could I have done to stop it? How can I stop it from happening to someone else?*" She leans against her friend. Beverley is so good at giving advice to others, yet so terrible at taking it herself.

"If you let the questions take over, if you let them become *everything*, you'll drown. Do you hear me, Bev? You'll drown. It will be the end of you. And I'm not going to let that happen. Not to me, not to you, not to Margot. We did a good job looking into Hank, okay? Getting the word out there. Putting the pressure on the cops. I know that had an impact. I know we made a difference. I know they'll find who did this."

"Well, what do we do now?" asks Beverley, her voice thin. "We're not going to give up, are we?"

"No, we're not going to give up," Elsie says, eyes cutting to the window and the shadows slanting across the backyard, cast by the lowering sun. She leans back, making herself comfortable on the couch. "Not when women here are still in danger." She clasps her hands together. "We're going to take a breath. We're going to reset. Then we're going to outsmart him."

THIRTY-NINE

THE WEATHER BREAKS and the rain finally comes, washing the pretty streets of Berryview in an insipid gray.

It's better this way, Beverley supposes. She doesn't have to explain to the kids anymore why she will not open the windows. This way she can keep them indoors and nobody will ask questions—not even her mother, who picks them up wordlessly every evening, an umbrella held above her head. When she leaves, Beverley retreats to the kitchen, pours a long slug of whiskey and turns to the pages of her scrapbook.

With her defenses down, like this, she'd let her secrets slip. She told Elsie about the pig, about the affair. She didn't have the strength to keep anything to herself any longer. Elsie had looked pained and dropped her eyes to the floor. Beverley knew she was finding it hard not to judge her for the affair, and she wouldn't blame Elsie for judging her. Beverley judges herself. She knows she is weak.

She called Sharon and told her that she, Margot and Elsie were no longer looking into Hank. Sharon seemed relieved, in a way, but Beverley also sensed something else in her voice: disappointment. If Hank was not the killer, that meant he would remain out of prison, free to harm Sharon, maybe even harm the kids. Beverley replaced the receiver and wept. It should have been good news. Instead, it was just another way she had let someone down.

She still hasn't spoken to Margot. Their coarse words play over in her head as she sits, her feet tucked up on the couch, watching mindless television. Hours slip by, a star-blurred emptiness, the mute passing of days. Weeks melt into one another in a slow, drowsy haze, gluey time stretching endlessly.

She thinks of the girls also. Of Kate, who loved horses, whose family said she had a wicked sense of humor and a childhood hip injury. Of Sarah, a talented majorette who by all accounts read romance novels by the truckload. Of Diane Howard Murray, about how her humble background never stopped her from going after her Hollywood ambitions, and about that dazzling smile, that confidence, just like Margot's. Of Emily Roswell with her cheerleading pom-poms, her talent for science, which made her want to be a professor. Beverley sees, in her mind's eye, Cheryl Herrera rising early and pulling on a hooded sweatshirt for training, kissing her father on the cheek before jogging out into the street, making her way to the athletics track.

Each morning, Beverley takes the paper and cuts out the articles she needs, pasting them into the book. It's like sinking into a warm bath. The police have established a task force to catch the "Central Valley Slaughterer." The papers report the latest breaks in the case. There are vague allusions to new suspects, new information from the families.

She has returned to other parts of her routine. She reclines now, in bed, her head on Roger's stomach. She knows she shouldn't have called him, that she should have the strength to move on by now. Their affair is disrespectful to Enid. Not only that, but it could also put his job in jeopardy. Yet there is something empty inside of her that only his kindness can fill. She needs his smoky scent, his touch, his low, soothing voice between the bedsheets. The fact that he has been a means to get more information about the girls and their murders is not lost on her. At one point, the fantastical thought crossed her mind that she might have been using him; that, were it not for her fixation on the case, had she not wanted to catch this killer so badly, she might have ended things long ago. It was an intoxicating feeling, and she had allowed herself to relish it briefly—to hold the power, to know what it's like to exploit. She could see why men have such a taste for it.

Tonight, they have been talking about the case again. Roger's team has identified a suspect out in Ventura, a man who spent time in jail for stalking and kidnapping a girl back in the fifties, when he was just a teen.

"Is he the one?"

"I don't know, Bev." Roger softly twists her hair between his fingers. The late nights at the station are showing on him. Dark crescents puddle beneath his eyes.

"I still think it's worth looking into the guy across the street." She indicates the exterior wall, imagining Chris Appleton's unkempt garden, his face at the window.

"Beverley"—Roger eases himself up on the bed, which tugs her neck into an awkward angle—"I've had a car on that guy for the past two weeks, okay? Because I care about you. But he barely leaves his house. He's a loner, not a criminal."

Beverley pushes herself out from under the sheets and crosses to the window, arms folded. Her skin itches with anger—but it is she who is the target of her own fury.

She *knows,* deep down, that it couldn't have been Christopher Appleton. And yes, if she admits it to herself, she is ashamed to have judged someone so quickly, this strange, isolated, unusual man. She's no better than the neighbors who spit in *her* doorway after news broke about Henry.

Roger calls her back from the window, and reluctantly she goes to him. He smooths his hand across her forehead, pushing back the hair. "Don't feel bad. A housewife can't solve a murder," he says gently. "Not even one like you."

A WHILE LATER, WHEN Roger is getting ready to leave for an impending visit from Enid's sister, Beverley leans against the hallway wall, watching him. It's part of their familiar dance, this long, drawn-out goodbye, Beverley scrambling to find reasons for him to stay just a little longer—a light bulb that needs changing, a bottle she cannot open, another twenty minutes in bed.

He pulls on his coat, and she reaches across to the sideboard to fetch his Lucky Strikes and a couple of papers she'd removed from his pockets when she was searching for his cigarettes earlier. She hands them all over, and Roger takes her face in his hands, tenderly kisses her on the forehead.

Once he's left Beverley sees a scrap of paper on the floor. It must have fallen from the pile when she handed everything else over.

She bends to pick it up, realizing it is a Polaroid photograph.

The flash of the camera has bleached out most of the details, but she can still see the image that has been captured. She flips the picture over. Scrawled on the back: *McKENZIE CRIME SCENE, SEPTEMBER 23RD.*

There is a wailing sound in Beverley's head. Her teeth feel as if they are vibrating. Captured in the grainy photograph, discarded on the grass at the scene where Kate McKenzie, girl number five, lost her life, is something Beverley has most definitely seen before.

FORTY

"What am I looking at?" Elsie asks, frowning up at Beverley, who arrived at the *Signal* office early in the morning, red-faced and radiating energy. Elsie had rushed downstairs to meet her. Beverley had never visited her at the office before—something had to be seriously wrong.

"It's the camera that was on Sharon's kitchen table when we visited." Beverley waves the photograph. "There's the checked strap. The cops found it near the McKenzie murder site."

Elsie stands, grabs Beverley's shoulders, pushes her onto the street.

"There's no way," she hisses as they hurry away from the office, passing looming *Think Small* ads for Volkswagen, posters of Bob Dylan with flaming, psychedelic hair. "We already discounted Hank."

There's a pause.

"Elsie, I'm not talking about Hank."

Now Elsie looks confused. Beverley holds the Polaroid aloft. "Whose camera is this?" she prompts.

It takes Elsie just a second.

"Shit."

FORTY-ONE

BEVERLEY PICKS UP the phone, turns the dial frantically. She needs to speak to Roger. The call rings out, unanswered. Frustrated, she slams down the receiver, casting her eyes around the newspaper office's lobby. Elsie is upstairs, gathering her belongings and making her excuses. They have to be quick. Beverley lifts the receiver again, dials the main number for the police precinct.

Eventually someone picks up. She doesn't recognize the voice.

"This is Beverley Lightfoot." She knows she'll get what she wants only by using her old name. "I have some information for Detective Greaves, on the Central Valley Slaughterer case. I need to speak to him. Urgently."

"Detective Greaves is not in the office right now."

Beverley grits her teeth. She knows what this means.

"Is there anyone e—" Beverley is cut off by the dial tone.

She groans. Now there's only one other option. She really doesn't want to do it. She knows it's risky—if Roger's off shift and at home, then Enid will be there with him—but she's going to have to go there to tell him what she and Elsie know.

He has never actually given her his address, but she knows where he lives. She has imagined his life with Enid so very often: a perfect whitewashed house with a couple of seats on the porch, where he'd drink a cool beer on a hot evening; a well-stocked kitchen, Enid making pies from scratch. If Beverley dwells on it too much, it makes her feel as if she has filth under her fingernails.

Enid doesn't deserve it. Beverley knows that. She doesn't deserve all the sneaking around and the lies, so very many lies.

And now Beverley is going to have to meet her.

Will Enid be able to tell? Will she take one look at Beverley and see her husband's kisses on her?

It's not a long drive to Roger's leafy suburb, and when she pulls up, the house is more modest than she expected. There are no lounge seats out front, but there is a large oak tree in the yard, its branches gnarled with age. A few leaves are starting to burnish to amber. Fall is on the way. Things are changing.

She steps out of the car but finds she cannot make her way in just yet. She leans briefly against the driver's door and considers the house, imagining Enid and Roger treading their way through the hallways, clasping fingers briefly as they pass each other.

She considers the large living room windows, imagining what happens behind them when the curtains are drawn. Does Roger kiss Enid when he returns at the end of the day? Does Enid even know about the killer they've been seeking? Does she know she is being so awfully betrayed?

Beverley wishes she could stay this way, on the periphery of a marriage she is about to ruin, but the police need this information right now. She takes a deep breath and pushes herself off of the car.

She can feel the neighbors' curious eyes on her back as she makes her way toward the door, raises her hand to knock. She pauses, puts an ear to the wood. Nothing. She grasps the knocker and beats the door loudly.

"Hello?" she calls reluctantly, knocks again, waits for footsteps.

Has Roger mentioned that he and Enid were going away? She doesn't think so.

She looks around her, assessing her options, then steps into the flower bed, eases her way past a rosebush until she reaches a window. She cups her hands together and peers through the glass. Everything appears normal inside. There is a large television, switched off, and a coffee table with a few magazines piled up on it and a pair of slippers by its side. Bookshelves line the walls, neatly ordered. There are no abandoned cups or plates to suggest that someone was disturbed and had to leave, no signs to suggest anything untoward. Roger and Enid must both be fine.

Unless . . .

Beverley's stomach twists. What if Roger already knew that Peter Farrer was the killer? What if he confronted him, went behind Cornwell's back to show him who was really the expert in this case, and things ended badly for him? Could Peter have been here, at the house? Could he have taken Roger and Enid?

She swallows. She knows she should wait, check that Roger and Enid are okay. But she has no more time to waste. The women will have to confront Sharon themselves and hope she believes them.

As she turns the key in her car's ignition, her brain buzzes with something undefinable, something tinny and nagging and persistent. She cannot afford to stop. She cannot afford to be pulled off track. She is so close to the final act; she cannot be distracted now. Peter Farrer is the killer. He has slaughtered five women, and if she doesn't get to Sharon's soon, he will be free to kill more.

FORTY-TWO

SHE'S FORCED TO make a quick stop at home to gather her bag and call her mother, check that she's okay to keep the children. Elsie has gone to Margot's to cajole her out of her mood. They started this together, and they should end it together, too.

But they don't have much time. They need to get to Sharon's as soon as they can if they are to stop Peter.

It makes so much sense now. This is why the police were never able to match the prints they found to anyone in their system—because the killer is little more than a kid.

Beverley quickly pulls her bag onto her shoulder. She takes a knife from the block in the kitchen and wraps it in a scarf, tucks it inside. They don't know how Sharon is going to react when they tell her that her son is a killer. They don't know how Peter will react if they confront him.

As Beverley reaches for the door handle, the bell rings.

She freezes.

She is not expecting anyone. Her mother is at home—she just spoke to her. She's meeting Elsie and Margot across town. Beverley pulls the door open.

"Ah." Christopher Appleton is standing on her doorstep. He looks sheepish, his shoulders hunched. Behind him, the sky curls with wisps of white-gray clouds.

At first, she is baffled. He is the last person she would expect to see on her doorstep.

Then she sees it—a hard shell, a small black eye. In his arms is Meatball the tortoise.

"He was in my front yard," the man explains shyly. "It's a miracle no one ran him over when he crossed the road."

"I'm so sorry!" Beverley reaches across and takes the tortoise from him. Her cheeks ache with the false smile. Her palms are growing slick. She needs to get out the door.

"Hey, he's just a tortoise." Mr. Appleton shrugs with half a smile.

There's a silence as Beverley waits for him to leave, her body charged with impatience. But there is something else making its grim way in, too.

Shame.

How could she really have believed this man—this *old* man—in front of her to be capable of murder? And not just murder, but grisly, ritualistic killings that are now so clearly the work of someone young and strong and troubled.

She eyes Mr. Appleton's knitted vest, his shirtsleeves swamping frail arms, the uniform of the retired. She is ashamed of herself. But she needs to leave. Now.

"Well, if that's—"

"I picked up your paper, too." He holds it out to her.

She pauses. Then, through gritted teeth: "Why don't you come and help me put him back in the garden quickly?" It will take only a minute. She lifts the tortoise like a football. Meatball responds by abruptly wrenching his neck into his shell.

There's something hanging in the air around Christopher Appleton. She knows its taste all too well.

Loneliness.

She sometimes senses it in her mother, too.

Just a minute, then out. That's it.

"Have you always lived alone?" she asks as she leads him through the house, thinking of the unkempt garden, the nights in front of the television, the twitching curtains.

He tells her that his wife died almost ten years ago, and that since then he's never really done well at looking after himself. "Holes in my socks, breakfast cereal for dinner, that sort of thing." He seems embarrassed to be saying it.

But Beverley is the one who should be embarrassed. She has been the subject of scrutiny herself, the fuel for rumors, the punch line to tasteless jokes.

With a wince, she remembers fleeing from him at the grocery store—seeing the cereal boxes in his cart and making the most elaborate of leaps. This is just a man who is trying to live after loss, a widower who can't work his oven—someone alone. She knows what that's like.

"I'd happily cook you a casserole for the freezer." It's a paltry offering, but it's something.

She senses him stopping behind her, so she turns. He stands there, blinking, visibly moved. "You don't have to do that," he stammers.

"Actually, you'd be doing me a favor." She forces a bright tone, wanting to hurry things along. "I'm a hopeless cook."

"Well, I'd love that." He smiles a genuine smile. "Shall I put this on the counter?" He raises the newspaper in the air.

She nods, then flinches when she sees the McKenzie girl on the front page. Kate. Stories about the potential killer run almost every day now. Will Peter Farrer be splashed across the front pages tomorrow?

"Well, if that's everything . . ." She has to get out, to tell Sharon what her son really is. It's the decent thing to do for a mother before she reports her son to the police. Even if it means doing it without Elsie and Margot, she has to leave now.

She places Meatball on the floor, picks up her bag again.

Then Mr. Appleton says something she does not quite hear.

She asks him to repeat it.

"Like something from a Hitchcock film," he says again, tapping the newspaper headline—STABBED IN THE SHOWER.

"What?" Beverley asks impatiently as Meatball plods away.

"Like Janet Leigh," he explains. "Marion Crane. Just horrible."

"You watch a lot of movies?" she asks through gritted teeth, eyeballing the door.

"I'm nutty about cinema," he says shyly. "I worked at Warner Brothers as a young guy. Props."

Suddenly her memory serves up something from its recesses: a dark room plastered with movie posters, piles of pack film stacked on the side. Something settles in her mind, heavy like snow.

She'd had the smallest space for doubt to inch its way into—maybe it wasn't Peter; maybe it was just some mistake, like how she had the wrong man with Hank. But she knows it to be truth now.

"In the film *Psycho*"—Christopher seems to have taken her silence as misunderstanding—"Marion Crane is killed while taking a shower."

He thinks that she doesn't get it, that it needs explaining. But things are rattling toward her now. Things are suddenly very, very clear.

"Would you wait here, please?" Beverley rushes to the back of the kitchen and opens the pantry door. From behind the tins of soup and packages of spaghetti on a shelf, she pulls out the scrapbook and carries it to the kitchen table. She places it flat, then quickly opens it to the required page.

"This," she says, tapping on an article. "Does this sound like any movie you've seen?"

He leans over and inspects the newspaper article. She knows she is close to unearthing something profound. She can feel it. Her blood knows it.

He looks up at her from the picture of Sarah Gunn, from Beverley's scrawled notes beside it, and he frowns. "Hanging from a hook..." he says quietly, as if he cannot quite believe what he is saying. "Well, it's how they find Charley's body in *On the Waterfront*, I suppose."

On the Waterfront. She knows that movie. Marlon Brando. She snuck in to see it in the theater, remembers the pictures of Eva Marie Saint in all the magazines.

She reaches down and hurriedly turns more pages, her fingers jittery.

"This one." She reaches a picture of Emily Roswell. "She was found at the bottom of a lake."

Mr. Appleton inspects the photograph. His shoulders drop.

"Is it from a movie?" she urges. "Is there a movie in which a young woman is found at the bottom of a lake?"

"I—I'm not—"

"Think. Please."

She is applying too much pressure—she knows it. He's just some guy who used to work in the movies.

"I'm sorry."

"A lake. A body in a lake," she prompts.

He shakes his head again. "I'm sorry. Not that I can think of."

Then she remembers. It comes at her like a brick through a window.

"Her hands were tattooed." She can taste the words, the horror of the detail. "Her knuckles."

"What sort of tattoos?"

"*Love* and *hate*."

"*The Night of the Hunter*." There's barely a pause before he answers. "Harry Powell, the killer, a religious fanatic—he had *love* and *hate* tattooed across his knuckles."

She cannot believe it. This is the link. This is what they need. This is the killer's inspiration, Peter's inspiration.

She tells Christopher about the two other murders. The first, he is able to assign after a while. Cheryl Herrera—strangled, then staked through the eye with an arrow. It leads him to a Sharon Tate film. The star's big-screen debut. *Eye of the Devil*, not even released yet. The art from its advertisements includes a skull with an arrow through the eye. The tagline: THIS IS THE CLIMAX IN MIND-CHILLING TERROR. People were excited about it.

Then there was Diane Howard Murray, strangled to death, positioned, postmortem, with her legs dressed in suspender stockings.

Christopher's eyes land uncomfortably on the floor. It's an image no one would want to have to imagine. He thinks for a while, shaking his head, scanning the small newspaper article repeatedly. The picture of Diane gazes out at Christopher and Beverley—just a young woman, a life full of potential, so demeaned after death.

"There is a film," he says eventually. "Mario Bava. *Blood and Black Lace*. It's Italian. The killer . . ." He shakes his head, as if the truth of what he is about to say is too strange even to be considered. "The killer stalks models. There's a scene in a park where he strangles a beautiful woman and then drags her through the trees. She's wearing black suspenders. It's very stylized, very visual."

"That son of a bitch."

"Are you saying this killer," Mr. Appleton quavers, "is some sort of Mario Bava fan? The Tate picture hasn't even hit theaters yet. This person must know their movies."

Beverley nods. Sharon mentioned film school. The camera. The posters. "There is a pattern. *This* is the pattern." She feels as if she wants to shake him, to squeeze him. The police can't contest this. "The killer is taking inspiration from what he sees on-screen."

Then it hits her. The letter—the one left in the grocery store parking lot, on the windshield of the truck. *Why can't you guys see the big picture?* The big picture. How could she have missed it? The clues were there all along.

Now she has it. She has what she needs. Peter Farrer will be arrested.

But for that to happen, she needs to ruin a life. She needs to tell a mother that her son is a killer.

FORTY-THREE

"WHAT IF PETER'S in there? Or Hank?" asks Elsie, eyeing the Farrers' house.

"You bring that knife, Bev?" Margot leans forward from the back seat.

"It's in the bag, but I'm not going in armed, like a cop. It's going to be enough of a shock for her."

"Did you call Greaves?"

"The cops are too busy to chat, apparently."

"And it was ever thus," Elsie quips.

"It doesn't matter," Beverley replies. "I want her to hear it from us before the cops wade in anyway. Maybe she'll agree to come with us to the station once she knows."

They approach the familiar driveway. There are lights on inside the house, but it takes a while for Beverley to work up the courage to knock on the door.

She cannot imagine being in Sharon's position. Knowing that your husband is a killer is one thing, but a son? Your own flesh and blood?

Someone you held in your arms and rocked to sleep in the middle of the night, his tiny eyelids drooping, his fingernails like the smallest, most beautiful translucent half-moons? She thinks of Benjamin and Audrey when they were newborns, their powdery baby smell intoxicating.

She almost doesn't want to do it, almost turns away, but then Margot steps forward and knocks.

They wait, the three of them abreast on the doorstep, Margot with her bold red hair, her lipstick; Elsie with her bookish glasses, her neat cardigan; and Beverley, who never really knew how much she had lost until she saw another woman going through the same pain as she had.

Soon enough, the door opens and Sharon is standing there, still in her pink sweater from the previous night's shift, her hair in rollers. She always looks so worn down and so childlike at the same time.

"What are you ladies doing here?" Sharon asks in that high, girlish voice.

Dread drops into Beverley's stomach.

"Gosh, I would have fixed myself up nicer if I knew you were coming around. You always look so glamorous." She's doing that thing with her scalp where she tries to give her hair volume at the roots, but she can't quite make it past the rollers. It makes Beverley want to howl with pity.

"Can we come in, Sharon?" Beverley asks.

"Sure, sure. Let me get you ladies a cup of coffee." She's going through the motions, but Beverley can hear the nerves in her voice. She must have sensed something in the way they held their shoulders, the way they waited at the doorstep, politely, to be asked in. People do that only when they are trying to put off giving bad news.

Sharon makes small talk as she sets about brewing coffee. She chatters about the weather, about the rowdy kids at the drive-in during her shift last night, asks the women if they've been watching *Dark Shadows*. "She's such a great actress"—she smiles hopefully—"Lara Parker, a real knockout."

"Come and sit down, Sharon," Beverley says softly. She knows those are the worst words to hear—the ones that come before the real thing, the ones designed to soften a blow but do the job of delivering it anyway.

Sharon nods like a scolded schoolgirl and pulls out a chair to join them at the table. Her eyes are jittery, pinballing between them as if she might glean some clues from their tight expressions, their avoidant glances.

"Has something else happened?" she asks. "Are you here to talk about Hank again?"

Beverley feels Elsie flinch in the seat beside her.

"No, Sharon, we haven't come to talk about Hank today. We've come to talk about Peter."

"Peter?" Sharon frowns, confused. "You want me to get him? Wait—let me give him a holler." She goes to scrape back her chair, but Beverley grips her arm, holding her tightly in place.

"I don't think that's a good idea." Beverley keeps her voice low. The last thing they want is for Peter to come out of his room. Sharon still seems confused.

A small part of Beverley had hoped, she realizes, that Sharon would do the hard work for her, that they would turn up with their grave expressions and their need to talk about her son and it would all fall neatly into place.

"Sharon." Elsie swallows. "We've discovered some things about Peter that you might find upsetting."

"What is this?" Sharon asks, growing visibly panicked.

"There are some things you need to know," says Margot, "some things that you won't like hearing, and we're sorry we're the ones who have to tell you."

Sharon swallows. Her eyes dart, willing them on, the way a doomed soul just needs to know its fate.

"There is evidence linking Peter to the murders of Cheryl Herrera, Emily Roswell, Diane Howard Murray, Sarah Gunn and Kate McKenzie."

There's a gawp, a bovine stillness, four silent seconds before it finally lands.

"No." Sharon lets out a dry, fractured laugh, shakes her head. "He's just a boy."

"Sharon, he's a man now. A dangerous man. I know it's a shock, but you have to stop protecting him. He killed five young women. We need to tell the police. We need to keep everyone safe now."

"What do you mean, stop protecting him?" Sharon asks, eyes saucer wide with alarm.

"I know it can be difficult, as a mother, to imagine your child being capable of these things." It smacks of hypocrisy. How would *Beverley* react if someone came to her house and accused her child of being a killer? "But we can never really know what people are capable of, even those we love the most."

"What evidence?" Sharon snaps. Beverley is surprised to see the scratch in her, the fight.

The evidence. Beverley draws a breath and looks to Elsie and Margot, who indicate that she should be the one to deliver it.

"First of all, there is the bracelet in the car, Cheryl Herrera's bracelet. Peter works at the garage with Hank and would have access to the same cars, so he could have mislaid the bracelet in there."

Sharon's jaw clenches as she looks to the table. Beverley can see a creep of red growing from the base of her throat.

"We now know that the killer took his inspiration from movies. The methods of killing, the way he posed the bodies after death, the rituals—they all relate to scenes from movies. And Peter—well, you said yourself that Peter is a cinema fanatic."

"But that's ridiculous—"

"And there's the camera." She cuts Sharon off. She doesn't want to give her a chance to bury herself in denial.

"What camera?" Sharon demands. The redness has spread to her face. Beverley can see her shaking.

"There was a camera found just yards from the murder scene eight nights ago, when Kate McKenzie was killed in her shower." Beverley reaches into her bag and pulls out the Polaroid. She places it in the middle of the table. Sharon immediately sweeps it toward her with chipped pink nails.

"Isn't that Peter's camera?" Beverley urges softly. "With the checked strap. It was here the last time we visited."

Sharon looks up at her, a furrow between her eyebrows. "But they took the camera."

Beverley holds Sharon's haunted gaze, but out of the corner of her eye she sees Margot and Elsie turn to her, just ever so slightly.

There is a pause, a beat too long, during which no one says anything.

"What do you mean, they took the camera?" Beverley asks.

"The cops," says Sharon, "a couple of weeks ago now. They took the camera away."

"Who?"

"The police." Then, slowly, "An officer came around to the house, said he needed our fingerprints to eliminate us, eliminate Hank, as suspects in a local case. But I knew it wasn't Hank, because you'd told me that, Bev. Then he took the camera from Peter's room."

Beverley's heart falters, the mechanism out of whack. What does Sharon mean, they took the camera? They can't have taken the camera. Peter left it there, at the last murder, probably when he got spooked.

"Which officer?" Margot asks, her back straight, looking intently at Sharon.

Beverley's eyes swivel from Margot to Sharon, back and forth. She's waiting for the answer but dreading it at the same time.

"Hank sorta knew him." Sharon's shaking hand goes to the back of her neck, pulls at the dark roots there. "Said he'd brought his cars in on and off for the past year. Hank had been working on those cop vehicles. I can't remember his name." She moves her fingers to her mouth, starts biting her nails, then withdraws them. "Gray hair . . . well, not gray, more like silver. Blue eyes. A Paul Newman type."

Beverley feels as if the ground below her is slowly fissuring, as if the chair she is on is beginning to sink, foot by foot. Then she remembers the receipts in Roger's pockets, the movie stubs.

"Was it perhaps Detective Greaves?" Elsie asks, avoiding Beverley's panicked glare. "Detective Roger Greaves?"

"That's it." Sharon's eyes snap up. "Good-lookin' guy."

"He took the camera?"

"Two weeks ago. Said he needed to run some tests on it, that he'd return it. Then he took our prints. It took days for me to get that damn ink off my fingers." She half laughs and trails off, looks between the women.

"When was the McKenzie murder?" Margot asks the room.

"Eight days ago," says Elsie.

They both look at Beverley.

"Why? What is it?" asks Sharon.

"Oh, Sharon"—Elsie's hand flicks to her forehead—"we're so incredibly sorry."

There's a wailing now in Beverley's head.

"What's going on?" Sharon asks, confused.

"Please." Elsie seems lost for words. "This is all just a big mistake. You'll have to forgive us. I can't believe we . . ."

Sharon frowns as Elsie pushes her seat back, followed by Margot, who gathers their mugs and takes them hurriedly to the sink. Sharon's head swivels from left to right.

Beverley cannot bring herself to move. Her mind is wheeling, clawing back through time, finding those sensations again: the way her body crumpled in half, entirely winded; the way she knew—*knew*—when she saw the first flash of red light arcing across her kitchen window that her life was about to change forever. Now she feels a sensation of being uprooted, the way the guts know before the mind makes the connection. There's something inside her, inside all women, that knows the truth before she is able to speak it. Denial—it's a physical force. There is a lot that can be dismissed before things start to harden into a shell of indisputable truth. She tries to stand but finds that she can't. If she gets up from this chair, that will mean that it is true. It will mean that she has missed it, that it has happened all over again.

FORTY-FOUR

"Do you think he's got Enid in there somewhere?" Margot sneers as they eyeball Roger's house. She has her baseball bat in her hands, the one she usually keeps in the footwell of her car.

Before them, the windows of the Greaveses' house loom like empty eye sockets. The branches of the imposing oak tree twitch in the breeze.

The day has grown morose, hot but sludgy with storm clouds. Duke strains on the leash at Margot's side. Beverley reminded her that she's never seen the dog bare its teeth at so much as a squirrel.

"But he looks the part, right?" Margot replied, shoving the Great Dane into the back of Elsie's Buick and taking a cramped seat beside him.

"What if she's dead?" Elsie asks grimly. "What if there are other women in there? Other bodies?"

Roger said for months—did he not?—that all he needed was a meaty case to get his teeth into. Beverley knew he was frustrated at being passed over for promotion, that he felt he deserved a fast track after everything he'd done for the service, after he and Cornwell caught Henry. She *never* thought it would come to this, that he—frustrated at not having a worthy case to solve—would create one himself, taking lives, attempting to frame a boy who had only just snatched his first steps into adulthood.

When he got the cars fixed at Hank's garage, was that the first time he met the Farrers? The first time he identified Peter's vulnerability, his fascinations, and realized he would be easy to frame?

Beverley knows now that she missed signs about Enid—the way Roger spoke so offhandedly about his wife, the way he dismissed her; the way Beverley never saw her, hasn't seen any evidence of her at all over the past few weeks. She pushed it away, into the recesses of her mind, shoved aside her impartiality, her unswerving focus on finding the one right answer. She has done Enid a disservice, so many times, but now she is going to find her, and they will make sure Roger pays for his crimes.

"We have to stay positive," Beverley replies, "for Enid's sake. She could be alive." She blinks away flashes of crime scenes—Enid buried somewhere, soil settling into the folds of her eyelids; her skin mottling at the bottom of a lake; her bones tossed around a forest.

But she might be here. They have to try to find her.

They pound on the door, not caring whether Roger's there and answers. There are three of them. It's daylight. They have a dog the size of a Shetland pony. Roger cannot overpower all of them, and at this point Beverley has come too far to let him. They could have called the police, asked for backup, but for the past six weeks the police have ignored them, disregarded their concerns and their instincts, pushed them aside. Would the police *really* believe them now if they told them that one of their own was responsible? The women know they have to prove it first. Still, Elsie put in a call to a friend at the *Signal*, told her what they were doing, so there is someone who knows they're here. Beverley clings to the security of it. Someone will come if things end badly for them in this house.

She puts her ear to the door. There's music coming from inside—a haunting country lilt, a man's voice crooning in a minor key.

"We have to get in," she orders. "Go see if there are any windows that will work."

Margot and Elsie split and circle the house. Beverley steps into the flower bed as she did before, to peer in through the living room window.

Now she can see things that she missed in her rush, things her brain discounted because they didn't fit the narrative of which she had convinced herself. Firstly, there is a mug on the coffee table, and beside it an ashtray full of the gray detritus of cigarettes. A plate holds the remains of an apple, the core so wizened and brown that it must have been there for a couple of weeks at least. Some of the shelves of the bookcase at the back of the room, she can see, have been disturbed. A few books lie, disinterred, at the foot of it.

Beverley hears Margot call out, so she rushes to the back of the house. Margot stands before a slim ground-floor window, gesturing with her bat. "We'll just have to smash it. Someone can climb in, then open the front door."

"Smash it?" Elsie asks, a note of hesitation in her voice.

"Yes, Elsie—smash it," says Margot. "If you're worried about getting into trouble for that, you might want to consider the trespassing, interfering with police business, impersonating figures of authority and general lawbreaking we've been indulging in over the past couple of months. Smashing a window is going the be the least of our—"

Elsie snatches the bat from Margot's hand and takes a swing. The glass shatters, trickling to the floor inside. The women wait, their breath held.

Only the unnerving wail of music comes through the gap.

"Who wants to do the honors?" Elsie turns to them both, her chest heaving.

"I'll do it." Beverley inspects the shards of glass that jut up in triangles from the window frame. She takes the bat from Elsie, knocks it against the fragments, clearing them as best she can, then tosses it aside.

"Here." Margot loops her fingers together and holds out her hands.

"Wait." Elsie joins her hands with Margot's. They all look nervously up at the window.

Beverley kicks off her shoes, places her right foot on the women's palms, grabs their shoulders and pushes herself upward. She gets traction but falls with her belly flat on the window frame. There's a sharp, hot scratch near her pelvis. She ignores it and pushes herself in through the gap, wiggling, her hands landing on some sort of cabinet inside.

Slowly, she worms herself in. The skin of her thighs drags along tiny glass teeth, but she doesn't care. She's in. She looks around her.

The air smells warm and cottony sweet, with a secondary scent of something sour. She's in a utility room, and what she's standing on, in an animallike crouch, is not a cabinet but a laundry machine. A wash basket stands in a corner, filled, from what she can see, with men's clothing. She recognizes the crumpled shirts, and a chill spears through her when she considers what Roger might have been doing when he was last wearing them. If she picks them up, inspects them, might she find blood on their cuffs? An unsuspecting victim's stray hair caught in the folds of the collar?

"What are you seeing?" Margot calls from outside.

"It's a laundry room. Nothing in here." She wonders if Roger so lazily left those clothes in the basket because there's been no woman around to wash them for him.

"Let us in!"

Beverley swings her legs around to drop down to the tiles. The movement sets alight a sharp pain just below her abdomen. She puts her hands to her stomach and runs them downward, feeling damp material. She glances down. Her pink dress has darkened to red, the fabric torn right through.

There is a hot, throbbing pain below her stomach. Tentatively, she lifts her dress, winces. A wound snarls just above her right hip bone. It looks deep. She can see a slight protrusion of tissue. It's bleeding heavily, but Beverley cannot let it stop her. She grabs a dustrag from a shelf, folds it quickly and holds it against the blood.

"Are you okay in there?" Margot calls, and her voice sounds warped.

"I'm fine," Beverley lies, tucking the dustrag into the elastic of her underwear and pulling her dress back over the top. "I'll come let you in."

She makes her way out of the laundry room, ignoring the sway of dizziness. It's cool inside the house, and strangely still, like a museum after hours.

The wailing music is still playing, the same haunting song on a loop.

"Enid!" Beverley calls as she moves through the hallway toward the front door. "Are you here? Enid? We're here to help you."

The women are waiting, eager, when she finally opens the door. Margot lets Duke off the leash and he slopes in, sniffing the floorboards, tucking his nose into the corners.

"Any sign?" asks Elsie.

Beverley shakes her head, holding her hand against her stomach, hoping they won't see the blood or the sweat on her skin.

She calls out for Enid again and puts her head into each room as they search. She makes a mental list: a small downstairs bathroom; the living room, with the coffee mug and the disturbed books; a kitchen where dishes lie, unwashed and caked in days-old food, in the sink. A single bluebottle drones through the thick, stale air, knocking itself again and again against a windowpane.

"Where is that music coming from?" Margot asks, her face scrunched in distaste. They pause, listening as the man's wail bleeds through the hallway. *"I wish I were glass,"* he drawls, *"so you could see through..."*

They follow the music, moving through the rooms as the bars grow louder and quieter, the same song finishing, then restarting.

"Over here," Elsie calls eventually, standing at the opening of a long, dark corridor. There is a door at the end, and the hallway is lined with old family photos. Beverley pauses to look.

Enid was beautiful—*is* beautiful—not the dowdy, nagging wife Beverley had allowed herself to imagine. It had seemed easier, more acceptable, to be the "other woman" if she convinced herself that Enid existed in a vacuum—without friends, without family, without her own interests, fears or aspirations—but the photographs are snapshots of the life of a woman with everything to live for: Enid laughing on a garden swing seat, head tossed back, pale neck exposed, free; Enid and Roger in swimsuits, pedal boats bobbing on the glittering sea behind them; Roger in his police uniform, badge gleaming, a proud Enid beside him, her hair salon-done.

Something warm drips down Beverley's leg and she moves her hand to it. Pulling her fingers away, she realizes they are coated in blood.

"Jesus Christ, Bev." Margot stares at her, eyes wide.

"It's nothing," she lies again. "I just got winded," she says, pushing harder at the place just above her hip bone. Her whole stomach is beginning to ache, and there is a faint, high-pitched sound in her head. She takes a breath and turns the handle of the door, expecting it to jam, locked. Instead, the door opens easily. The music blares out, hitting them like a wall, and they step in.

FORTY-FIVE

"I WANNA GO WITH you . . . to that other world."

"Someone shut that off," Elsie calls, and Margot moves to the eight-track player.

The silence rings out. The women's eyes widen as they take in the room.

It looks like some sort of fanatic's lair. Along one wall there's a long desk, above which ripped-out newspaper articles have been taped to the paint. On the opposite wall are sketches; Elsie moves to inspect them. "He was planning how to do it."

Beverley rushes over. Diagrams are sketched in ballpoint pen on the lined pages of an exercise book. They depict the way in which each of the five women was killed.

She raises a hand to touch them. One diagram shows a body swinging on a hook. Parts of the diagram are numbered, small notes scribbled beside them. *Should be a cargo hook but can only get a winch hook,* one of them reads. She pulls away, her fingers leaving a smear of blood on the paper.

To others, the room might be passed off as a place of investigation, something put together by someone looking into every detail of the crimes. But Beverley, Elsie and Margot can see it for what it is, a place where abhorrence is designed, a place of planning.

It makes Beverley sick, the fact that he was so deliberate, so painstakingly precise, this man she has let into her home. There's horror in the meticulousness of it all, the ease he must have had with killing.

She realizes then that the pig must have been Roger's doing, too—not a warning or a taunt, but a means of confusing her, of throwing her off any scent of suspicion that might have lingered around him.

She swoons and grabs her stomach. How could she not have seen it? How could she have let this happen again?

"Seems like he was pretty obsessed with these girls." Margot picks up a yearbook that has been left open on the desk and holds it out. Sarah Gunn's picture is immediately recognizable.

"No, he wanted to make it look as if the killer was obsessed with them," Beverley replies.

"What do you mean?" Elsie asks. Her eyes flick down to Beverley's palm, which is clasped to the bloody pool on her dress.

"Bev, you look—"

"He wanted to make it appear as if the killer was someone who would naturally target girls fresh out of college, pretty girls, popular girls."

"Like someone with an axe to grind?" Elsie asks, frowning at Beverley again with concern.

"Like some sad loner, someone odd, someone who'd just been dumped."

Beverley's skin is becoming very cold. She touches her cheek with the back of her hand; it has the clamminess of old, abandoned meat.

"He did his research and chose his victims based on who he thought someone like Peter Farrer would target." She says it through a fog. "He chose methods that would draw the attention of the press eventually—once he'd decided there were enough victims—making the killings high-profile while also using them as a way to move suspicion toward Peter."

"What about the bracelet, then?" Elsie casts her eyes around at the diagrams. "Cheryl Herrera's. How did that get into Hank's car?"

Beverley allows her back to lean against the wall. There are flashes of light in front of her eyes.

"Roger used Hank's garage to get the cars from the precinct fixed up," she says—that's what Sharon told them. "He must have seen Peter there. Maybe they chatted. Maybe Peter had his camera with him. Maybe they got to talking about movies . . ."

"It would make sense for him to presume that Peter and Hank drive the same vehicles," Margot says. "All he'd need to do was toss the bracelet in."

"But why the hell did he do it?" Elsie asks.

"Because he wanted to be the best," Beverley answers. The walls of the room are all leaning in. "He was frustrated at not being promoted after Henry's arrest. He wanted to be the one to solve the case of the decade, so he created it himself."

"Jesus—" Elsie whispers, but she is cut off by the sound of barking.

FORTY-SIX

Margot's head whips up, and she runs out of the room, followed by Elsie and, eventually, Beverley, who staggers down the hallway behind them.

Margot finds Duke in the kitchen, scratching at the bottom of a door. The dog whines, sticking his nose to the crack.

"Is it a pantry?" Elsie asks.

Margot pulls the dog away by the collar and tries the handle. "It's locked," she says, turning to Elsie and Beverley. Duke immediately returns to the gap and recommences his whining.

"No," Beverley says, the realization a storm cloud tearing open. "It's a basement."

She stumbles to it, beating her fist on the white-painted wood.

"Hello!" she shouts. "Hello?" Louder. "Is there anybody down there? Enid?" Her fists leave bloody curls on the paint. The other women join in, pounding their fists and leaning their weight against the door, trying to force it open.

"What if there are others?" Margot asks breathlessly. "What if there are bodies?"

"Someone needs to break it down." Elsie pummels. "Not you," she adds quickly, casting a glance at Beverley, who is now bent double, clutching her abdomen.

"How the hell are we supposed to break down a door?" Margot cries.

"Can't we pick the lock?" As Beverley cranes her eyes upward, her friends look blurry, shimmering.

Suddenly Elsie raises her foot and kicks.

Beverley grits her teeth against the pain as she watches her quiet, determined friend raise her foot again and again, slamming it against the wood, trying to loosen the lock. Elsie sweeps the hair back from her face, her eyes darting, the exertion emblazoning her cheeks with crimson. "I think, if we all tried, we could get it," she urges.

The three women step back, positioning themselves in line with one another, left shoulders pointed forward, eyes fixed firmly on the door. Briefly, Elsie clasps Beverley's fingers, and does the same to Margot's.

"Ready?" Elsie says. "One, two . . ."

On three, they charge, their bodies smashing against the door in unison.

Pain sears through Beverley's entire body.

But it works.

The door springs open and reverberates on its hinges, slowly creaking wider to reveal a dark set of stairs leading down to a place of absolute black.

"Holy crap." Margot peers through the gloom.

"Enid!" Beverley cries as more pain daggers across her stomach. She feels her eyes begin to roll back, her body wracked, as she falls to her knees at the top of the stairs.

"Bev! We need to get her an ambulance," Elsie urges Margot, but Beverley shakes her head fiercely, gesturing down the stairs. They have to see if there is anyone down there, to see if there is anyone they can save from this.

"I'll go," Margot says, shoving Duke aside and placing a foot on the first step.

"Jeez." She buries her nose in her elbow. There is a stench rising from down below—not like death, or what Beverley imagines death might smell like, but like bodies, like cattle squashed together in their muck.

Margot continues down the steps, with Elsie close behind her. Slowly, Beverley pulls herself upright, sees their heads disappearing down below and makes a decision. She will not give up now. She will not be left bleeding on this kitchen floor, so close to the finishing point. So, with a trembling body, and in a pink dress soaked through with blood, she lurches forward and begins to descend slowly.

The temperature drops as the women move belowground, and the rancid smell intensifies. Beverley's senses are on high alert, her nerves strung tight; she is a prey animal moving through the forest at night. There is a *feeling* down here, a sense of something inhabiting the space even though they cannot see it.

The air is thick and stale, profoundly dark. There is a ticking sound, like the working of pipes, and then something else, a scrabbling noise, a scratching, like rodents squabbling—or, Beverley realizes, like something trapped trying to get out.

"Did anyone bring a flashlight?"

"Maybe there's a light pull somewhere . . ."

"Where do these steps end?"

A strained, bestial sound comes from somewhere in the basement.

The women freeze at the bottom of the steps.

It comes again.

"Shit. Somebody find a light."

The women frantically search in the darkness, hands scouring clammy walls, finding nothing but infuriating smoothness until Beverley reaches across something hard and metallic. She runs her fingers over it, searching for a switch or a button.

Light suddenly fills the basement space.

It is stark, artificial, yellow. Margot stands with her hand still grasping the bottom of the light pull, but each of the women is staring at the same thing, for a split second when there is only silence and horror and held breath.

At the center of the room, a large pipe runs down into the floor. Attached to that pipe by the wrists is Enid.

She has been tied with her arms above her head. Her mouth is gagged and her head lolls in exhaustion, but her eyes . . . her eyes are wide and animal and frantic.

Then the silence breaks.

Beverley reaches her first, tugging uselessly at the cable ties around her wrists.

Elsie bends, pulls the gag down from Enid's mouth, asks her again and again if she's hurt, if she can breathe. She orders Margot to go and fetch water from upstairs.

With the gag removed, Enid's wail is vulpine, an inhuman distress call, a sound of sheer terror.

"It's all right. It's all right," Elsie coos in the soothing tones of a mother. "We've got you. We're here now. You're safe." She turns quickly to Beverley. "Find something to cut these cable ties."

Beverley drags herself into action, grateful to have someone tell her what to do, order her own delirious thoughts for her. She stumbles around the cluttered basement. Among the household storage and the tins and the boxes are signs that Enid has been here for a long time.

There are two buckets, one of them the source of the stench, in which she has clearly been forced to perform her daily functions, and another with water and a sponge, presumably used when she has been allowed to clean herself. There's a pile of newspapers and a chair, which has been positioned directly in front of the pipe. Briefly, she imagines Roger sitting there, chin in his hands. Would he watch Enid as she suffered? Did he taunt her?

She continues searching for something that might cut the cable ties. She did have a knife, she thinks helplessly. She'd brought one but foolishly left it in her bag, on the front seat of the car. She realizes that there are ropes and wrenches scattered about, and a hammer on top of a cabinet, stained with something sticky and black.

Suddenly she feels light, too light, and her knees crumple beneath her. She is forced to cling to the cabinet to stay upright. A very bright star lodges itself in a corner of her vision. The sounds of the room—Elsie's muttering, Enid's ragged breathing—start to seem as if they are very far away.

She moves her hand to her stomach and feels that the blood has started to dry out. Perhaps that means she has stopped bleeding. Or perhaps it means she has no blood left to shed.

She can hear Margot moving about upstairs, running the taps. Then, suddenly, she sees them—a pair of garden shears propped up against a wall. She grabs them and staggers toward Elsie.

"Why did he do this to you?" Elsie is asking. Enid appears skeletal, a grim contrast to the woman in the photographs upstairs. She looks up at them. Beverley flinches as her eyes briefly meet Enid's. Does she know who Beverley is? Can she tell, just by looking at her, that her husband has had his hands on her?

She is so cold. The shears fall to the floor.

"Bev?"

She wants to find the strength to answer, but she can't.

"Bev!"

That's when the sound comes. A car approaching, the crunch of tires on concrete.

Beverley, Elsie and Enid look between one another, hot with panic.

"Shit!" Margot calls down from the top of the steps. "It's him."

FORTY-SEVEN

ELSIE GRABS THE shears from the floor and cuts the cable ties. Enid's wrists are raw and weeping where the plastic has gnawed into her skin.

The car's engine roars closer.

"We need to get out of here," Elsie cries frantically. "You're going to have to help me get her up, Bev."

"Hurry!" Margot screams down from the top of the stairs.

"Margot, get out of here!" Elsie yells. "Leave the back door open for us."

There's silence as Margot hesitates. Then they hear barking, footsteps moving through the house, pausing briefly before there's the sound of the back door opening.

The engine noise has come to a stop, and Beverley prays not to hear the car door slamming, the key in the front door.

She and Elsie take Enid under the arms, holding her weight on their shoulders. She is frail, and it takes a while for them to lift her and get her to the bottom of the steps, but they have to hurry. Roger will be in the house soon.

"I can do it." It's the first thing Enid has said, and her voice is hoarse but determined.

Elsie goes ahead, telling Enid to rest her hands on her shoulders. Beverley follows behind, wincing with each step as they slowly make their way up to the first floor of the house.

Beverley watches as Elsie reaches the top of the stairs, then turns and holds out her hands for Enid. Beverley's feet are wet, she realizes, glancing down to find them slippery with blood. Everything is losing its edges. She wonders for a woozy moment if she might fall backward, but she looks ahead, forces her focus to sharpen, commands her muscles to move.

Then she slumps. She cannot help it. It's as if the bones in her legs have crumbled to powder. Every ounce of strength has abandoned her. Her vision swarms with red. At the top of the stairs, through the haze, she sees Elsie call out to Margot. Then she conducts Enid toward the back of the house, yelling at her to run.

Elsie returns to the top of the stairs, silhouetted by the sunlight spilling into the house, frantically holding out an arm, beckoning for Beverley to move—*screaming* at her to move—up the stairs. But Beverley cannot shift a centimeter. The whining in her ears blares more loudly, reaching a hypersonic pitch. She feels her heart—*feels* it—pulsate, slower, slower. Her vision is ringed now with black. She moves her head up slowly. She can see Elsie, still screaming at her, still holding out her arms, but she cannot hear her. She cannot hear anything but the strange, discordant whining.

Elsie's head whips around then. Beverley can see the fear in her posture, her hands raised in defense. She sees another figure appear at the top of the stairs, sees it raise an arm and land a blow directly on Elsie's skull. She sees the eyes roll back in her friend's head as she tumbles backward, out of sight. Then Roger turns and fixes his sights on her.

Beverley tries to scream, tries to beg him to leave her alone, to tell him that she knows who he is, what he is. No sound comes out but the wet mewling of a kitten. Roger is descending the steps, drawing closer. She has never seen him like this, never seen him so cold, so reptilian.

She imagines what the girls—what Cheryl, Emily, Diane, Sarah and Kate—must have felt when they realized what was happening to them.

Roger says nothing. He simply bends and seizes Beverley's arm, hurling her body clean off the step. As she tumbles backward, seconds seem to pass, drawn out by the motion of falling, until the crash. Her body lies limp, functionless on the cold basement floor.

FORTY-EIGHT

When Beverley comes to, eyes blinking groggily, she realizes she is being dragged somewhere by her feet. Her arms are trailing behind her head. She opens her mouth to scream, but nothing comes out. She tries to kick her legs, to thrash her arms, but it is as if she is no longer the owner of her body, she no longer has a say in her skin or her organs. *He* is in control of her flesh. He can do what he wants with her. He always could.

He will kill her. She is sure of that. She just does not yet know how.

She hopes that Margot came back for Elsie, that they got Enid out, that they are safe somewhere far away from here.

She knows she has only minutes left in this body, only minutes more of this hell.

Her children flash into her mind: Benjamin and Audrey chasing each other around the pool; Benjamin grabbing his tiny feet, his gorgeous little toes, on his changing table; Audrey dancing so unselfconsciously while Beverley sits, grinning, on the sofa. She smells her mother's perfume, feels the soft crepiness of Alice's skin, sees the light slanting in through the church window onto Henry's face on their wedding day.

She didn't think it would end like this—with her becoming a victim herself—but she supposes, through the final fogs of her life's breath, that there is some poetic justice to it.

Through warped swells and pulses of sound, she can hear Roger muttering something.

She strains her ears, although part of her wants to give up, wants to close her eyes and let the calm roll in.

But she should know what he says before he kills her. She owes it to the girls to hear those words.

She catches only partly formed scraps of sentences as Roger hauls her toward a pile of boxes, then bends to lift the top half of her body into a seated position. He wants her to watch what he is about to do.

"... ruin it all ..." she hears him say. "Nosy bitches ..." Each time she blinks, she is amazed that her eyes open again, that her body is still fighting.

Blink.

Roger is moving across to the pipe at the center of the room.

Blink.

He is holding the shears, the ones Elsie used to cut Enid's wrists free.

Blink.

He lets them dangle at his side as he inspects her.

Blink.

Is it pity she sees in his eyes?

"You should have realized, Bev, that no one knows how to think more like a criminal than a cop."

Blink.

He stands at his full height and takes the handles of the shears, opening the arm-length blades and waving them close to her neck.

This is it, then, is it? This is how she dies, her neck severed like one of the sunflowers in the garden?

There is a noise coming from somewhere else in the room, but Beverley cannot locate it. Her thoughts are drifting—to sunshine, to flowers, to air.

There is a bang, a loud one, and Beverley wonders if it's that, a bang, and not angels' singing, or children's laughter, that one hears when one dies.

It comes again, like a car backfiring. She can still see Roger above her. She can see his face, the cold shock upon it. He looks down at his chest. There is a black spot there, opening and opening and blooming red. He turns his head slowly. Beverley's gaze follows his.

There is someone standing at the foot of the basement steps.

Enid.

She is holding a gun—presumably Roger's. She must have known where to find it, Beverley realizes with her last breath—under their bed, in the top drawer of his desk, in a safe in the living room . . .

As Roger crumples to the ground, Enid speaks, the words rattling but strong enough.

"And you should have realized, Roger, that no one knows how to think more like a cop than his wife."

FORTY-NINE

"Two liters of blood? You never did like to do anything by halves, did you, Bev?"

The hospital room is stark and sterile. A whir is in the air, caused by the workings of unidentifiable machines along the walls. The space smells of ammonia, disinfectant and Margot's woody Diorissimo perfume. Lingering on the peripheries: the scent of hospital dinners—boiled potatoes and apple pie.

Beverley is half propped up, she realizes, several pillows stacked behind her back. Her mind is foggy. Needles are in her arm. Everything is bruised. Everything is fiery and sore. Her hair, she can feel, is matted to her forehead, her skin sweaty. Her mother would be horrified.

But they are there, the three of them. They survived it. Beverley wonders, with a beat of hope, of guilt, if Enid is in one of the neighboring rooms.

"Elsie!" Beverley calls suddenly, alarmed, the words hoarse in her throat. "Your head."

"No real damage done." Elsie moves a hand to the bandage. "It's you we're worried about. Do you want water? More pain relief? I can call the nurse."

Beverley blinks slowly, takes a moment. Then warm tears spill over, winding their way down the sides of her nose.

"Oh, quit that," Margot soothes. "People who catch killers don't have time for tears—too busy saving the day."

"How'd you get out?" Beverley asks them. "Are you both okay?"

"We're all fine," Elsie assures her. "Margot came back for me." She says it proudly. "Enid's okay, too."

"Well, I didn't want to miss out on all the drama," Margot jokes, but a smile doesn't follow. They've been through so much. Beverley wonders if they'll ever be the same again.

"Is Roger . . . ?" She almost doesn't want to ask.

"He's alive," Elsie replies flatly. "We saw the ambulance take him away. The cops are in his room with him now."

Beverley's face crumples. "I'm sorry." She shakes her head. More tears. "I should have seen it. I didn't see it."

Mass killers are master manipulators. She knows that. They're experts at hiding in plain sight. That's exactly what Roger did.

"Are we really doing that again?" Margot sounds tired. "No one can stop these people, Bev. No wives, no sisters, brothers, cops. But we got him—*in the end*. We got him, Bev. He's done."

There's a sudden knock at the door, and the women freeze. A young nurse stands at the doorway, a worried look on her face. "Sorry to interrupt, but there's a reporter here to see you."

"Oh Jesus," says Margot, fixing her hair. "Here come the press."

"It's okay," says Elsie softly. "Send her in."

A woman appears at the doorway, and Beverley turns her head toward her. She has wild hair, a steeliness in her eyes and the languid posture of someone who knows her own worth.

"This is Patti," Elsie says as the woman smiles calmly, then takes a seat, pulls a notebook from her purse.

"Ladies"—she looks among them—"you ready to tell your story?"

FIVE DAYS FREED

Foiled by Women. Oh, it pleases me deeply to know how much he will detest that.

He always thought he was so clever. He thought that we, women, could never see him for who he really was. But of course, as with so many things over the years, he was wrong about that.

I was planning to leave him. I knew about the affair. I knew he had another woman. I never hated her, though, and now I know she was just a pretty, young, vulnerable woman he felt it was his right to take advantage of. I owe her my life, I suppose, my husband's mistress. Irony has such a wicked sense of humor.

I'd packed a bag, but he hadn't noticed—he rarely noticed anything that didn't concern his career. I'd stashed it in the back of the closet, with the golf clubs, made inquiries about a little apartment on the coast. I'd rather have been alone than with a man like my husband, a man who slung his dirty shirts in the laundry basket at the end of each day, not even considering that I might see the lipstick smears, smell the perfume. What an insult. How embarrassing, a cop who couldn't even have an affair convincingly.

When I found that my coat was missing, that was when I got angry. I thought he had given it to her, my best Burberry. Now I know, of course, that he put it on that poor Calabasas girl, Diane—all part of his twisted show, part of his quest to be "special," to be remembered.

The police told me that he confessed. Five girls. My God, it's far worse than what he'd taunted me with when we were down in that basement.

I could call him evil. I could call him poison, a monster, a maggot, a beast. But to put a name to him, to what he has done, would give him the sort of power that he could never deserve.

I did love him once, a long time ago, when we were young and hopeful that life would deal us a good hand of cards. But I fell out of love years ago, long before he became a killer. And now I am going to wash my hands of him forever.

To me, he's nothing, and I hope that for those girls' families he will become nothing one day, too. Simply a footnote. An afterthought. A meager insignificance. Shut away, forgotten, cast into the shadows so that the light of their daughters, sisters, friends, can shine through, bold and bright.

FIFTY

SIX MONTHS LATER

Beverley steps out of the car and peers up at the house. The air is crisp, cut through with a chill, the sun glassy and bright, a sign that spring is coming.

Does it look any different, her home? She doesn't think so. But what it represents has changed for her now. No longer is it a prison to be barricaded before she goes to sleep each night.

A flock of birds passes overhead, black silhouette curves streaking across the lucid sky. The cool breeze nips at her skin, and she pulls her jacket tightly around her.

Mrs. Akerman, the neighbor, walks by with her dachshund.

"Afternoon," Beverley calls cheerily.

The woman casts a disgusted glance behind her and hurries along. Some things never change.

Bev shuts the car door and makes her way up the path but stumbles on the heel of her new shoes. Margot told her these were the very best shoes to wear in court. She even sourced them for her from a dealer in Golden Point. Beverley bends to remove them, then walks barefoot toward the trash can at the front of the lawn. She lifts the lid and tosses them inside. She won't be needing them again.

Roger seemed so small, so powerless, as he sat in the dock during the trial. He'd recovered from the gunshot wound, but the injury had left him with a rasp in his chest, which was audible across the courtroom. Stripped of his uniform and his badge, and with his once-strong hands in cuffs, he looked old, tired. It was a letdown, really. She'd felt nothing when she saw him there, in his prison uniform.

He had taken a plea deal, agreed to confess to everything to make the proceedings as easy as possible for Enid, the very wife he had kept prisoner in his basement for weeks. Beverley was disgusted, but she'd expected nothing less. Even now, Roger is trying to manipulate people's perceptions of him, to make them see him as a good guy who wanted to spare his wife the shame of what he did. He was always so very eager to be the hero, whatever the cost.

There are still people, she knows, who believe, with the focus of the righteous, that all you need to do to understand a killer is crack the code, that all that's needed to foil a murderer is to place things in order, to find the signs and decipher them. But evil, she has learned, is not order. It is chaos.

She avoided Roger's glare as she delivered her own evidence, as she told waiting ears the details of her affair with Roger, and Roger's ruthless desire to prove his own excellence as a cop, to replace Cornwell when he retires. There was a question that troubled her for months, though. Why had Roger chosen Peter, just a boy, to frame for the murders? Why not Hank? Hank would surely have been an easier target. The answer, it seemed, was testament to Roger's grandiose pride, his desire for power. A killer like Hank, he admitted, made sense, but was unoriginal, uninspiring. A killer like Peter—a troubled, violent teen, a young killer, someone different from the run-of-the-mill Hanks of this world—would garner more attention from the press, more headlines, and the person to catch him would, therefore, get more attention, too.

How differently things could have played out. If it weren't for her and Elsie and Margot, Peter Farrer could be in a prison cell right now. Roger could have won. No one would have suspected a thing.

Roger had attempted to control it all, thought he was clever enough to dictate the whole narrative—a conductor before an orchestra of fallen bodies. It's a shame for him that Beverley, Margot and Elsie bested him, that Enid bested him ultimately. Now he'll spend the rest of his life behind bars.

Beverley told the court how he'd spoken for years about his desire to get his teeth into something meaty. How he felt overlooked at the department. How he would have done anything to change that, to take Tom Cornwell down, replace him—absolutely anything at all.

When the sentence was read out, Beverley did not feel justness or victory, only sadness—sadness for five lives cut short; five girls on the cusp of adulthood who would never get married or have children or have cocktail parties in their fabulous kitchens with their Margots and their Elsies; five families whose lives would forever be marred by fear, by wishing things weren't as they were.

Enid was there in the courtroom, and that was the first time the women had seen her since it all happened. They had not spoken to her before that, although Beverley had sent a letter apologizing for everything. Enid hadn't replied, but on the first morning of the trial, Beverley received a bunch of flowers—gladioli—and a card with Enid's signature and only one other word written on it: *strength*. Enid gave evidence against her husband, poised and calm and commanding. She had confronted Roger; that was why he'd attacked her, kept her tied up in the basement. She'd noticed his elusive behavior for a while, his avoidance, his erratic moods, but when a coat went missing from her closet—a Burberry trench she'd picked up on her last visit to England, the coat she now knows was used to dress Diane Howard Murray's lifeless body—she'd decided to ask him about it. She hadn't expected the fury, the violence, the blood.

Beverley's eyes met Enid's on occasion in the courtroom, but Beverley knew it was not her place to smile. She will forever regret how she dismissed the existence of Roger's wife because it was convenient for her to do so. She had convinced herself, in some strange way, that she needed him more—but she didn't need him. Neither of them did.

Now Beverley lets herself in through the front door and hears laughter coming from the backyard. Through the open screen door, she can see smoke dwindling upward and into the gauzy early evening. Elsie and Margot are already there. They have things to celebrate, too—endings to commemorate, new beginnings to mark.

Elsie recently learned that the stories Hunter allowed her to write about Roger's victims are being turned into a book. Hunter eventually recognized that her talent extends far beyond stocking spirit cabinets and typing up minutes. She's the newest reporter on the *Signal*'s crime desk—working beneath Patti, who is proving to be a fair and encouraging mentor.

Margot finally succumbed to Beverley and Elsie's pleas and sought a shrink. She was making real progress on her vulnerability and her fears. She is also seeing a new man. She waited awhile to tell Beverley and Elsie that she had seduced her own therapist, but had they *really* expected anything less?

Beverley steps through the double doors and joins the women on the patio. Margot pours her a cocktail from a pitcher, something sweet and orange like the sun. The kids are tearing about, causing havoc, but Beverley doesn't blink when they wander out of sight. She can hear their shrieks and their hollers. She knows they are safe. She knows that she must let them forge their own paths through life.

Bad things, she now knows, are not the universe's way of punishing those who have made mistakes. Bad things don't happen because we think the wrong thing, make the wrong choice, miss opportunities or misstep. They are not things that can be predicted, or planned for, or braced against with locked doors and cut-back bushes, and trying to prepare for them will not make them any easier to deal with when they eventually arrive. Bad things have happened to Beverley and to her children, and it's likely that bad things will happen to them again—just like good things will happen again. The sun will rise and the rain will fall. She cannot stop any of this by doing penance, by attempting every day to atone for the actions of someone she had no control over.

The doorbell rings, and Margot disappears to answer the door, reappearing a short while later with a small, hunched figure in tow.

"Look who it is!" she calls out, beaming.

Christopher Appleton has a cake in his hands. It is slightly lopsided and, from what Beverley can see, rather burned around the edges, but he holds it aloft as proudly as a father holds his newborn. The women cheer.

This is what friendship is, she thinks—not boastful cards from those who can't trouble themselves to ask after *her* children, *her* life, the things that she has nurtured. Friendship is when someone will knock down a door with you; sit for hours in a car, watching a dangerous man with you; hold your hand in a hospital bed as life-giving fluid is pumped into your wrecked body. Bake you a cake.

Beverley encourages Christopher to sit.

"Oh, I couldn't possibly interrupt," he stammers. "I was just dropping this off."

"We insist." Margot pushes him down by the shoulders onto a seat and gives them a squeeze. "And I'm making you a margarita."

"Are you ready?" Elsie asks Beverley, gesturing to the fire crackling in an old ceramic plant pot.

Beverley nods and stands, then retreats to the kitchen and returns with the scrapbook in her hands.

"Feeling good?" Margot asks.

They all watch her, kindness and understanding in their eyes.

She nods.

She takes the book—filled with words of blood and violence and horror; every story she could find that was written about Henry, Albert or Stephen; every story that was written about Roger and the four women who brought him down—and holds it over the fire. After a second, she tosses it into the flames. They quickly engulf the pages, warping years of fear and guilt and sending them up into the sky in a twist of silver smoke. The children's laughter fills the air again. Margot, Elsie and Chris Appleton raise their glasses. Beverley turns to them all, takes a deep, clear breath and smiles.

ACKNOWLEDGMENTS

My profound thanks to an indomitable team of editors—Kerry Donovan, Rosa Schierenberg and Janice Zawerbny. You took this book (and me) and fought tooth and nail to make us as brilliant as we possibly could be. I feel so lucky to have been a small part of such an impressive team.

Thank you to Genni Eccles, Lauren Burnstein, Tara O'Connor, Anika Bates, Elise Tecco and the wider staff at Penguin/Berkley, Penguin/Viking and HarperCollins Canada. Huge thanks as well to all the international publishers who have come on board to become part of this book's journey around the world. To the publicists, art teams, editorial staff, assistants, translators, copy editors, production editors, and anyone else who was involved in the making of this book, I'm dizzyingly grateful to you and in awe of the work you do (due to the long timelines involved in publishing, I haven't met you all yet, but very much look forward to doing so!).

To my incredible, unstoppable, absolute comet of an agent, Maddy

Milburn. Thank you for taking this book from me when I was vulnerable and a bit bashed about by life, and for shooting for the stars. I'm so, so grateful to have you. Thank you to Rachel, Meghan, Valentina, Liv, Hannah L., Hannah K., Georgia, Josie Freedman and everyone at the wider Madeleine Milburn Literary, TV & Film Agency for the endless enthusiasm and kindness.

To my writer friends and soulmates—Nikki, Emilia, Ally, Amy, Saara, Collette—life would be far less fun (and certainly a lot more anxious) without you. I love you all.

My love, as always, to the Kirbys, the Arnotts, Tom, Loo, Martha, Rufus, Sam, Phoebe, Max, Laura, Robin, Harriet and the rest of my friends and family.

Dad—I think you would have liked this one. I miss you every single day. To mum, thank you for being by my side for all the highs and lows of life. I love you so much.

To Bobby, the rock of my life, the best of the best, the gentle giant who makes everything safe and calm. I love you always. To Rose, the other half of me, my reason for it all—I could not do any of this life stuff without you. And to my wild, hilarious, lionhearted Joni. You are everything.

Finally, the hugest thanks to three special women: Beverley, Elsie and Margot. You saved me.